TWINS
OF THE
PROPHECY

JASON M.
BROOKS

Cross Point
Publishing

JASON M. BROOKS

Published by
Cross Point Publishing
United States of America

The Carsonian Chronicles: Twins of the Prophecy
Copyright © 2014
Jason M. Brooks

Cover Painting by Mike Green
www.darkgreenarts.com

Cover Image by Angie Green
www.angiegreen.com

Final Cover Layout by Indie Pub Central
www.indiepubcentral.com

Printed in the United States

ISBN-13: 978-0692201114
ISBN-10: 0692201114

Young Adult/Fiction/Fantasy

Visit Cross Point Publishing on the web at:
www.crosspointpublishing.com

Connect with author Jason M. Brooks by visiting his website at:
www.jasonmbrooks.com

OTHER TITLES FROM JASON

The sequel to Twins of the Prophecy – Fall 2014
Subscribe to Jason's newsletter to stay up to date on the
release dates and other news:
www.jasonmbrooks.com/newsletter/

CONTENTS

DEDICATION

To Becky. My wife, my best friend and my champion
who has encouraged me to see this book to completion.

1

The hooded figure darted across the courtyard, eager to get to her destination yet also determined not to be found out. To go into the wing of the academy students was forbidden – yet her message was vital. She had to find him and reveal the news she had just learned. The future of two worlds rested in their next decision.

She was lucky that the clouds of the fall night had concealed the light of the moon. The courtyard wasn't equipped with lights and so it was much easier to move within the shadows. A cool breeze stirred up and grabbed hold of her hood and began to pull it off of her head before she reached up with her left hand and caught it. She tugged it down over her forehead and didn't miss a stride as the entrance to the tower was now at hand.

She skipped every other step as she bounded upwards to the main door. As she reached the door she darted off to the left and caught her breath behind the concealment of a stone pillar – contemplating what she would do once she entered the chamber. Her hand instinctively reached to the heavy stone embedded in gold that hung around her neck.

It was a necklace that he had given to her a few months after they began to date. Having it in her possession, made her feel his presence. She drew strength from having it near her heart. Yes, it was almost childish to think that an object could replace flesh and blood when they were apart – but this family heirloom that he had entrusted to her so soon after they fell in love was a testament to something greater. A love like no other. She didn't care if she was acting like a teenage girl engrossed in puppy love. With him away on missions and training assignments so often, it was what she needed to feel connected to him when she couldn't hold him. She cast her mind off the thought of the necklace and focused back to her task.

She knew what floor he was on. She knew which room was his – or at least she thought she knew based on descriptions he had given her. Truth be told, she had never actually visited his dorm room. As a non-student at the academy, she wasn't allowed to go into the student's tower, especially not the room of a student. While her father was a professor at the academy, it didn't afford her any special privileges. Her very actions would result in expulsion for the man she loved and humiliation for her proud father. Yet all had to be risked for the news she carried – and much more.

With her breathing now steady, she readied for the next leg of her journey. Surely she would have to avoid some of the professors who were up and patrolling the halls. She was certain that she was crafty enough to get around a few of them. Once she got up to his floor, she wasn't sure she wouldn't arouse the wrong person and bring her whole dire mission to a screeching halt.

Yet she had to move on.

She slipped away from the safety of the pillar and grabbed onto the handle of the door. Slowly she pushed it open, peeking through the opening gap and looking into the vast entryway in search of anyone who might be stationed there. After verifying that her current viewing area was clear, she inched the door farther open and scanned the next available area that came into view, pushed further and scanned the next and then pushed it open enough to slide through once she was sure the room was clear.

She kept her cloak pulled tightly around her body and hurried for the security of a large stone statue just to the right of the door. She knelt down and then took in the room. She imagined the room as one large clock face – just as he described it to her. The door she entered was the six o'clock position. Straight ahead at twelve o'clock was the door that led to the classroom wing. At the two o'clock position was the stairs that went up to tower of the level one students. At the four o'clock position was the stairs for the tower of the level two students. The stairs for the third and fourth level students were at the ten and eight o'clock positions respectively. It was the stairs to the level three students that she needed to climb.

She calmed her nerves and concentrated through the sound of the pounding of hard pumping blood in her ears, listening for footsteps. It all seemed rather safe for her to make her mad dash for the stairs.

She choked down her fear, sprung out of her hiding position and broke into a dead sprint for the ten o'clock position of the room. After running across the soft grass of the courtyard, she was taken back by the clicking of her shoes on the marble floor.

"Is somebody there?" she heard a voice call out. "Who's up and about?"

She nearly stopped in her tracks, yet her fear overrode that impulse and she exploded for the safety of the staircase. She could hear footsteps clicking on the floors of the hallway in the classroom wing. They were drawing in fast. They stopped. The handle of the large oak doors clicked and began to squeak open as she jumped over the first three steps, rounded the first corner and then pressed her back up against the wall and stood still. Her heart thumped harder than ever before. She feared it was about to burst through her chest at any second. Worse, it was loud enough for someone else to hear.

The footsteps marched into the room and she could almost sense where the person was. They seemed to be moving for the center of the room where they all of a sudden stopped. She could almost picture the person standing there and scanning the room slowly – eyes piercing into the shadows in search of a student who was disobeying the rules and not tucked away for the night.

The footsteps began to echo in the chamber again. She chanced a glance around the corner and could see a glowing light moving towards the fourth level tower. She considered making a mad dash up the steps in hopes that the person was going to scale the tower in search of the culprit – but they didn't. The glowing light began to make its way towards her tower. She didn't dare make a sound. The light was soon at the opening to the level three student tower and she just barely escaped the light that shot up into the staircase to illuminate anyone who might be hiding inside.

The person was going to come up. She just knew that they could sense her presence. The light seemed to dance around and then jump up. It was rising! She was positive that they were coming up the steps. Somehow, they knew she was there. Had the Creator spoken to them? Had he revealed her location? Was she doomed to fail on this night?

The light jostled upwards some more. They were slowly making their way up, she had no doubt of that now. If she took off up the stairs, she would eventually be caught. The person in pursuit was no doubt a highly trained knight. They were conditioned to scale a pitiful flight of spiraling stairs. In truth, most of them ran up and down the tower stairs just for exercise. She would never outrun them.

She heard the heavy steps of the person as they drew close to the first bend. Once they turned the corner, they would be eye to eye with her. She took a deep breath. All was lost. She was about to be found out.

A cat hissed from somewhere in the room from where she had come. The light stopped approaching. "Zelda?" the voice of the man said. The light turned and she could tell he was going back down the steps. "Zelda, is that you I heard making all that noise?" She let out a slow breath and then smiled when she heard the man making kissy sounds with his lips. "Come on girl... you need some petting, don't you." He made a few more kissy sounds and then she finally felt free to continue on her mission.

Perhaps the Creator had reached down and changed her fate once again – like he seemed to be in the process of doing with the important news she had to bring to her man. Up the steps she began to go. She moved slowly, placing her foot softly on the stone steps to be as soft and quiet as possible. She didn't need any more close calls.

She got past the first floor, the second, the third and the fourth. She had five more to go and then she would reach his level. Once inside his chamber, she would have to figure out which one of the six bedrooms was his. She knew that he had a window that faced out on the East side of the valley, but with the tower being circular, almost every room on that level would face the East in some way. If only he would have described it as a clock face like he had the great room that served as the main entryway into the student wing. But how was he to know she would one night be sneaking up to find him.

Yes they were married, but it was forbidden for a student to be married and in training at the same time. They had to keep it all secret in order for him to complete his training and be knighted. She couldn't cause him to be expelled and lose out on his dream of walking in his father's footsteps. She couldn't risk the embarrassment it would bring on his legacy and her family. Under normal circumstances, there was no reason she would ever have attempted this – yet tonight, normal wasn't a way of life. She was making this up as she went along.

At last she arrived on his floor. She slowly opened the door and revealed the large room that was shared by all the student's in this apartment chamber. A dying flame crackled in the fireplace and illuminated the room just enough for her to see without the aid of a lantern or glow rod. Seven doors – six led to the bedrooms and one to the bath.

Which was his? If she opened the wrong door and woke the student on the other side, what would happen then?

She closed her eyes and concentrated. She focused hard on him, hoping that through the vastness of the Light, he would sense her presence and wake up. Hoping that the Creator would bless her with just one more wish. She had no other options but to hope for a bit of luck.

She focused harder, almost to the point of imagining herself with him. *She could see him lying in bed. She could see herself walking across the room, standing over him while he slept. She grabbed a hold of this feeling and focused harder on it. She could see herself standing over him and then whisper his name. He didn't respond. She whispered his name again, this time with more urgency.*

He stirred.

Did he sir in real life or only in her concentrated thoughts? She pushed that question out of her mind and refocused her effort. *She whispered to him and then reached over and shook him gently. His eyes fluttered and suddenly jolted wide open as he was visibly startled into full alert.*

She heard a bed squeak in one of the rooms. There was a rustling of covers and a snort of someone who had just been spooked from a hard sleep. It had worked! While she had never displayed the ability to use the Great Powers of the Light, she knew of them because her father was a master of those abilities.

He was now a Seventh Level Knight and a trusted professor to her husband. He had once invited him to their house for dinner while tutoring him on a subject. That was how they had first met. Her dad would be appalled to learn that an act of kindness to his student would be the culprit to the humiliation of having his daughter marry a student against the wishes of the academy.

She heard the patter of footsteps coming from the third door from the left. She took a chance – sure that it was him – and ran over to meet him when his door opened. He drew back at first and she used his backward momentum to push him into the room and close the door behind them.

"I'm pregnant" she said, wasting no time.

His mouth dropped open.

"I'm pregnant" she repeated in hopes that he knew this was real and not some sort of dream.

"How? We've only been together one time since we ran off to be married."

She smiled as she wrapped her arms around his neck and embraced him in a long, overdue hug. "It only takes one time silly."

"Do you know how much trouble I'll be in? Do your parents know?"

"No... I just found out myself – but there's more. More you need to know."

He gently pushed her back and rested his hands on her shoulders. Holding her out at arm's length, he looked in her eyes. "Were you seen coming up here?"

"No. I made it without being caught. But that's the least of our worries."

His eyes grew dark and he began to lick his lips. His hands trembled lightly and she knew at that moment that he knew why she had to find him tonight. He didn't hesitate. He rushed over to his bed and dropped down on the floor. Reaching under his bed, he dragged out a suitcase and threw it on top. He undid the leather latches and flung it open and then went over to his small wardrobe closet and pulled out shirts, pants, boots, socks and underwear and began to stuff them into the small compartment.

"Are you certain?"

"I saw a seer. She looked inside my belly and was guided by the Light. The future was blocked from her but she confirmed that which she couldn't have known. I trust her."

"She's never been wrong before. She's the most trusted seer in the Kingdom," he said without breaking from his work. "Did you pack provisions?"

"A few. Grabbed a few clothes. But the mountains are cold. I don't know if we dare risk it. Maybe we just confess what happened and move to the village. We can live happily there."

"They won't let us. As soon as the babies are born, they will take them. They will take them from us and we will never see them again."

"You don't know that," she protested. "The Knights of Liberty are not like that."

"I would agree with you if I didn't already know how close they watch me. I'm surprised we even had an opportunity to run off and get married without being caught. For all I know, we have been discovered and they have been keeping quiet about it all this time – just waiting to see what type of offspring we might have."

"I know what the prophecy says, but do you really believe they will over react like this? I mean really... do you truly believe they will take the boys from us?"

"They're afraid. My mentor warned me about how the council watches me. They fear that the day is drawing near. Nobody really knows how the prophecy will play out and they won't take the risk of not having some sort of safety measures in place. The best way for them to control the fate of the boys is to have total control of them. They will push us out of the picture. So much fear... so much uncertainty... that's what my father used to tell me. I have to protect them. This is the only way to do that."

"You're making too much of this. Maybe it isn't going to really be like that."

He stopped packing and turned back to her. He gave her a reassuring smirk and then said, "We can't take that chance, Love. We need to leave here. Leave the Kingdom and go to the other world. We will be safe there. The twins will be safe there. Best of all, we can be together under our terms. We can live quietly and leave this prophecy behind once and for all."

"It will be a dangerous journey. We might not make it to the gateway – and if we do make it, how do you plan to get us past the guards? And what if you die? You're the last of your family."

"I know a few people at the gate. I'll get us through – I have no doubt of that. But while I am the last to carry the McGregor name... I'm not the last to have McGregor blood in my veins. If I die, then it's safe to say that the Creator had a different plan – one that didn't involve us and involved one from a different branch of the family."

"What about me? How will I live without you?"

She came up to him and with trembling hands reaching out to his. His hands shook just as much as hers, yet she still found a deep strength within his touch. On the outside was fear but on the inside he burned with confidence and faith. He was committed to seeing them get to safety and she knew what he was determined to do would never fail.

She shook her head up and down and bit down on her trembling, lower lip. At that moment she put all of her trust in him, believing that he knew the best course of action to take. She was surrendering to him and trusting that he would get them to safety and that they would indeed bring into the world twin boys. They would be the center of their life and they would together – the four of them – be a family.

As soon as he was packed and dressed, they hurried back the way she had come and worked their way back to a bush on the far end of the courtyard where she had stowed her packed suitcase. He attached a strap to it and then tossed it over his shoulder. With both cases strapped to his back and weighing him down, they made their way to a stream that passed under the exterior wall of the castle grounds. To go through the front doors would be preferable, but with sentry guards at the post, they would be caught instantly.

They both jumped into the icy water and began to fight their way up stream and under the wall until they came to the iron gate that kept the temple grounds secure from outside intruders. However, the gate could be raised from the inside and that was what he went right to work on.

He turned the metal wheel with all of his might, causing the rusty pulley system to squeak and creek with every turn. The noise pierced both of their ears and he was certain that someone within the temple grounds would hear the racket. He couldn't risk raising it all the way up and so when he was confident that he had raised it enough to swim under, he stopped turning.

"Go," he whispered as he pushed her gently under water.

She took a last gulp of air and then jettisoned down and away from him, soon popping up on the other side of the gate.

"Who's down there!" came a cry from behind. She could see dancing lights coming towards the opening to the courtyard. There was the sound of clinking metal and she instantly knew that they were drawing weapons. Would they attack? Of course not. They would put two and two together and bring them both back to the High Master who would then have to deal with them and their actions. But if her husband was right, they couldn't allow for the babies to be born here.

"Come on!" she rushed him as the lights grew brighter. There was a series of loud splashes and she knew that they had entered the stream and were beginning to swim towards the gate.

With a last gulp, he disappeared under the water and made his way for the other side – yet he didn't pop up when he should. Bubbles rushed to the surface from somewhere in the dark cold water.

"What's going on!" she cried out, not caring that the guards could hear her. "Where are you?" knowing full well that he couldn't hear her while he was under water. She reached down with her hands, searching for his. She took a deep breath and dived under, her hands waving back and forth searching for her lost husband.

Was he stuck? Was he drowning? Was she destined to raise these twins of prophecy on her own?

A great light began to glow somewhere in front of her. She opened her eyes in the cold, rushing water and could see a light wrapping around him. A tentacle of light extended from him and pushed hard at the gate while he worked with his sword to cut the shoulder straps of the suitcases that had become caught on the tips of the metal bars. Once free, he used the tentacle of light to rocket him forward and up towards her. He reached out with his hand and grabbed hers and the momentum carried them both to the surface.

On the surface, the glowing light that encased him disappeared and darkness filled the tunnel again. The splattering of water as the pursuing guards swam against the current drew closer. He gasped for air and hacked out the water that had found its way inside his lungs. "Go!" he gasped. "Swim!"

They began to swim hard against the current until they broke out of the darkened tunnel and emerged in the dark night of the mountainous valley. They climbed up on the banks and the cold fall wind nipped at their wet bodies. He quickly got to his feet and pulled her up with his left hand, his right hand held his sword.

"What happened?" she asked.

"The suit cases got snagged on the gate. I had to cut them loose with my sword."

"But all of our warm clothes? Our provisions?"

"Come on!" he said and he began to urge her along.

"We can't go without those things — without something. We need a change of clothes, food, supplies!"

He didn't stop to discuss their dire situation. He continued to pull her along with him as he broke into a sprint. She fought to keep up.

Soon they were a long distance from the castle. She cast a glance back while they took a quick break to catch their breath. The silhouette of the fortress rose up from the flat plains of the valley. The walls offered safety, security and familiarity. In contrast, as she looked in the direction they were headed, she saw danger, uncertainty and possibly death for both of them and their unborn children.

"We're not going to make it," she said through the shivers of cold that rattled her body.

He grabbed her and pulled her close to him. He rubbed his hands over her body in an attempt to provide some warmth. "It's a long way out of here, Love. But we can make it. We are supposed to make it."

"How can you be so sure?"

He held her close and continued to rub her with his hands. Together, tightly pressed together, she felt warmth cutting through the cold of the night. She also felt a sense of destiny and new determination flood into her. He didn't have to answer her question. She could feel the answer in his strong arms.

When they knew they could no longer stay in the same place any longer, they began to make their way into the mountains. The trail would be long and winding. Their destination was a very long way off by foot and even longer with no supplies or extra clothing. The chances of survival was little to none.

From here on, their journey would all depend on how deep their love was and how far that love and commitment could take them.

2

Seventeen Years Later...

"I have their location, Master. The Grand Master has at last revealed the truth that we already speculated. The Order has been watching them for seventeen years."

"Now you understand why I left you where I did."

"I have waited seventeen years to avenge my failure, Master. I will personally deliver them to you."

"No. Again you must be patient. As you learned before, fate can turn us in the wrong direction. We must have our people in places where they can take needed actions. You are in a very important position for me. I will not risk losing my one foothold in the Order. You have your mission. You know that which I desire."

"For seventeen years I have been planting the seeds of destruction, Master. How much longer must I be among these infidels? How much longer must I pretend to care about their trivial pursuits of peace and order?"

"For as long as I desire you to. For three thousand years I have waited for my time to return to power and escape this shell. I have reason to be anxious. You do not. You have waited seventeen years and you will wait seventeen more if I so command it."

"Yes, Master."

"I have more work for you to do. But first, I need the location of the boys. I have my loyal servants waiting to extract them."

"But the Cold War has not been favorable to your knights, Master. The Knights of Liberty have a large presence in the World. They will overpower your efforts to capture the twins."

"I have already calculated that. I have put into place a plan that will effectively bring the boys into the Kingdom and restore me to full power. This time, there will be no mistakes."

* * * * *

Caleb shook the cobwebs from his head. That last hit had put him in "dream world" as they liked to call it when there was a good hit on the field. He bounced up and joined his team in the huddle. He looked up and caught the signals from his coach. He relayed the play on to the other members of his team and they broke their huddle and went to the line.

The ball was soon snapped into his waiting hands. Caleb dropped back and began scanning the field for open receivers. The crashing of pads and the grunts of strong teenage men who were fighting for supremacy of the field, was the only sounds he could hear.

He had long ago figured out how to push the crowd noise out of his head and focus only on the sounds from the game. He could hear the walls of his passing pocket as it moved. He could hear the cries of a lineman who was losing his ability to block. He almost seemed psychic in the way he could tell when a defender was about to wrap him up in a sack and then duck under the move and scramble off to pick up yards or complete the pass. Caleb rarely got sacked and for the opposing teams, it became a priority to contain him and take him out of the game. With Caleb in command, anything could happen and colleges were beginning to notice.

Caleb was just getting started with his junior year of high school but he was already well aware of the bright future his football skills were opening up for him. If he could continue to master his abilities and attract the right schools, anything was possible. Leaving this dinky, rural town of Tarrin, Wisconsin behind, was his number one goal. He didn't want to become like his father and have no dreams of greatness. He wanted more. He wanted it all.

His football skills were sure to give him the world, and while his dad cautioned him against wanting more than he needed, Caleb was already positive that he knew what was best for himself. Maybe his twin brother Lucas could be happy in a job at the lumber yard working alongside their dad, but that wasn't the life for him.

Channeling that confidence and determination, Caleb ducked down just in time to avoid a defender that had zeroed in on him. He spun out of the grasp of another defender and then he broke into a dead run to the right – leaving his pocket of protection behind.

He scanned down field, searching for anyone who had the opportunity to get open. He saw Corey Russell breaking free of a safety and getting a two-step lead on him and that was all Caleb needed to see to know he found his man. Without planting his feet on the ground, he relied on his rocket arm to propel the ball down field and into the waiting hands of his receiver who took the ball the rest of the way into the end zone.

Another touchdown and another notch in his belt towards a full scholarship and a place on an NFL team making millions of dollars.

The rest of the game went like clockwork. The defense did its job and then Caleb marched out and brought his team down the field for the score. It was mechanical and almost predictable. The final score reflected the efforts of the Tarrin football team and the smile on his face as he exited the locker room said it all.

"Great game, Caleb!" he heard some of the cheerleaders call out to him as he made his way for the doors. He looked at them and gave them a smile that said "Thanks, did you expect anything less?" and continued on his way to the parking lot. At his car he could see a blond headed girl with a perfect figure and decked out in her cheerleader outfit waiting for him. She was always there. He was certain she always would be.

"Not bad number twelve. Gunning for the state record books are we?" she said with a huge smile across her soft face.

He smiled at her remark with a slight chuckle. It wasn't the cocky smile he had given the other girls. They only got to glimpse the exterior of Caleb McGregor. They only got to see the football jock who was the pride of the city. The "Young Gun" who had put Tarrin on the map in the high school football world. They only knew the kid who had the potential to be a great – and rich – pro football star. But this girl, the one who had control of his heart, she got to see the real Caleb.

She knew his inner fears of never amounting to anything. She knew how he wanted to make his parents proud yet not be stuck in this rut of a city. His parents always nagged him about being content with what he had, but he wanted more. He knew he deserved more and he wasn't about to dampen down his love of the game or the gifts of his ability and settle for cutting wood or pumping sewers or whatever else this town had to offer. He wanted to experience life at its fullest – and he wanted Andrea to be right there with him.

She knew that the ego he presented to his friends and

schoolmates wasn't the real him. She knew his love of his family. She knew how he wanted the best for them and the best for her. She had seen him cry – something they never would see. She knew how he loved peace and quiet after a big game over going to a party – though he always tried to make an appearance at the post game parties to keep his jock image alive.

Those things fueled his fire to compete but they left him drained. At the end of the day, he wanted to be with those he loved most. She was the only person that wasn't related to him by blood that truly knew him and was a part of his inner circle.

As he walked up to her, he dropped his duffel bag to the ground and wrapped his arms around her waist and pulled her in for a soft kiss. From a few cars away he could hear some of the kids from his team cheering him on. He ignored them and just enjoyed the moment – and the fact that they were jealous of him being with a stunner like her.

"Off to Ricky's party?" she asked.

"After we take my brother home. I promised mom and dad I'd give him a ride back."

"But by that time the party will be half done. Why not just bring him along?"

"He's not into that scene. He's a loner like my dad. Always has been... always will be."

She gave him a frown and then said, "There's nothing

wrong with wanting to have a quiet life. You're not much different from them."

"I hope I'm a lot different than them."

"I like your parents. I like Lucas. I'd like you even better if you quit cutting on them all the time."

She was defensive when it came to him cutting down on his parent's way of life and his brother's lack of ambition. Perhaps it was the fact that both of her parents were killed and so she relished being a part of a family system. Sure she had her grandparents, but they had long ago left the parenting phase of their life. They were good at being a sounding board but lacked the intimate understandings of how she worked that only her parents could know. While they provided security, they lacked all the other skills that she needed at this juncture in her journey.

When Caleb and Andrea began dating last spring, she immediately grew attached to the McGregor family. Her parents and his were best friends for as long as he could remember, and so she grew up playing at their house many nights. With her parents passing, she was comforted by their willingness to take her in and love her as their own. Sometimes it made him worry that she was more in love with them than with him.

"We don't need to go out tonight," she said as she took his keys and unlocked the car door. "We'll hang out at your place."

"Really?" his hopes dropping a number of levels down.

Nate Sanders had his duffel bag over his shoulder and happened to be walking by the car when he overheard the conversation. He was a great safety and place kicker but he was becoming increasingly annoying. He was new to the school so Caleb could understand his desire to fit in and make friends, but being nosy and listening into conversations that didn't involve him was a bit too much. He seemed to have a knack for showing up at the right place and at the right time to pick up on key parts of conversations. He just happened to be wandering by at just the right time once again. It almost seemed as if he was spying on him. It was how he had gotten the name "Nosey Nate."

"Hanging out with mom and dad tonight?" he said with a smile. Caleb couldn't wait for him to graduate and leave Tarrin. He longed to be free of this busy body.

"For a while maybe. I would rather pop over to Ricky's for the party."

"Listen to your girlfriend. Stay home. It's safer for you there," he half chuckled as he walked over to his car, climbed in and then just sat there and stared off into the night.

He sure seemed like a troubled person. For someone with such great concentration on the field, he spent a lot of time just lost in space – apparently thinking about nothing and being alone. He talked a good game, often convincing people that he was some sort of party animal, but he didn't seem to really interact with anyone and was never seen by anyone at parties – unless of course Caleb happened to be there. Nate's parents never came to any games or to his knowledge, any school events. It was as if he had nobody *but* himself.

Not that it's any of my business, Caleb thought to himself.

"Hey!" Lucas' voice called out from somewhere in the darkness of the vast practice field. "I'll be right there!"

Caleb searched the black space and soon saw the silhouette of his brother emerge in a dead run. He was tucking a glowing disc into his disc golf bag and breaking away from a pack of three other people. "Another round of night disc golf?" he asked.

"Best time to do it. Everyone's at the game so we have the course to ourselves," Lucas said as he patted his brother on the shoulder and then winked at Andrea. She bent down and popped a lever on the side of the seat that caused it to move forward and Lucas crawled into the back seat. "Where to?"

Caleb rolled his eyes. *Anywhere but home... but I guess my choice doesn't matter.*

Caleb waited for Andrea to get in and then he gently closed her door. He scooped up his duffel bag, went around and opened up the driver's door and stuffed his bag into the back seat next to Lucas.

"I thought we'd hang out at your place," Andrea said with a grin. "Play some cards, pop some popcorn and drink some Dew."

"Seriously?" Lucas seemed thrilled. "Sounds like a perfect night to me."

"Yea, perfect night," Caleb sulked.

Lucas seemed to have an attitude on life that mirrored Andrea's. Maybe it was for that reason that he couldn't understand why she was with him and not his brother. She was bubbly and got excited by the little things. Lucas was much the same way while Caleb was more serious, more focused on himself and thought the little things were boring. Perhaps his greatest fear of hanging out at home with Andrea and his family was the fear that she would realize that she was dating the wrong guy and dump him for Lucas.

* * * * *

As they pulled out of the parking lot, Caleb was unaware that Nate pulled out behind them. He stayed back quite a few cars. He mirrored every turn that Caleb made but did so at a far enough distance that he never became aware of his presence.

Caleb turned right at the stop lights and was soon on his way out of town. Nate turned right as well and followed them out of town and deep into the country. When Caleb turned into the driveway of the family home, Nate continued on by, but at some point he circled back, drove to a side road that ran along the east side of the family property and then killed his lights and turned off his car.

In the darkness, with the cold fall air cooling off the car quickly, Nate sat in silence and let the night hours tick on until dawn. Inside the McGregor house, nobody was aware of Nate's presence. They went about their business.

3

Caleb's dad, Gavin, grabbed a few bags of microwave popcorn and tossed them into the "nuke box" as they often called the microwave, and popped up the salty snack while their mom, Catrina, went to work on getting the drinks ready. Lucas was quick to gather up *Trivia Pursuit* and Caleb just watched in horror as his family and his girlfriend, drew together for a night of fun and games.

Somehow, this didn't seem like the thing a football star should be doing after a big win. He was fairly certain that he should be out drinking or something – keeping up the image of a jock. However, it didn't take him long to get engaged in the game and forget about his own concerns or desires. He was lost in the moment. He was actually enjoying the company of his family and his girlfriend and he started to feel a pang of regret for his earlier thoughts.

"Heck of a game tonight, Caleb," his dad said as he washed down a mouth full of popcorn with a chug of *Mountain Dew*. "You lit up their secondary. Everything they threw at you, you just stepped up and picked them apart. Beautiful game."

Caleb's love of the game of football came from his dad's love. While he had never played in high school, he very much enjoyed spending his Sunday afternoons watching the NFL games. He didn't seem to have a liking of one team over another but instead seemed to have individual players that he enjoyed rooting for.

He loved seeing them use their skill sets to raise up the performance of their respective teams. He enjoyed the personalities displayed during the games and in the post-game interviews. It was the joy of watching grown men play with reckless abandonment that really fascinated him the most. They put it all on the line each Sunday for nothing more than the love of the game – and maybe the chance to touch the trophy at the end of the year.

"Coach heard that a couple of scouts from Ohio State were in the stands tonight. If I can finish off the year strong..." he trailed off when he noticed his dad and mom go from gleeful smiles to concerned looks that they exchanged with each other. The mood had shifted quickly.

Andrea chimed in, "How was your disc golf game, Lucas?"

He perked up a bit and then went into a long explanation of the intricacies of a few of his best shots and how Peter had lost one of his disks in the creek and then on to other aspects of the night's game that Caleb just tuned out. He was fixated on his parent's apparent change of attitude. They went from happy to... he wasn't sure what it was. It wasn't the first time he had seen it happen, but it seemed the more he talked about going big time with his football dreams, the more nervous they became.

Lucas did a good job of shifting the conversation back to joking and having a good time. The family laughed and played on through the night until it was time for Caleb to take Andrea home. He always hated to part with her. If they could get married today, he would. But at seventeen, he had a few years to wait for that dream.

As he put the car into park, he turned and looked at her soft features in the moonlight that lit up the interior of the car. She was gentle and loving. She cared about others and had this natural gift of reminding him of what was truly important. As he reached over and gently touched her cheek with his palm, it suddenly hit him and he said in almost a whisper, "You planned this tonight... didn't you."

She drew back as if she were in shock of his accusation and yet the sly curl to her lips betrayed her. She rested her head in his hand and closed her eyes as she drew in a deep breath and captured the moment with all of her senses.

"I get to thinking I'm Mr. Big Shot and you make me do something lame to keep my ego in check," his smile grew big and he almost laughed when he finished with, "You really get me. You understand me."

"I know you want to be successful and become this great

star, Caleb. That is a great thing. I want to be with someone who has plans for their life and not just plans for being a bum. But don't forget where you came from. Don't forget your family, because when you forget them, you forget the important parts of yourself. I would give anything to have my parents back..." she trailed off as her eyes left his and she seemed to go to another time and place. No doubt she was reliving the accident that changed her life. She shook the memories from her head and then refocused her eyes on him, "You need them... you need family and connection..."

"I need you." He leaned over and their lips came together. Her warm breath, her soft skin, her hand as it came up and touched his cheek, connected him to a place of total belonging. He loved his game of football, but it was here that he found his real purpose. It was with her and his family that he could truly feel his place in the world clearly defined. Just hours ago he was lost in a fantasy world that consumes and destroys many people. Now he was back on a firm foundation – anchored by her.

"I need to get in before my grandpa comes looking for me," she said as she reluctantly pulled away. She got out and gently closed the door, peeking in the window one last time and giving him one last smile to take home with him.

"I love you," he said.

She gently kissed her fingertips and then blew it in his direction before turning and heading up the walk to the front porch. He put the car into drive and then headed for home – leaving a piece of himself behind with her.

She did understand him. She saw his need to break free of the delusions of what he wanted to become and instead return to who he was. Caleb shivered as he thought back to his earlier thoughts of wanting to leave Tarrin behind. He almost puked when he thought of how much he resented his dad's job and Lucas' lack of desire to become something better than their dad.

He was a good man. He was an excellent provider. He was everything a dad should be and beyond. Andrea had cut through the fog that clouded Caleb's mind and showed him the truth – the greatest person he should aspire to be is not one of the hot shot pro football players who are a dime a dozen, but to have strong character and moral substance like his dad, a type of dad that seemed to be a dying breed in the world.

As he pulled into the drive, he had a restored view of his dad. It brought a smile to his face and a warmth in his heart. When he opened the front door and saw him sitting at the table reading a book with a cup of coffee, he was glad to have this chance to talk with him.

"Thanks for coming to the game."

He placed the book face down on the table to mark his page and then looked up to Caleb. "No place I'd rather be on a Friday night. You've got some serious game. You really think you want to go to Ohio?"

"I don't know," Caleb said as he shrugged his shoulders. "I really haven't given it much thought. I've actually only dreamt of going pro. I never thought of playing college ball first."

"You can't get to the NFL right away without going college first," his dad took a slug of coffee after telling Caleb something he already knew. "I kind of thought you might go to Wisconsin. Maybe Miami – never saw you as a Buckeye."

"Why not? What's so bad about them?"

"It's not that something's wrong with them. I just didn't see you playing in Ohio. They're more of a power running team. So is Wisconsin, but they are opening up their game a lot as of late. Ohio wouldn't know what to do with your arm."

Caleb smiled as he pulled out a chair and sat down at the table. "To be honest, I'm not even ready to think about college. I still have this year and next. When the colleges start knocking on my door, then I'll get serious."

"It won't be long before that happens," he said with an unsteady tone. His face started to grow serious and the football talk seemed to be over. "This isn't easy for me to say Caleb, so I'm just going to throw it out there. I need you to scale back a bit, Caleb."

"What do you mean?"

"You're drawing too much attention. It's not just people in our town or our state. Your name is spreading. Media is picking up on you. You're a high school sensation... won't be long before ESPN comes knocking on our front door. There's a buzz about you and I don't think you're ready for it."

"I'm ready for it Dad. I want this."

"I know you want it... but you're not ready for it. You're head gets big. You forget yourself and become someone else entirely. If you're not careful, you'll self-destruct and then everything you've fought for, everything you care about will be lost. It will all be for nothing."

"Where is this coming from?" Caleb's voice raised up and his dad drew back – apparently startled by the negative reaction of his son.

"It's my job to guide you, son. It's my job to make sure you stay on the right path..."

"It's my life to live. It's my path to take... not yours. Maybe you're satisfied being a guy who sells wood... but that sure won't be me!" *Where did that come from?* Caleb regretted the words as they came out of his mouth. He saw the instant pain in his dads face. He knew he had made a huge mistake.

"It pays the bills, Caleb. It keeps a roof over our head and food on our table. That's all I can ask for. Besides, there are far greater things to live for than fame, and sometimes fame isn't all it's cracked up to be. It puts you in danger... and worse... it could put your entire family in danger."

Gavin got up from his seat and took a quick glance in his coffee cup. Any thought of finishing it off left him and he just slid the cup to the middle of the table and left for bed. Caleb wanted to apologize, to reassure his dad that he was proud of him and loved him — but stupid pride clamped down on his throat and prevented him from saying the words he should have said at that moment.

Why did I say that? He asked himself again. Andrea was wrong about him. He was sure of it. Maybe she didn't know him after all. If she had seen his outburst, what would she think of him now?

"She'd probably leave me for Lucas," he mumbled to himself.

He would fix things in the morning. Luckily it was going to be Saturday and everyone would be home when the sun rose. He would have a good night's sleep and all would be well. He probably wouldn't even have to apologize for what he said. His dad would wake up refreshed and wouldn't even give Caleb's words a second thought. It was the way he was. Quick to walk away and not say something he would regret later, and quick to forgive.

Two traits that Caleb needed to learn   .

It was hard to get to sleep with the thoughts of his argument with his dad still running through his mind. But at some point he closed his eyes and drifted off, only to have his lights turned on much too early in the morning for his taste.

"Get up, Caleb. We've got work to do," Gavin said as he pulled the covers off of his son.

Caleb rubbed the sleep from his eyes and looked at his dad who was hovering nearby with a cup of coffee in his possession. He had his flannel shirt, jeans and work boots on which meant only one thing, "We're cutting wood today, aren't we?"

"Think of it as bonding time."

Gavin walked over to a chair in the corner of the room and scooped up the clothes that Caleb had worn into the woods the previous weekend and tossed them on his bed. He held up a steaming cup of coffee that he was holding in his left hand and used his eyes to gesture that he had poured it for his son, who offered a simple nod of the head as a sign that he understood who it was for. Gavin set it on the dresser and walked out. From the other room he could hear that it was now Lucas' turn to wake up.

After a quick breakfast with little chit chat, they hooked up trailers to two of the three four wheelers and made their way into the woods. While they had forty acres of woods behind the house, it was a thin strip of woods along the side of the property that hid a side road from view that Gavin was focused on working in. A storm over the summer had knocked down a number of trees in this patch and he wanted to get them cleaned up before any unwanted varmints moved in and claimed them as homes.

After selecting the perfect place to begin work, Gavin shut down his machine and climbed off. The boys followed suit as they pulled on their work gloves and did some light stretches to get the blood flowing.

"I wanted to apologize for last night, Caleb."

"I shouldn't have ripped on your job, Dad."

"No you shouldn't have, and I'll take that as an apology, but that's not what I need to apologize for. I actually have to apologize to both of you. There's something I have been keeping from you both – something both your mom and I never wanted to discuss. The problem is, Caleb, you're making a lot of noise with your football skills and it's putting our entire family at risk."

Immediately, Caleb became excited. He was expecting an apology and instead his dad was back to accusing him of putting the family at risk, "What are you smoking, Dad? What risk does me becoming famous bring to the family?"

"Power brings corruption, Bro," Lucas chimed in. He was squinting from the strong morning sun that was shining directly in his eyes.

"No, it's not that," Gavin said as he set the chain saw down on the back rack of the four wheeler and began walking through the woods in the direction of the road. The boys followed suit. The sun was bright and warm and the frost covered leaves glistened as the sun danced off of them. A gentle sprinkle of water came down as everything woke up on this chilly morning. "I'm not even sure how to tell you both what I need to say. It's barely believable – but you *need* to hear it."

Lucas looked over at Caleb who looked back at him. They exchanged blank stares and continued to walk behind their dad. Lucas was the first to speak up, "You didn't bring us out here to cut wood, did you?"

"No. I came out here to tell you something that is going to wreck your world. Change how you look at things and hopefully," he looked back, directly at Caleb, "make you understand why we need to keep a *very* low profile in this world."

He stopped and turned to look at his sons. He opened his mouth to speak and then quickly closed it. He tried again and yet another misfire. What was on his mind, Caleb wondered. What about his football skills had brought this much worry to his dad?

"This is going to sound crazy, but you both know me. You know that I have never lied to you about things that are important. I can tell a good campfire story, but as you can see, we're not around a campfire. So..." he paused again. His mouth opened, then closed. He turned around and began to walk some more. With his back turned to the boys, he began to speak, almost at a whisper, "We're not from around here, guys."

"What?" Lucas asked. Neither of the boys could fully hear what their dad said.

He turned and looked at them and then repeated, "We're not from around here. We're not even of this world."

Caleb chuckled and then said, "We're aliens?" He was sure that his dad was having a bit of fun with them, yet it didn't make much sense to be this serious if it was all a joke.

"Kind of... but not really. What if I told you that there were multiple planes of the world in existence? That what we see is not the only world *to* see. That you can go between worlds through a rift in time. Kind of like a sheet that divides two rooms. You know that other room is there but you can't get to it because you are on the other side. You put a tear in the sheet, and now you can get into the other room."

"I would guess that you're a bit nutty, Dad. What are you talking about?" Caleb asked.

"Have you ever asked yourself, why don't I have any grandparents?"

"You told us they were both gone. That you didn't have brothers and sisters," Lucas said.

"Yes, well... neither your mom nor I have brothers or sisters, but we both have parents. My dad is dead, but my mom is alive and well. So are your mom's parents – or at least the last time we saw them they were."

Caleb and Lucas both stared at him with disbelief. "Where are they?"

"Seventeen years ago, we left them behind to protect you two. We left them in the other dimension... if you want to call it that. It's really called, Carsonia. A world of living and breathing humans, Angelians, Qualians, Warox, trolls, goblins and more. A world of awesome beauty… but on the verge of total destruction. It's where your grandparents, cousins and relatives all live and where we once lived… before we had to escape."

"Dad," Caleb began. "This is the most insane thing I have ever heard. You really have gone over the edge… haven't you?"

Lucas remained silent. He often was a processor of information. He weighed what he knew before opening his mouth to speak. This was all a bit crazy, but he wouldn't cast judgment until he knew for sure. Caleb was admittedly angry that his brother wouldn't just side with him and call his dad out for his apparent insanity.

Gavin took a few steps back from his kids and then closed his eyes. He began breathing deep and smooth. Suddenly, from somewhere above, a gentle ball of light began to descend. It hovered over Gavin for a second and then began to move over him, encasing his body in a soft, glowing light. The twins drew back – almost ready to run and scream for their mom – yet curious of what was covering him.

From the light that surrounded him, tentacles began to come out and they danced around him. He opened his eyes and looked over to his boys. "They call it 'The Light'. It's an energy force that The Creator allows certain people to tap into and use for protection of yourself, or to protect the innocent… the oppressed. It's His gift that we use to protect His creation."

A tentacle stretched out and grabbed a fallen tree and began to lift it up. Gavin strained to control this arm of light, but with more deep concentration, he was able to lift it up and move it over to where they had parked the four wheelers. He set it down gently and then the tentacle returned to him. He sent two more arms of light out and scooped up the boys in each one.

"AHHHH!" Caleb screamed. "Put me down! Put me down!"

Lucas screamed briefly but then seemed to be enjoying the ride.

The beam of light wrapped around Caleb's ankles and dangled him upside down and weaved him in and out of trees, barely missing them at times.

"Are you trying to kill me?"

"Enjoy the ride, man! This is great!" Lucas was always the one who loved reckless fun. Caleb was all about the calculated and planned events. Lucas was all about the impulsive actions.

The tentacle pulled Caleb over to his dad and held him upside down but low enough so he was eye to eye with his dad.

"I didn't go nutty, Caleb. Do you believe me now?"

His first instinct was to be defiant. He didn't like surprises and he despised being lied too for all of his life. However, seeing this power in action did evoke a touch of awe and the ability to forget the anger and a desire to hear more. Not to mention it brought a sense of believability to the whole story. Yet he still wanted to ignore what was being said. He feared what all of this new revelation may mean in regards to his future. It was clear to Caleb that he was a stewing pot of mass confusion.

Reluctantly, while dangling upside down in front of his father, Caleb gave in, "Go on."

The tentacle of light slowly lowered him to ground, his head touching the wet, leafy surface and then the rest of his body slowly being laid down until it released his ankles and retracted into the glowing ball of light that encased his dad. Caleb sat up on his elbows as Lucas came over and extended a hand to help him up. Caleb took his hand and with one tug, he was back on his feet. They both watched as the light dissipated and their dad was returned to normal.

"That... was really cool!" Lucas said.

"There's more to the Light than just that. But it should prove that I'm not playing a game. What I'm about to tell you both is the absolute truth and it's why I am afraid of all the attention you are drawing to the family, Caleb."

"I'm one McGregor in a world filled with McGregor's. The chances of anyone finding me are slim to none."

"Really? Have you considered how easy it is to find anyone on the internet? Nobody is free from eyes that want to find them. Why do you think we do not allow the internet here?

Why no social media access? Why no email? Because we're weird?"

"Well, the thought crossed my mind," Caleb was serious.

"I always figured you guys were afraid of technology," Lucas added.

"We are. We're afraid it will be used to find you boys. We can't allow that to happen. The more people write about you, the more people talk about your name, the greater the chance we will be found. It's a matter of time before someone connects the dots. You may be one in a million of McGregor's, but how many McGregor families have twin sons in the world?"

"Probably a few. But why would twins matter?"

Gavin didn't answer. He continued with his assessment of the situation, "How many twin boys with the last name of McGregor have no known grandparents or other living family members outside of their mom and dad – who by the way, have no records of ever being born – *anywhere* in the world."

"This isn't looking good," Lucas chimed in.

"How many McGregor twin boys with no family and parents with no records to speak of, have a mom and dad whose names are Gavin and Catrina… the exact two names of two people who ran away from their homes over seventeen years ago?"

"But why would anyone narrow it down to twin boys with

the name of McGregor? Why would that fact be so important?" Caleb asked again.

"Because of the prophecy."

4

"This entire charade has been about the Prophecy," Gavin said. "The prophecy of twin boys born of the family line of McGregor's. One is destined to restore light and peace to Carsonia. One will undo all of the evil that the Dark Master Natas has established in the kingdom. Only this one boy can bring to an end the war that has lasted for thousands of years. The other brother… the other twin brother…"

Gavin choked back pain that had worked into his voice, "…is connected to the Dark Master. As long as he lives, so will the Dark Master Natas. The blood of this twin will free Natas from the Shadow World. The blood will bind the two and they will live an immortal life, endangering the fate of both this world and Carsonia."

"One of us has to die in order to stop… Natas?" Lucas asked.

"And now you see why we ran away. The Knights of Liberty… those who use the Light to protect the innocent… were and probably still are fearful of the danger the Twins of Prophecy pose on the kingdom. They… like your mom and I, could never choose to kill one of their own to defeat evil. We didn't know how they would react if they were to learn that the twin boys were born.

"Would they lock you both up? Would they let the whole charade play out? Would they take you away from us and raise you themselves and in the process make the choices for you and against your will in order to keep the prophecy from coming true? The High Council of the Knights of Liberty were too risky to deal with. We had to make a decision and to do it fast.

"To protect you, we ran away. We believed that nobody would ever find us in this place. We believed we were safe and that you both could just live a normal life and the choice would never have to be made."

"And then I became a football star," Caleb looked down, now fully aware of how his selfish ambitions had put everyone – including Andrea, in danger.

Gavin came up along him and laid his hand on his shoulder. "It's not your fault. You're just being a kid, discovering your passions and living out your dreams like we always wanted you too. We just didn't know you were that dang good," he smiled as he patted Caleb on the back and then pulled Lucas in and held them tightly. "Everything we've done was to protect you both. But maybe we were the selfish ones.

"Why did the Creator choose me and my family to call

to fulfill this prophecy? Who am I to ignore His wishes? I guess we have to leave it all in His hands and see how this all plays out. I'm still praying that you can both be spared, though. Maybe someone long ago misinterpreted the prophecy and none of it has to shake out the way we have always believed it would. All we can do is pray."

He squeezed them harder and nearly suffocated the two of them before Caleb wiggled loose. He was uncomfortable right now. Everything was spinning and the life he had planned out was suddenly being taken away from him. He searched for some sort of answer to how to take back control and wasn't really sure if it was possible to do so.

Lucas broke away from his dad and seemed to be drawn to a path in the woods. It was a well-worn path and probably one belonging to the deer. Caleb wasn't much for hunting, but Lucas and his dad were avid woodsmen. "Take a look at this, Dad. It looks like the deer are passing through this patch."

Gavin walked over, kicking back the long ferns that hung over the trail. "They've never really used this stretch before. They always cross over from the Cormican property into the back forty."

"I wonder why they shifted down here. They'd have to pass through the yard and walk right by the house to get back there."

Gavin said something louder than he had intended and

both the boys caught it, "This isn't a deer path."

Caleb hustled over as their dad broke into a slow jog, following the path through the narrow strip of woods and right up to the old farm road on the other side. The road was dark and moist from the frost that night – all except one rectangular patch.

"Someone was parked out here last night," Gavin said. He walked back to the path and knelt down, moving leaves and long blades of grass aside to see what the ground could tell him. Lucas and Caleb walked up behind him and watched him work. They saw it before he even had a chance to say it, "Boot tracks!"

He got up and broke into a dead sprint, following the path. Caleb and Lucas kept up, twigs and branches snapping them as they lumbered through the dense patch and came to a small stack of wood that had belonged to a tree their dad had cut down two summers ago. Behind it sat one stump and a cleared away area. "Someone's been sitting here and watching us."

Caleb felt the world closing in on him. He was angry and confused. Scared and yet fighting to remain calm. Everything was going to be alright. The prophecy was going to just go away. This was all just a coincidence – though having a pervert staring through your window all the time – probably checking out your mom – wasn't exactly a calming feeling.

"They're here. They already found us," Gavin said slowly. "I thought I was better prepared than this. They snuck right up through my own woods. How the hell…"

"Who? The Knights of Liberty?" Lucas asked.

Caleb almost wanted to throttle him for even suggesting that possibility.

"Let's hope so. If it's not them… it's a whole lot worse than I thought."

5

The weekend seemed to drag on forever.

After informing their mom of what they discovered, she became agitated and worried. Everyone was on edge and maybe a bit too paranoid. With thick tension came arguments and a disharmony that often didn't come into the McGregor household. It had boiled to such a point that Lucas was glad when Monday morning arrived and he could go back to school.

Lucas had decided that he wouldn't get wrapped up in all of this. He was actually excited by the idea of learning how to use this power that his dad had used. He even wanted to learn more about their history, their family heritage. He wanted to understand where he had come from and what he and his brother were destined to become.

The prophecy really didn't worry him much.

Why worry about it? It seemed in his estimation that there was very little anyone could do to control the outcome. If this was all a divine matter, it was out of their hands anyways. It was like his view on death. You can't escape death so why try to avoid it. Often, trying to prolong your time on Earth by being ultra conservative, led to a dull life and the missing out on exciting adventures.

Everyone worried about his reckless pursuits. He wasn't a gifted athlete, but he had a deep sense of adventure and that is where he thrived the most. He loved to rock climb without gear. He liked to explore caves with deep crevices and harrowing walls to climb up and down on. He longed for his yearly white water rafting trips that the family would take out west each summer. He enjoyed living on the edge of life. This whole prophecy thing was just one more adventure waiting for him to go on.

"Mr. McGregor. Do you have something for me?" The voice of Mr. Voldakov had broken up his thoughts and even sent a shiver up his spine.

Mr. Voldakov was an older man who still was built like a brick wall. His heavy Russian accent led to many jokes by the students that he was probably some ex KGB agent who could kill you in a million different ways you didn't think were possible.

He was the newest teacher in the high school and not someone you played with. Nobody wanted to go one on one with the professor in his office if you didn't turn in your homework. His icy glare and his big hands were enough to make you consider jumping out the window and ending your own life, because dying at his hands would probably be painful.

Lucas stammered as he opened up his book and rummaged through all of this papers that he kept together. He knew the make-up work from his bombed test was stashed in there somewhere. He had to find it quickly before he ended up in his office for a lecture.

"Do you have it or not?"

"I have it, Sir. I know it's here somewhere. I did it last night."

"You absolutely blew up your test this week, Son. You should have put more work into it than just one night. How can you learn this stuff if you don't study it?"

"Bombed it, Sir."

"Excuse me?"

"Bombed it. You said I blew up my test, but we don't say 'blew up' – we say, 'bombed it'. You completely bombed..." Lucas looked into the icy glare of his teacher and then cowered, "...you can say blew it up. That works too." He yanked the paper out of his folder and passed it to his teacher who snatched it away with a quick swipe of his hand – his eyes still boring down on him.

"Find your seat, Mr. McGregor."

Lucas didn't hesitate. He scrambled to his desk and sat down as one of the boys behind him snickered. He looked over and caught the crystal, light blue eyes of Andrea locked on him. She smiled and said softly, "If you were having troubles in class, why didn't you mention it to me? I'm at your house all the time anyways."

"No offense, but that's a little embarrassing. Being tutored by my twin brother's girlfriend? Thanks, but I think I'll pass," he offered a warm smile back as he dug out his notebook from his backpack and got ready for class.

He was appreciative of her offer but afraid at the same time. Lucas had a hard time understanding what she saw in his brother. In so many ways, she was so much like him and less like Caleb. As kids, the three of them would be playing in the yard while their parents talked about "parent stuff" and he always had this crush on her. At night he would dream of holding her hand. Going on adventures together. He wanted to be the one to marry her one day – yet it was Caleb that she was with.

Sure it was high school and the chances were that one day they would be broken up and maybe his dreams would come true, but that would be too weird. There was no chance that he could ever date her. No chance of ever being with her. As much as he loved her sweet personality, her loving life to the fullest attitude, and her gentle compassion, he could never fall in love with her. That just didn't seem natural.

While he would always have a strong bond and respect for her, he also had made it a firm decision to never entertain thoughts of them falling in love. Having her at his house all the time was hard enough. Having her sit next to him and teach him how to pass his chemistry test in a close environment like that, would be downright murder. It was better to keep that door closed completely than to have it cracked open at all.

Lucas already knew that there was someone out there for him. Since Saturday morning when his dad talked about this other world, he was finding himself daydreaming about this beautiful girl that was there waiting for him. She was adorned in an all-white dress that flowed down, hugging all of her curves. There was this bright light set behind her making her look like an angel. Even now as he thought about this girl of his dreams, he began to push out all thoughts of Andrea and felt a warming sensation flood over him.

"Do you have an answer, Mr. McGregor?"

Lucas could hear the chuckles in the room. He was busted for daydreaming and he had no idea what answer Mr. Voldakov was looking for.

"I could guess, Sir. But I'd be dead wrong," honesty was the best policy.

"Right you are, Mr. McGregor. I will see you after class in my office."

He felt a shrinking sensation – as if he just became three sizes smaller than everyone else in the class. He slid down in his desk, hoping to disappear behind the other bodies in the room. Out of sight, out of mind was now the policy that would keep him alive until the final bell. What dreaded assignment would Mr. Voldakov give him for not paying attention in class? He could think of a number of tasks that would ruin his plans for the evening.

The bell seemed to sound rather quickly that day and Lucas was off to face his punishment. He took a few calming deep breaths and then walked into Mr. Voldakov's office. His fear was gone and it was replaced with confidence maybe even a bit of swagger. He was determined not to appear intimidated by the old Russian.

"Most students walk in here and mumble and cry from right where you are standing," Mr. Voldakov was quick to say. "You actually looked scared when I told you to see me after class. I am impressed. You can control your fear with thought. That is a powerful trait of a true warrior. You are to be commended."

Lucas raised an eyebrow. A warrior? What made him use the term of warrior? Who even used that word these days?

The professor handed him an envelope and Lucas slowly reached out and took it. "What's this?"

"A letter for your parents. Make sure they get it."

Now fear returned. He could control his fear of Mr. Voldakov, but his fear of his parents was an entirely different matter. No doubt that this letter contained a written account of all of his bombed tests and late homework assignments. He was doomed once his parents read this.

"Mr. Voldakov, is there any way I can avoid giving this

to Mom and Dad?"

"I think not. I should have given this to them when I got here, but I did not. Now they must have it. They must know. Now go away. You have more classes."

I am in such deep trouble, Lucas thought. *I am a dead man walking.*

But when his parents read the letter that night, they never spoke to him about it. They didn't ground him, they didn't lecture him. They just read the letter, folded it back up and placed it in the envelope and tossed it in the garbage. There was an uneasy glance exchanged between them, but nothing more. It was not their typical response to trouble at school.

"So…" he said with a puzzlement, waiting for the fires of God to rain down on him. He hated to unleash the punishment on himself, but he had to know. He couldn't just wait for them to dish out what he had coming. He knew about the bombed tests and the missed assignments. He knew he hadn't put everything into the school year and he would rather face the consequences now than to have that cloud hang over him all night long. He just wanted to be done with it.

"Don't make any plans tonight. Plan on being here with us," Gavin finally said.

"I'll do better. I promise."

"It's not about your grades, Lucas," Catrina said. She walked over and wrapped her arms around him, pulling him in tight. For a slender figure, she had muscles that practically could squeeze the life out of an elephant. Typically he enjoyed a hug from his mom, but this one had something dreadful to it. It was a hug that also came with a dark omen.

Lucas wrapped his arms around his mom and returned the hug. He looked up and caught the eyes of his dad looking right at him. Gavin gave him a slight nod of his head, but Lucas still wasn't catching on. "What?" Lucas finally asked.

"They're coming and there's nowhere for us to run."

6

Caleb was working with one of the coaches on some of his throwing mechanics when the first scream came from somewhere near the school. Two more piercing screams echoed through the yard and everyone turned to see what was going on.

Four men in long, flowing robes, took gradual steps towards the football field. Their faces were concealed beneath the hoods and in their right hands they held gleaming objects that appeared to be swords – though they were still a ways off and it was hard to tell. For all intents, they seemed to be a few weeks early for Halloween.

Suddenly sirens began to howl somewhere in the distance. Police cars? Did these guys have anything to do with the police sirens? Caleb wondered.

The head coach of the team was the first to sound the warning bells, "Guys, get behind me."

Nobody took heed. Like Caleb, this just seemed like four men dressed too early for a Halloween party or some sort of prank. It didn't ring as if it could be truth.

The coach called out to the men, "We're having practice! I need you four to clear the field. For your own safety!"

From the group of the men, a sly cackle could be heard. The first warning of danger pinged in the back of Caleb's mind and sent a shiver down his spine. Something was wrong. This was all wrong. "Coach, get back!" Caleb let the words slip out of his mouth just seconds before one of the cloaked men raised his hand and unleashed a ball of brilliant fire.

It roared through the air and slammed into the coach, throwing him back and to the ground. The fire seemed to melt into his chest and then from inside it began to do its work. Smoke began to come out of his ears and mouth. His skin bubbled and darkened and soon exploded into flames as did his eyes as they dissolved in their sockets before flames jumped out and reached into the air. In seconds his body was engulfed in flames and it burned down into ash.

Like that, it was over.

The brave players of the Tarrin football team became terrified children as they screamed and finally took the coaches advice and ran for their lives. Three squad cars jumped over the curb and screamed towards the four attackers. Caleb was frozen still.

In his head, the warning gave way to voices. They were hissing voices and all of them were saying in unison, "We have the answers, Caleb. We have what you seek most. Fame, fortune and the pursuit of your dreams. We have the answers, Caleb. We have what you seek most. Fame, fortune and the pursuit of your dreams." The hissing voices continued the same statements over and over, holding him in place. He was attracted to this danger that approached him.

Three of the attackers broke off and each one seemed to be focused on one of the three police cars while the middle one continued to walk straight forward – towards Caleb. From under the hood, he spoke, "We can give you true freedom, Caleb. Come with me and I will free you from what you fear most."

This voice wasn't a hissing voice. It was a cool, warming and pleasant voice. The voice was truthful and had a deep concern in his tone. From behind him, Caleb saw one of the cloaked men fire multiple balls of fire at one of the police cars which flipped end over end before exploding in a shower of debris. The other two dark figures followed his example and did the same thing, sealing the fate of all three squad cars and their drivers.

"Come with us, Caleb. Your true destiny awaits," the figure said as it drew close. He no longer held a sword in his gloved hand. Instead he was extending it out towards him, in a gesture of, "Come with me. I'll take you where you need to go."

Caleb took a step forward. The offer was too great to resist.

"No, Caleb! Don't move!" it was a familiar voice.

Reluctantly, Caleb broke his stare off from the

approaching man in a black cloak and sought for the source of the new player in the game. To his surprise, it was one of the team players. The helmet came off from his head and he threw it with great force into the skull of the approaching cloaked figure who stumbled back. Caleb looked closely at his teammate and realized that it was Nate Sanders.

Of all people, it was Nosey Nate that was coming to his rescue?

Nate reached into the back of his football pants and pulled out a metal rod that almost looked like a sword hilt. He gripped it firmly in his right hand and then flicked it down towards the ground. From the top of the handle, little pieces of metal seemed to roll out, but instead of crashing to the ground, they grabbed on to one-another and began to pile up, extending outward until they had formed a long sword blade. With a quick glow, the seams all came together into one straight and solid metallic weapon.

"Get behind me," Nate said as he jabbed his sword straight into the chest of the tempter. The cloaked figure screamed with a high pitched cry as death overtook it. It wasn't a natural human scream. It was something demonic — a cross between an eagle's cry, a small child screaming at its highest pitch and the screech of fingernails down the chalk board.

As it collapsed to the ground, its hood rolled back just enough to reveal a human like face that looked as if it hadn't eaten food in days. The skin was pulled tight against the bone structure of the skull, the eyes glowing red. The stringy white hair was twisted in knots and matted down. With a hiss, it exhaled its last breath and died.

Caleb shook the fog from his head and suddenly realized the danger he was in. He seemed to have fallen into a trance. The voices were gone and the comforting feeling he had once had was now replaced with icy fear that he could taste in his mouth. He shook, cold from the shock that had overtaken him. He tried to get control of his emotions and of his own body but he was having a hard time discerning reality from hallucination.

Was that really Nosey Nate who just drove a sword through the chest of something in a black cloak? Did he really just watch his coach be reduced to ashes? Are there really three police cars in burning heaps lying on the practice field?

None of it seemed real. He submitted to Nate as his teammate grabbed him by the arm and began to pull him away from the final three cloaked figures. Deep inside he knew that he needed guidance to get out of this mess. He simply did his best to keep his feet moving fast enough to keep up with Nate as he guided him back towards the parking lot.

"I need you to snap to it, Boy!" he could hear Nate hollering through the loud ringing that still kept him in a daze. "We need to get you home. We'll make a stand there until help arrives."

Caleb tried to answer him but his mouth just dropped open and no words would come out. He stumbled and nearly fell to the ground on numerous occasions, but Nate was there to offer a helping hand and brace him from collapsing.

"You're going to be okay, Caleb. We'll get you and your brother out of here and to safety. The Order is already sending in the big guns."

What did that even mean? Who is the Order and what in the world are the big guns? He slightly recalled a conversation with his dad over the weekend but somehow, none of it was connecting together. It was as if his brain was short circuiting and he was getting a series of error messages. Did those creatures do something to his mind?

He couldn't recall the point at which he climbed into Nate's car. He didn't even remember the ride home. All he could see was the sight of his coach being incinerated and a dazzling display of explosions as three police officers died from balls of fired hurled from the hands of these mysterious cloaked men.

Nate was quick to usher him into the house and slam the door tightly behind them. If it wasn't strange enough to have one of his football teammates come to his rescue brandishing a sword, it was even stranger when he realized that someone else was holding a sword and standing in the middle of his living room.

Caleb blinked rapidly a few times, shaking his head and

trying desperately to make sure he wasn't seeing things. He looked again and sure enough, the man from his school was still standing there.

"Mr. Voldakov?" Caleb asked.

"It is going to be alright, Caleb," he said in his heavy, Russian accent. "Help is on the way. In the meantime, you have me, my student and your dad."

Gavin walked in with a sword in each hand. He held them as if they were natural extensions of his body. He seemed to be as comfortable with them as he was his own gun, or the television remote. Did the world that their dad told them about on Saturday, just come crashing in through their front door? The very people his parents had run from, had suddenly showed up and were now their allies?

"I thought you didn't trust them?" Caleb said. His strength was beginning to return and the warnings that he heard in his head, now were making sense.

"We're going to be seriously outnumbered, Caleb. We're going to have to trust Master Vladamir and his Apprentice," Gavin said as he walked across the room and brushed back the curtain. He looked off in every direction, searching for something – probably more of the crazy people in black robes.

"And what do we do when we push back the bad guys and suddenly we find ourselves surrounded by the Knights of Liberty?" Lucas asked.

Vladamir slowly pulled on a pair of brown leather gloves and didn't look up when he answered, "You will have no choice but to trust us then as well, young Lucas. We have been watching you and your family since the day they left The Kingdom. If it was our intention to take you away from your parents or lock you away in some sort of dungeon, we would have already done that. You can no longer be safe here. We can no longer watch in hiding."

"What does that mean?" Caleb asked. He looked to his mom and dad for answers, but their eyes only told him what he feared most.

"It means, young Caleb," Vladamir pulled his last glove tight on his hand and then looked over at him, "The McGregors are returning to where they belong."

7

"Something's moving out there!" Nate said. He was watching the front yard through the bay window in the darkened living room.

"This is silly," Catrina said as she walked into the room and handed Nate a new cup of tea – it was his fourth cup in that hour. Lucas was concerned that If the fight were to break out in the next few minutes, he would be too busy peeing to help defend the family.

Catrina continued, "We could have already packed up the car and gotten out of here – a long way from the prying eyes of the Draith."

Ignoring her comment, Vladamir came alongside his young student. "What do you see?"

"Someone's coming down the road. Not dressed in a robe but definitely not one of ours. It's getting really hard to tell."

Vladamir took his turn pressing his face up to the glass. He used his left hand to shield the glare coming from the kitchen light behind them. "I see him... coming in from the

East."

Caleb jumped up from his spot next to Lucas, "Its Andrea! She walked over." He started to go for the door but Vladamir stepped in front and pushed him back toward the couch. "Hey!"

Vladamir looked over to Nate and nodded his head, "You know the girl?"

"Yes, Master. I had a few classes with her."

"Good. Go out there quietly and see if it is her. If so, bring her home."

"No," Caleb protested. "Bring her here. I need to explain to her what's going on."

"That's not happening," Vladamir replied.

"But if you're going to just whisk us away when this is all done, she needs to know what happened to me. She needs to know I didn't just leave her... like her parents. She already lost her parents. She can't take that again!"

"She'll be okay, Caleb. She has her grandparents. They'll help her get through it." Catrina tried to sooth him but it didn't come close to working.

"I'm not risking the lives of civilians," Vladamir said. "She needs to be a long way from here before..." Vladamir stopped and moved quickly for the window.

"I feel it too, Master," Nate said.

Lucas was startled out of his seat. His eyes frantically searched the room for the source of the voices that he was suddenly hearing. They were more like hisses than voices really, and they came from all around him. The one sentence they seemed to repeat over and over was, "Come with us, Lucas. Come with us, Lucas…"

"He's hearing them!" Gavin called out when he entered the room. "Just like Caleb did. They haven't learned how to shut out the voices."

"We shouldn't be here!" Catrina cried out. She was clutching the stone of her favorite necklace in her right hand. She worked hard to put on a brave display but fear was written in all of her slight movements. Her stroking of the stone, her lips moving in silent prayer. Lucas turned to her to find strength and instead he found a wreck.

"What voices am I hearing?" he asked. "Where are they coming from?"

"Your head," Caleb said in a raspy whisper as he stood in the shadows of the room with his eyes almost glazed over. He wasn't making any movement to rush out and rescue Andrea. He seemed engrossed in listening to the voices. "They are speaking the truth to us."

"NO!" Gavin yelled as he shook Caleb by the shoulders. "They are lies… whispered by the Draith."

Lucas looked over to his brother who continued to be zoned out. The voices continued to speak into his head, yet he didn't seem to be stuck in the same trance as his brother. What was different between the two boys that Caleb would be consumed by the words while he was finding himself agitated and desiring to get them out of his head?

"Andrea!" Lucas called out. "She's still out there!"

"Get her in here, Nate. We'll have to take our chances with protecting her as well."

Nate scrambled around the furniture and ran out the front door. Lucas walked over to his dad and then asked, "Dad, I want these voices out."

"Vladamir is right. We don't have time to teach you how to block them, but you seem unaffected anyways. Help me get your brother to the couch. It's going to be your job to make sure he stays there. Don't let him go out searching for the voices. Can you handle that?"

Lucas nodded his head up and down. Through dry lips he asked, "Who are the Draith?"

Gavin opened his mouth to answer when suddenly Nate came into the room with a kicking and screaming Andrea in his arms. He tossed her into the room with force and then slammed the door behind him.

"You bit me!" Nate said.

"What do you think you're doing you creep? Have you turned into some sort of stalker..." she looked around the room and became quiet.

Lucas touched her lightly on the shoulder and she jumped away in fear. She turned and for the first time caught a glimpse of Caleb.

"Did they get him?" she called out as she dropped by his side and began to rush her hands over his face and through his hair. "I heard what those men did at the school. Did they get Caleb?"

"He's fine… I think," Lucas said as he knelt beside her.

She looked back at Gavin who was armed with swords. Her eyes darted from the swords, to his face and then back at the swords. She seemed to be turning the image around in her mind for answers. When she was certain that she wasn't going to guess what was going on, she turned to Lucas and asked, "Why does your dad have a sword in his hand? Why does it seem so creepy in here?"

"I don't even know where to begin," Lucas replied. None of this was even remotely believable or explainable.

"It's bad… really bad," Nate said as he scrambled in from the back rooms.

"The bite?" Andrea asked.

"I wish it were just about a bite," Vladamir said in his thick accent. "Coming in from the East?"

Her eyes locked on the tall man who was a teacher at the school but now seemed to be standing in the McGregor house holding a sword. Her mouth opened as if she were about to ask someone to clarify why he was here and then she just seemed to give up and turned her attention back to Caleb.

"More like every direction, Master."

"They all have swords," Andrea observed as she looked over to Lucas with wide eyes. "What is going on?"

"Keep your head down and stay with me," Catrina said as she wrapped her arm over Andrea's shoulder. "When it's all over, I'll explain everything," she huddled Lucas and her over Caleb's motionless body while Gavin disappeared to the dining room to look out the back door. Vladamir went into one of the rooms on the East side. Nate remained with them in the living room.

All was silent. The calm only made the voices in Lucas' head even that much louder.

The darkness gave way to a glowing blast of hot, orange light as the glass of the large picture framed window exploded and balls of fire ripped into the wall behind the couch that Lucas, Catrina, Andrea and Caleb were huddled over. The flames licked the back of the couch and Catrina was quick to pat them out with her hand while the fire moved up the wall and began to dance along the ceiling. More balls of fire rushed into the room, each one increasing the intensity of the heat and each one blasting through the walls and engulfing the room in flames.

"They're not wasting time. They're trying to burn up our only protection," Nate observed.

"I told you we should have left as soon as we could. What made you think we'd last a second in here against them?"

"What makes you think we'd last a second out there? They're Draith. If we accidently bumped into one, the rest would teleport to the exact location and we'd be finished."

"Who are the Draith?" Andrea asked.

"Good luck getting an answer," Lucas replied.

"If we hold out long enough, the reinforcements should get to us and we'll have them outnumbered."

"You hope."

More balls ripped into the room. The recliner erupted into flames while the lamp on the end table exploded into a shower of porcelain and glass. The carpet began to go up in flames. The house shook as more balls of fire slammed into the house. The darkness had given way to the dancing glow of flames that continued to consume the house. Lucas started to feel as if he was too close to a bon fire as his eyes watered from the heat.

"We can't stay in here much longer!" Nate called out to Vladamir. "We need a new plan!"

Vladamir and Gavin both came into the room with their swords at the ready. Gavin looked over to his family near the couch. He motioned with his head for them to get up and then pointed at Caleb as well, "Get him up. We're making a break for it. We'll go through the back door and make straight for the woods. The three of us should be able to buy you four enough time to get into cover. Lucas, go as deep into the woods as you can. Get back to the old Peterson barn and get into the basement. We'll join you as soon as we can."

"Dad, with Caleb like this, we won't be able to move fast."

"Find a way. You need to do this, Son. I need you to do this."

"Yes, Sir. I'll do my best."

Vladamir walked over and scooped Caleb up from the couch. He draped him over Lucas's shoulders and then gave him a pat on the back to move him towards the dining room – also glowing with heat and fire. "We don't have time to talk anymore. We will blaze a path. You get them to the place your dad spoke of."

Without even a second to protest, Vladamir and Nate dove out the frame of the shattered glass sliding doors and began to swing their swords wildly. The pinging and clanking of metal echoed from outside. Gavin kissed Catrina on the forehead and jumped out after them.

"Go!" Andrea cried out. "Follow them!"

With a quick adjustment of Caleb on his shoulders, Lucas lumbered forward and nearly collapsed to the ground when he smashed his brother's head into the side of the frame and was jerked off balance. Catrina stabilized him and they struggled across the lawn.

Gavin locked blades with a cloaked figure. He swung his sword high for the head but the opposing warrior was quick to block. He then went low and was blocked again. With a quick twist of his wrist, he slid his sword over the top of the enemies and then came up with a deadly hook that took the cloaked figures head clean off.

Gavin then darted ahead and continued to guide his family forward. The glowing light returned and encased his dad like it had the other day in the woods. The tentacles began to dance around and then they reached out and began to scoop things up and hurl them at other cloaked figures. At one point one of the tentacles picked up one of the warriors and tossed him into the night sky.

As Lucas risked a quick glance around, he caught the sight of Vladamir and Nate using the same power of light and dispatching their enemies quickly.

Bolts of lightning tore through the air. Some of these hit trees that exploded in a shower of splinters and bark. Others connected with the blades of Gavin, Nate and Vladamir. Balls of fire came in and they used their tentacles of light to smash them back at the person who created them.

Hisses and screams of anger awakened the wildlife in the woods. Birds cried out as they scrambled into the air. Lucas barely missed the first tree as he entered into the woods with his mom and Andrea with Caleb weighing him down and making him move clumsily through the forest.

"Don't smash his head into anything," he heard his mom call out.

He took a quick look back and he could see the glowing

white light of three men battling with dark figures as the glow of the burning house lit up the night sky. What would the people of the town think when they read about this in the weekly paper?

The farther he got from the house the quieter the voices became in his head. He could finally think straight as he gained new strength and continued to keep pace with the girls. "Mom, I'm not sure, but I think you need to angle more to your right. It feels like we are going too far to the West!"

She must have heard him and made an adjustment because his internal compass seemed to be happy with the new bearing. If it wasn't for the full moon above, Lucas was sure he would have killed himself on a tree, but he knew these woods better than anyone and the moonlight was just enough to help him navigate through it safely.

Suddenly the voices returned, but they were different. They were more like squawky human voices instead of the hissing demonic tones he had heard before. He also didn't feel the confusion that he had heard back at the house. The voices got louder and then he could hear the snapping of twigs and the crunching of leaves. Added to that was the clomping of what sounded like a stampeded of horses.

"We're not alone!" Lucas cried out. "Run faster!"

Catrina stopped and reached back to help pull Lucas ahead and move him along faster when she was suddenly snagged and pulled into the darkness.

"MOM!"

Andrea turned to look back. She suddenly became aware of a noise just off to her right and turned just in time to catch the sight of something that horrified her. She let out a scream just before the shadows of the woods gave birth to creatures that let out wicked cries of glee as they scooped her up on the run and then disappeared into the same part of the night that had swallowed up his mom.

"ANDREA!"

The ground shook slightly as thundering footsteps drew close. Lucas skidded to a halt and laid Caleb down on the ground. "Dad?" Oh how he had hoped that his dad and the others had arrived. He searched the ground and found a thick branch lying within arm's length. He picked it up and turned to the direction of the footsteps. "Where's my Mom?"

"Silly boy," a deep voice growled in the darkness. More thundering steps as it drew even closer and now Lucas could make out a silhouette in the shadows. It was a massive bulk of a two legged creature that was coming close. His head seemed to be the size of a large truck tire with horns sticking out on top. "What do you plan to use that for?" it asked him.

"If you don't give them back... you're going to find out."

The beast seemed to chuckle at that thought and continued to move forward. "I smell your fear, boy. I smell your self-doubt. You are not a warrior but just a little boy." It drew closer.

It just began to emerge from the darkness when a beam of white light tore through the night sky and scooped him up off his feet and tossed him into the woods. Branches snapped and trees shook as he plowed through the tops and landed with a rumble somewhere in the distance. Gavin, glowing white, rushed up alongside his son with his sword drawn and ready to attack.

"Where's your Mom and Andrea?"

"Something got them. A bunch of things got them."

Vladamir and Nate joined them, also glowing as the balls of light encased them. Vladamir peered into the dark. "We don't have much time before they catch up. We need to keep moving. Where are the girls?"

"Gone," Gavin said as he pulled Caleb up to his feet and threw him over his shoulder. "They got them both. Which direction did they go?"

Lucas pointed into the darkness.

"We can't worry about them now, Gavin. We need to protect the boys. I need to protect them. I promised your father long ago that I would watch over his heirs. Tonight is too dangerous. Tonight, I need you to trust me that I am loyal to the McGregor family and to the Order and that I have both you and your children's best interests in mind. I can't have your loyalty divided."

"My loyalty?" Gavin drew up face to face with the taller Vladamir. "She's my wife... my family. We all get out of here or none of us!"

"You're willing to let your own son's be destroyed at the hands of the Draith? You're willing to sacrifice them for the life of your wife?"

"And Andrea," Lucas added. "She's not a part of any of this."

The woods began to come alive as the enemy drew near. Trees erupted into flames and lightning weaved through the foliage, searching for someone who might be out in the open and be struck by surprise.

"If I had to venture a guess, I would say the girls are safe," Vladamir said as he observed the destruction coming their way. "For the prophecy to be fulfilled, they need the boys to return to the Kingdom. The girls will be their insurance. We have been played for fools."

"What do you mean?" Gavin asked as he surveyed the night before them – probably calculating where the barn was.

"The Draith know that we have them outnumbered in this world. They knew we would overwhelm them with the power of the Knights of Liberty here. So they grabbed some insurance to make sure we would follow them back into the Kingdom. I know your thoughts, Gavin. As soon as we defeat the Draith, you and your family would have slipped away and went back on the run. There can be no doubt that the Dark Master knew this as well. He is using your wife and Caleb's girlfriend as bait to make sure you return."

Gavin gestured for everyone to follow them and they made their way through the woods. He looked back briefly to direct his question at Vladamir, "You're saying that the boys were never the intended target?"

"Oh, they were *a* target, but not *the* target. Not yet at least. If they would have captured the boys, they would have never made it out of this world with them. They divided their forces, knowing we would put everyone on the twins and then they used a second force to grab the girls. Now they can slip into the Kingdom with their captives and know without a doubt that we will pursue them."

Gavin was puffing hard as he jumped over logs and brought them into a clearing filled with tall grass. The old barn was just ahead. "Why would they assume we would bring the boys with us on a rescue mission?"

"Because you are predictable, Gavin. You don't trust the Order and you know they are not safe here. You'll bring the boys with you in order to protect them... but in fact, you will be doing exactly what they want you to do."

As they drew near the barn, Gavin stopped and turned around. His eyes danced between Nate and Vladamir, his anger showing from the contortions on his face. "We were all fine until you two showed up. We wouldn't be in this predicament..." Gavin's face relaxed, no doubt realizing that it wasn't their fault that all of this was happening.

Suddenly, the slight bit of calmness that they had found

near the barn gave way to a screeching whistling sound. Like an artillery round, balls of fire came howling from the sky and slammed into the ground, showering the four men with earth and shards of flaming plasma.

"Back!" Vladamir called out and they scrambled closer to the barn.

"She's loaded with old hay," Gavin said. "If you thought the house burned down fast…"

"The others will be here soon. We will have to hold our place here."

"They won't hesitate to kill us," Gavin said as he crouched down by Vladamir. "But the boys must leave here alive. They won't risk their lives… yet they're lobbing this stuff in here like they don't care."

"They are being rather reckless. Perhaps the safest thing for the boys is for us to leave them here and we take the fight to them."

Gavin nodded his head up and down. What they would do next, they would do for the safety of the boys.

"Dad!" Lucas called out. "You are safer with us. Use us as shields and protect yourselves… well, at least protect yourself." His eyes looked over to Vladamir and he caught a faint glimpse of a smile come across the cold hard face of the Russian like man.

"Young Lucas is right. Nathan and I will handle this. Your place is with your boys."

More balls of fire exploded in the barn behind them, raining down pieces of wood and shingles with blades of straw floating down to the ground. The ground shook as lightning cracked into the surface and the deafening snap of electricity pierced their ears. The world seemed to be collapsing around them.

Gavin crouched down next to his boys and Vladamir and Nate took off for a last stand. Gavin glowed as the bright light that encased him seemed to grow brighter. As balls of fire came close, the tentacles reached out and batted them away from the boys. For the first time in all of the chaos, Lucas felt safe. He looked up and watched as his dad do things he had never seen him do before.

He commanded the arms of light to deflect debris, to catch a falling concrete wall and push it safely to the side, to grab a Draith that got to close and hurl him off into the woods. From time to time he would jump back up onto his feet and use his sword to deflect a ball of fire back at its sender, using his sword like a baseball bat. He was calm and in perfect control as the destructive power of the Draith showered them with deadly force.

Was Vladamir and Nate still alive? Lucas chanced a glance up over the tall blades of grass and caught a glimpse of two glowing balls fighting their way through a crowd of cloaked, black figures – all dancing among the fires in the field. The hissing voices grew louder and more prevalent but soon they collectively let out a screech that caused Gavin to drop to his knees, plugging his ears with his fingers the same as Lucas now did.

Caleb was still in a zombie state and didn't seem to care. Lucas was glad that the screaming wasn't coming from his head like the hissing voices did. He started to notice a new sound in the arena. There were voices of men and the clashing of metal. The screams began to diminish and with it the voices in his head started to be silenced.

He slowly looked up and saw that the field was now filled with white glowing figures that were decimating the Draith who refused to surrender. Swords were driven into the chest of some and they shrieked and died. Others had their heads cut off or were picked up by a tentacle and hurled into the night sky. One Light bearer, scooped up a Draith, twisted him in the air and then drove him head first into the ground.

The balls of fire were no longer being hurled at them and the battle seemed to be dying fast. Gavin reached over and helped Caleb and Lucas to their feet.

"We're getting out of here!"

"But what about Mom and Andrea?"

"We're going after them – without the help of the Knights of Liberty. We'll go and find them and get them back here. Then we are going to disappear forever."

Lucas couldn't contain the smile that grew over his face. He loved adventure, but this evening was more than he ever wanted to experience again. Keeping these creeps out of their lives sounded like a great idea. But he did have one concern, "What about Nate and Mr. Voldakov?"

"They've earned my trust. They will meet up with us on the other side but we need to act as if we escaped their watchful eyes."

"Was this their idea? Don't they trust the Knights of Liberty?"

"Oh, they trust the Order. But Vladamir made a promise to my father many years ago. He will do as I ask because of that promise. They may have found us, but they won't be controlling us."

With that, Gavin took the lead.

They crouched down low and began moving away from the battle as they used the tall grass for as much concealment as it could provide. Caleb was still in a bit of a fog, but he was at least able to walk on his own and follow the occasional instruction.

The three of them quietly slipped out of sight and headed deep into the woods. They moved quickly, navigating through a large swamp that would keep the Knights of Liberty and any Draith stragglers from following. Only Gavin knew the lone safe and dry route through the swamp areas of Tarrin. He had discovered it during his many years of hunting back here and now he was using it to get a leg up on those who might pursue.

"Dad," Caleb asked as the sun began to rise and light their way through the thick bramble that grew on the edge of the swamp land. "What's going on?"

It had taken a long time to clear his head of the influence of the Draith. He was just now realizing that his world was much different than when he had fallen under the trance.

"It's a long story and we have a long journey ahead of us. I'll explain everything. Just be patient and keep moving. We have a long way to go and we can't risk being seen."

"Where are we going?" Lucas asked. Sure he knew that they were going back to the Kingdom that the McGregor family had come from, but what route they would take was still unknown.

"Back to the gate that brought us here. Back to where this all began."

8

"They have all been destroyed, my Master. Every last Draith that you sent has been destroyed."

"It is an acceptable loss… one I knew must happen for my plans to be furthered. Their deaths have actually increased the powers of my remaining Draith. It is a victory on many levels. The loss of life is the beginning of even greater power. You will one day see this."

"But the boys have fled with their father."

"Yes, but as I told you… I had another plan in play. My Draith have long been outnumbered in that world. I knew they could not withstand the sheer number of Knights of Liberty and therefore I created an incentive for the father to return to our world."

"And you are certain they will come here?"

"Mideon has succeeded in his work. He has brought the wife of Gavin into our world. Gavin will never trust the safety of the twins to the Knights of Liberty. You have seen to that for me. Instead, he will bring them along for a rescue mission. Thus, bringing them to me."

* * * * *

Caleb was famished. He had lost nearly an entire day of his life being in some sort of zombie state and during that time he was sure that nobody took the time to make sure he got something to eat. His stomach twisted and cursed him for letting it get to this point. Moving through the woods and then sprinting across open fields was quickly draining his energy.

"Dad, we've got to stop and get something to eat!"

"We can't risk it right now. I need you to toughen up and keep moving for a while longer. I have a safe place for us to stay for a quick rest. We can get some food, a change of clothes, and some transportation to get us to the gate."

"What do you mean by a safe place? Are we talking a house?" Lucas asked.

"No… kind of. It's a bug out shelter. At least that's what I call it. In the event that the Draith or the Knights of Liberty found us, I built an underground bunker with enough supplies to sustain us while I worked out a long term solution. It's a piece of land that a family friend gave me. A piece of land that I am sure nobody knows we have in our possession."

Caleb felt a wash of strength come over him knowing that there was hope for a rest in the near future. He was curious about the bunker though. He could only think of one family they had ever grown close to in his lifetime – and other than their daughter, they were all dead. To keep his mind off of his roaring belly he asked a few more questions, "Who was the family friend?"

"Chuck and Lisa – Andrea's parents. Chuck was a doomsday prepper and he convinced me to invest and help him build a bug out shelter for some day in the future when nukes rain down on America or the economy collapsed or whatever apocalyptic crisis might come. While he built it for that reason, I wanted it in case of this type of scenario. I had hoped to never have to use it."

"Andrea's parents were those type of people?" Caleb was taken aback by this revelation.

"Well… there's more to it than that… but yea. Chuck saw the world in a different light. Besides, there's nothing wrong with being prepared for the worst. It's like the ant and the grasshopper. The ant was ready for winter because he prepared…"

"The grasshopper stole from the ant and the ant ended up dying anyways," Lucas chimed in.

"I'm not sure where you heard that part of the story, but that's not how it went."

"He's messing with you, Dad. I can tell by the stupid grin on his face."

Gavin stopped and took a few deep breaths and then turned and looked at his two sons. For the first time, Caleb saw a strength and resolve that he had never seen before. His dad was moving with purpose and a plan. He wasn't the weak lumber yard worker but was instead looking more like a determined warrior.

"I figured he was either messing with me or I did a seriously poor job teaching you guys the basics of life. How are you both doing?"

"I'm confused," Lucas began, "How did this all happen so fast?"

"I'm starved."

"If we keep moving, we'll be there in an hour or so. I need you both to be super strong for me. We are just getting started on this journey."

"How do we get there... you know... Carsonia?" Lucas asked.

"I mentioned that gate, right?" Gavin picked up a long, thick stick that was lying on the ground and used it as a walking stick as he began to lead them forward. "There are five known gates in Carsonia. Each one can allow a certain number of people to pass through it to come into this world. Once the maximum number of people pass through it, it becomes impassable until someone dies in this world or someone returns to the Kingdom."

"So obviously, not just the Knights of Liberty have control of them. The Draith have access to some of them as well."

"It's been a source of an ongoing war for many years – but that doesn't answer your question. The answer to your question is, there is a sixth gate that only a handful of people know exists. And there is one more that happens to belong to our family. Only we know of its existence. The one we will be using is the sixth one that only a few know of.

"On this side of the gate it is in the Rocky Mountains. On the Carsonian side, it comes out in a small village in the North where the McGregor family originally came from – before destiny made us royalty."

The three of them lumbered on as they crossed an old country road and then sprinted across an open field and dove into the safety of the woods. They continued to press on, but exhaustion was catching up to all of them. Gavin was even beginning to slow a bit and from time to time he stumbled over his own feet.

"So our family is of noble blood?" Lucas asked.

"Yes," Gavin answered between huffs as they climbed a steep hill. By this point in their journey, it had felt more like a mountain. "Our distant ancestor, Callam, came out of the North and settled in the land of McGregor. He joined the King's Army and over time became a trusted knight; eventually earning the title of First Knight. He later fell in love and married the Kings daughter. After a successful assassination attempt on the King, in his dying breath, he left McGregor in Callam's hands. So began the reign of our family. Callam brought peace throughout all of Carsonia as he united the Twelve Kingdoms into the Carsonian Council. He presided over it for many years until he was betrayed by one of his most trusted. From there, the rise of Dark Master Natas began and the Age of Peace came to a bitter end."

"Who's sitting on the throne now?"

"Nobody. After a dark and destructive war between the Bearers of Light who came to be known as the Knights of Liberty and those who mastered dark magic known as The Dark Order of the Draith; the people began a witch hunt and cleansed the land of both. The people chose to reject The Light and instead chose to embrace its own destiny."

"And it didn't pan out?"

Gavin shook his head no and they trudged on — finally reaching the top of the hill and beginning a steep descent.

"So how do we fit in? How did this prophecy begin?" Caleb asked.

"King Callam was able to drive back the forces of the Draith. In his final stand, Dark Master Natas embedded a part of his life force into the King's wife who was pregnant. He prophesied that one day, from the bloodline of King Callam, twin boys would be born. The blood of both would free him from the Shadow World and the blood of one would be linked with him and sit at his right hand as he conquered both worlds. He pledged to make them fall at his feet. In the three thousand years that have passed, you the first twin brothers to be born."

"Is the prophecy true?" Lucas asked.

Gavin didn't answer right away. He seemed to mull the

thought over and from time to time he grunted and opened his mouth as if he were about to speak, but the words just wouldn't come out. They went on in silence for a while. The cracking of twigs and the crunching of leaves under their feet was the only sound.

At last Gavin answered, "I don't think it has to be. I think we all have the ability to choose right from wrong. Maybe one of you can be tempted easier than the other, but I don't think that means you have to choose evil over good. I've always believed that the only true prophecies are spoken by the seers who are called into duty by The Creator. I'm certain Natas isn't a chosen seer so I would say that his prophecy isn't really a prophecy. I think it's more like a spell that he cast. Spells, like all dark magic, can be broken by people who are strong and call on the Light."

He looked back at Caleb and Lucas and gave them a warm smile. "We've raised you both well. I would say that if anyone can break the curse of Natas, it's you two. Be strong and courageous and call on the Light when you are in the darkest of times."

"And how do we do that?" Caleb asked.

"When we get to Carsonia, I'll show you. For now..." he was breathing very hard, "Let's get to the bunker and get a bite to eat and a little shut eye. Once we are in Carsonia, it's going to be a long journey to find your Mom and Andrea."

The last thirty minutes of their trek was done in silence.

They soon arrived at an old logging road that had a rusted chain connected between two poles and a "Do Not Trespass" sign hanging in the center of it, blocking the entrance.

"My stomach is excited," Caleb began as he took the lead.

He walked quickly but soon realized that he didn't hear the crunching of the dry ground by many feet but only by one set – his set of feet. He turned and looked and found that Gavin and Lucas had stopped fifty yards back. They seemed to be waiting for him. As he turned back to join them, Gavin raised his arm in a limp manner and gingerly pointed across his body in an Easterly direction.

"It's that way, Genius," he informed him.

"Well, if you want to go that way, I guess we can." Caleb caught up and followed the two of them until Gavin came to a stop by a series of stumps. He stood alongside of them and then turned to the North. Taking twenty large steps, he came to a stop and then slammed his foot hard into the ground. A metallic clank rang out.

Caleb's face lit up, a smile consuming his handsome features. The pains of the past twenty four hours were gone. Inside he was rejoicing and the thoughts of his Mom and Andrea were sadly far from his mind.

Gavin kicked away leaves and branches until he revealed a metal door. Taking a key that was strung round his neck, he unlatched the lock and opened it up to reveal steps that disappeared into a dark hole. He reached under the lip of the passageway and flicked a switch and florescent lights flickered on and the path down became clear.

"Where is the electricity coming from?" Caleb asked.

"We have a few solar panels concealed in the trees. The wires run into the ground to a secret chamber where they are connected to batteries which in turn, powers the bunker. Now get it. I'm starving."

The boys quickly made their way into the bunker and Gavin closed the hatch and secured the latch behind them. Soon all three were gathered in the small kitchen area, eating cans of corn beef and hash and slices of warmed Spam, devouring some sort of cracker/bread hybrid thing and guzzling countless bottles of water. To the boys, all worries were gone. It felt more like a family hunting trip than the reality that they were on the run for their lives and eventually would need to become rescuers for their loved ones.

They were able to drift off to sleep and after a restful twelve hours, they geared up for their journey. Caleb was in charge of packing food.

Taking an old military ruck sack, he packed it full of packets of dehydrated meals that would last them for a week. Of course they would supplement some of the rations with the fresh game they would surely find along the way. In theory, the packs of food should last for three weeks if the hunting was as good as their dad claimed. He also packed three full canteens of water and three packages of water purification tablets that should last them for a month if need be.

Again, their dad was bragging about the water – claiming it to be the most crisp and pure drinking water anywhere. It still didn't hurt to have the tablets, Caleb figured. With a few more odds and ends, he had their food supplies ready to go.

Lucas was in charge of security and hunting supplies. He found a shot gun that he broke into three smaller pieces to fit into a ruck sack. He also loaded up four boxes of ammunition. The sack could take much more but it was the weight that Lucas was weary of carrying for a long distance. Besides, the gun was for hunting only – maybe as a weapon for protection in a severe emergency – but their dad assured them that his skills of using the Light and his swordsmanship abilities would be enough to protect them all. This kept Lucas from loading up with two full automatic rifles that had been stashed in the shelter. If they should get pulled over, it was probably best not to have these on hand.

Gavin took care of the rest, loading up his ruck sack with whatever he felt might come in handy during their quest. He planned to gather clothing and other supplies once they reached the other side, but he still wanted to have a few of the conveniences from this world with him when they returned to Carsonia.

They set out that day with full belly's and fresh spirits. The bug out truck was a miles walk into the woods and locked away in what looked like an old hunting shack with a car port attached to it. Gavin found the keys where they had hidden them and then fired up the vehicle, which ran rough from sitting idle for three years. Caleb grabbed three cans of gasoline and tossed them in the back and then they were off.

It took a solid day and night of driving to get into the Smoky Mountains and then they abandoned the truck and hiked into the hills. By day break, they came to a skinny waterfall that concealed Gavin's secret gate.

"How is it that so few in Carsonia knew of this gate?" Lucas asked.

"Callam's father had discovered it. He feared what could happen if people from their world stepped into this world or vice versa, so he never spoke of it to anyone. He only charged the McGregor family with the task of keeping it protected and using it only in the event of dire need. Unfortunately, the Draith discovered new ways to open new gates. By the time the Knights of Liberty thwarted their efforts, they had opened five new ones."

"So this is how you came to this world?" Caleb asked.

"It wasn't my first choice... but yes. The gate I wanted to use was closer to the academy, but I couldn't risk being caught so we took a longer route and passed over through this one."

Gavin walked up to an over grown area and began to pull back shrubs and vines. When Caleb and Lucas realized he was doing it for a reason, they began removing the camouflage as well and soon, rude yet functioning steps that were carved into the rock, were revealed. The climb was dangerous as the three of them crawled up the steps on their hands and knees.

"You brought a pregnant woman down these steps?" Caleb asked.

Gavin didn't answer at first. He just struggled onward. Finally, between breaths he said, "She wasn't that far along."

"Lucky she didn't go into labor right here in the mountains. We'd probably be a couple of hillbillies right now."

"It's easier going down than back up. Besides, your mom's a natural adventurer. You get that from her, Lucas."

"She doesn't seem like someone who likes adventure."

"Trust me… there's a side of her you have never seen. Adventure is definitely in her blood. You see a bit of it when we are out rafting. If she wasn't trying to be a mother hen, we'd be going down the most treacherous of white water rapids."

"I'd like to see that one day," Lucas said as he wiped the spray from his face. As they drew closer to the falls, a fine mist began to settle on them and made the steps slick.

"You'll get to see that, Lucas. We're going to get her back."

It suddenly hit Caleb that there was a bigger problem that they didn't address before leaving home, "Andrea's grandparents! They have no idea where she is. They're going to be in a panic. They probably have half the county out looking for her."

Gavin stopped climbing and looked back at the panicked face of his son. He seemed to twist that revelation around in his mind and finally he said, "There really is nothing we can do about it, Caleb. When we get her back, they'll just have to rejoice and hold her tight. There's no way we can call them now and tell them that she was kidnapped and taken back to Carsonia."

"Back to Carsonia?"

Gavin looked surprised. He was about to say something, paused, then finally huffed and said, "You know what I mean."

But Caleb wasn't sure. Why did he get flustered over misspeaking?

He figured it must have been nothing and that his dad was just feeling the weight of all the recent days' struggles and simply misspoke. He was reading into something that wasn't there. Yea, that had to be it.

This whole thing seemed crazy and unbelievable. His life would never be the same no matter how hard he tried to imagine repairing the damage that's been done by all of this.

How would he explain to Andrea that he wasn't really from Tarrin, Wisconsin? How would he explain that he's really some freak from another world and that he can't live out his dreams because even bigger freaks of nature would find him and hunt him down like a dog? How could anything ever be returned to the way it was – let alone, how would they explain all of this to her grandparents who will have been worried sick for who knows how long before she is found and returned to them?

"Come on guys. The sooner we get this done, the sooner we get back to living out our lives in safety."

"How do you figure, Dad?" Caleb said in a gruff tone. "They'll just come back, hunt us down like before and we're back to running again."

"Because I'm going to do what I should have done the first time. I'm going to destroy every gate except this one. We'll come back through and then seal this one forever as well. Once we come back, they'll be no way for them to come after us. And those that are already here will have nowhere to go. I'm ending this the way I should have all those years ago. If I would have known that all this would backfire..." he left that one unfinished.

But his words rekindled hope in Caleb. Perhaps there was a chance for him and his dreams yet.

They crawled up behind the waterfall and found an entrance to a small cave. It wasn't very far back to go before they found a glowing light that ran from the ceiling of the cave to the floor and was just wide enough for someone to slip through if they turned to the side.

"Listen, guys. Carsonia will be very dangerous. I want us to keep as low of a profile as possible. I want to slip in, find your mom and Andrea and then get you guys back here and out of there. I'm going to stay back and seal off all of the gates."

"By yourself?" both asked in unison.

"No. Vladamir promised he would help me protect you both. I'm guessing he will help me seal them all up. It might take a while so I'm going to train you both in the arts of using the Light and using swords. My dad was a fine swordsman and I was far more advanced than the other students my age. When we get to Carsonia, we should have time for me to teach you what you need to survive. Then I need you to protect your mom while I seal up the gates."

"That's crazy, Dad," Caleb said.

"That's the deal. I need you both to grow up and follow my orders like good soldiers. Everything depends on it."

Caleb reluctantly nodded his head up and down while Lucas seemed to give it more thought.

"Lucas," his dad said. "I need your promise that you *will* follow orders."

"Yea. I will."

Gavin nodded his head up and down and then motioned for Caleb to step up to the light. "You'll feel yourself sucked in once you enter into the light. Just go with it. Don't fight it. You'll rip yourself in half if you do."

"What! What type of crazy is this?"

Gavin broke into a full roll laugh and then choked out the words, "It's a joke. Just let it take you and you'll pass through a lot quicker."

With Lucas nearly on the floor laughing, Caleb slowly let his fingers touch the glowing light. He could feel what seemed like little lips of goldfish coming up and nibbling on his fingers in search of food as the light tried to latch on and pull him in. Slowly he let his hand go into it and now he felt a full tug. As his arm went inside, he could feel his body being pulled forward and soon he was completely inside. Just as fast as he went into the bright light, he stumbled out the other side.

His ears exploded with the sounds of screaming and shouts of rage and he was completely disorientated as he staggered into a tree. An arrow lodged into the bark just inches from his face. He turned and saw a metal blade come straight for his head. His quick instincts kicked in and he dropped to the ground as the sword bit into the poor defenseless tree.

The green, scaly creature with pointy ears, raised his sword into the air and came down with a hard chop – but another sword blocked the blow. It was his dad who came through the gate just in time.

Gavin used his sword to push the attacker's blade up and away and then he came around with his second sword in his left hand and sliced the creatures head clean off. With two swords at the ready, Lucas helped Caleb up to his feet and they found protection behind their dad.

"Goblins," he calmly informed them. "Looks like a quiet entry is out of the question.

9

Darkness.

Peace.

Slow and steady breathing and dreaming of being in her bed, tucked in tight with the fan lightly blowing a soft breeze over her face.

Then came a sharp pain to the side of her face that tossed her head to the left and left a burning hot sting on her cheek.

Andrea's eyes darted open as she tried to focus and find the source of the pain. From the corner of her eye she saw a dark green object approach without warning and jolt her on the other side of her face. Now her head swung to the right.

She looked up into the wild eyes of the green scaly beasts that had snatched her and Catrina out of the woods... how many days ago?

It had all become a blur. The days were rushing by so quickly and it was hard to tell how long they had been forced to be dragged along the never ending, narrow roads in these rocky hills.

The sun was hot and baking them where they sat tied up

to a tree in the middle of nowhere. Andrea was tired of these rude awakenings.

"Food. Eat," the beastly creature said as it dropped a bowl of mush at her feet. It had a rancid smell and looked like oatmeal that had never been cooked and was sitting in too much water for much too long a time. It was bloated, slimy and nothing that she wanted to even attempt to choke down again.

"Are you okay?" she heard Catrina say from behind her.

"I'm alright. You?"

"Thirsty. Eat your food. We're going to need the nourishment."

Andrea's eyes looked down at the bowl of garbage in front of her. "You call it nourishment?"

"It's better than starving to death and it has water in it which we are in desperate need of. Choke it down for me, please?"

While her one arm was chained tight to the tree, her other one had a longer extension of chain which allowed for her to reach in front of her and grab the bowl. She slowly lifted it to her lips and then with a grimace, took a swig of the chunky concoction.

Her face twisted as the aftertaste sent shockwaves to her brain telling her to avoid drinking anymore of this garbage. From behind she could hear Catrina glugging it down and so she went back to work on the bowl, choosing to drink it all down with one large gulp.

She fought the urge to throw it all back up.

Tossing the bowl aside, Andrea sat in her place in silence. She looked around at the busy goblins that roamed here and there. They would fight with one another from time to time. They didn't seem to have any one purpose. They were all looking busy, but none of them were accomplishing anything of any importance. It all seemed to be for show.

As if reading her mind, Catrina said, "They follow orders really well, but they are otherwise worthless. They had a great importance at one point in their history, but then they betrayed the Kingdom of Man. They joined with Dark Master Natas and for their betrayal, they ended up being exiled and becoming of little importance to anyone. Slaves to whatever master would make the best offer to them."

"The bounty hunter?"

"Probably. I haven't seen him today. I wonder where he's gone?"

Catrina had begun to reveal bits and pieces of what had happened back at the McGregor home. She revealed who Caleb and Lucas really were and how the family had been on the run from a dark prophecy.

All of it seemed like a fairy tale as she described it, yet Andrea knew that this woman would never lie to her. She was as much a mother to her as her own mother once was.

"How are we going to get out of here?"

"Patience," Catrina said in a soothing manner that Andrea was quick to believe. "Gavin will come for us. You should have seen him in his days as a knight..." she let that thought die as she seemed to reflect on those days.

"Pretty amazing, huh?"

"Absolutely. Runs in the family I suppose. If anyone will fight through the depths of hell to save us, it's him."

Andrea smiled.

She was sure that Caleb would do the same. She was certain that they were already on their way to rescue them. She had this feeling that had become strong deep inside her.

Even as they goblins carried them through the wall of light and brought them into this strange land, she had felt a warm light wash over her. It was as if a veil had been removed from her eyes and soul. She felt a power grow inside her and the deeper into this land they went, the more connected to it she felt.

She was certain that the feeling came from knowing that Caleb would come for her. It was assurance and confidence that all would turn out alright.

"Where do you think they're taking us?" she asked.

"There is a massive mountain system in the center part of Carsonia. We seem to be skirting along the side of it and moving into the plains region. It's kind of a wasteland where very few humans live. Mostly the goblins call it home. I'm guessing they're taking us where they feel they can best hide us."

The air was warm as it flowed over the plains and blew

over them. She could feel the water being sucked out of her body. She looked for shade because this pathetic, dead tree that they were chained to did not offer any. As her eyes took in the terrain, she came to believe that Catrina was probably right.

She could see the tips of mountains far to the southwest. To the east she could see nothing but ever expanding nothingness that they were currently navigating.

"It's hopeless," Andrea said.

"It's not hopeless. Gavin, Caleb and Lucas will come for us. We just have to wait."

But waiting was not something Andrea was fond of doing. She was already growing tired of the inhumane treatment that the goblins continued to offer up.

The slaps across the face for no reason. The garbage they called food. The eyes filled with malice intent that bore into her as they circled her – intimidating her.

"The sooner they get here, the better," she said.

She looked around and fought against the growing urge to cry.

10

Gavin had both swords at the ready as the goblin forces closed in around them. One, who seemed to take the lead over the others, ran his tongue hungrily over his lips and then with a curling voice said to the McGregor's, "Three tasty little flesh packets have just walked right into ours camp, boys. I says we eats them!"

"We builds new bangers with them bones," another one cackled. He was decked out with weapons of all sorts of shapes – all made out of the bones of humans and other types of creatures.

"We peal the flesh from the meat and dry it for new boots and coats!" another crazy goblin said as he danced around with a torch in one hand and a club made of a long leg bone connected to a skull in the other.

"Dad..." Caleb asked as he cowered behind the only person with weapons. He was shocked at how weak he had become in the last few days. He was at a serious disadvantage and none of it made him feel good. He was angry at being weak and scared to die and yet a fire burned inside of him wanting to fight back; but not at all sure how to do it.

"These rascals are mine," Gavin said as the Light surrounded him.

The goblins jumped back. Their laughter turned to rapid cackles and the stir of conversation among them. The leader didn't want to seem too afraid and only took one step back while the others fell back quite a few feet before standing their ground. Gavin didn't give them a chance to regroup.

Lunging in, Gavin drove the blade in his left hand through the belly of the lead goblin while the blade in his right hand hissed across his body and chopped off the leaders head. He spun in a complete circle and with his blades extended away from his body, he caught two more goblins and dropped them in death. The mob grew angry and all of them swarmed in for the kill – and Gavin began to systematically destroy them one after another.

Caleb couldn't breathe. He had never seen his dad perform in such a way. He was full of confidence, oozing with skills and ability and he was ruthlessly powerful – removing goblin heads left and right without missing a beat.

"How does he do that?" Caleb asked.

"He's an assassin Bro. Our dad is a freaking assassin."

The woods came alive as more goblins poured into the battle. From the shadows they ran out with their clubs of bones and the occasional glint of a metal weapon. They didn't seem to notice the defenseless boys against the tree. The goblins seemed to be fearful of dying, but angrier over the loss of their fellow band of brothers and willing to do whatever it took to avenge the deaths of those Gavin had killed.

Heads and limbs fell to the ground with sickening thuds as Gavin blazed through the pack of wild animals with precision accuracy. It was like watching a tornado rip through a trailer court. The little houses tried to hold their ground and yet the wind just pealed them apart piece by piece before picking them up and tossing them around like rag dolls. The meat eating animals in these woods were sure to have a feast tonight.

But the numbers began to stack against him. They continued to pour into the playing field and Gavin was starting to have a hard time keeping up the lethal pace.

He would send out a tentacle of light that would scoop up a goblin and toss him back into the woods. He would then use other tentacles of light to pick up tree branches and other debris and hurl it into the mob of attackers.

Caleb was done standing by as a spectator. He searched the ground for any sort of weapon that he could use. He found a club and figured it was better than nothing at all.

Lucas caught on to what his brother was doing and followed suit. Soon they were both ready to enter the fray and their movement caught the attention of one of the many goblins who broke off from the pack and shuffled down towards them.

"Well, we're in it now, I guess," Lucas said as he drew back his club like it was a baseball bat.

"AHHHHHHH!" Caleb screamed as he rushed forward. His cry of attack drew the eyes of a ton of goblins and now that they realized there was easier prey to be had, they broke away and rushed the boys.

"You idiot," Lucas said as he hurried to catch up to his brother. They met the first goblin and together they wacked at him until he dropped to one knee. They continued to whack and hack away until he fell to his death.

Caleb stumbled back – his stomach sick as he looked at the lifeless body at his feet. Each time he smacked the green beast it hurt worse than the first. But his anger fueled him to continue. Now the sight on the ground made him turn and puke.

Lucas moved to try and comfort his brother, but instead he had to swing his club to fight off the next goblin to reach them. "I need your help, Bro."

Caleb fell to his knees as tears rushed down his face, "What did I do?"

Lucas pushed back one goblin but was soon tackled to the ground by another – his club sliding away into the leafy ground. He was defenseless and looking straight into the yellow eyes of his soon to be killer.

It raised a piece of bone that had been whittled down

into a sharp point and prepared to drive it home for the kill. Lucas closed his eyes – but instead of felling pain, he heard the hiss of a sword fly through the air and the crunching of bones and the tearing of flesh as the goblin was sent to his grave.

Lucas opened one eye and caught his dad standing over him, back in a defensive position and using his two swords to protect his kids.

"Get up, Son. I'm going to need you both real soon."

Soon all three were back to back and completely surrounded by goblins of all sizes and shapes. The goblins stopped their attack for the moment while they sized up their competition. Gavin used the tentacles of light to push back ones that got too close and would crack other arms of light like a whip in the air, sending out a warning to keep them at bay.

"Will Vladamir and Nate be here anytime soon?" Lucas asked.

"I doubt it. Very few know of this gate and I'm guessing the one they used will be a long way from here. Besides, we we're going to meet at a central location in a few days. They wouldn't be out here looking for us."

"Lets us finish thems," one of the goblins called out. "I am hungry! We haven't eatens in days."

"We'll eatens. But first we must kills them without more of us getting dead," another one hissed.

Glowing balls of light suddenly lit up the night sky. As they drew closer, Caleb began to think that he could make out human forms inside of the light – yet it wasn't like his dad who was encased in the light. They seemed to be fuzzy forms of glowing beings.

They swooped in and landed around Gavin and his boys. As they landed, the fuzzy light drew together and soon slender, human beings clad in flowing blue robes and long golden hair, stood around Caleb, Lucas and Gavin. They had their swords drawn and were defending the three of them.

More beings landed on the outside of the attacking goblins and now the goblins were outnumbered. The tallest of the new arrivals turned to Gavin and said, "Stay back. We will handle this, Gavin."

"How does he know your name?" Caleb asked.

"For Carsonia!" The leader cried out and his blue clad warriors rushed in and began to slash their way through the goblins – leaving not one standing. As the last of the screams subsided, the leader returned to the three of them and fell to one knee before the boys. The other beings of his group did the same.

"The Twins of the Prophecy have arrived. The dawn of the revival has begun," he said with his head bowed.

"This is Marcause," Gavin said to his boys, "A friend of mine from my days in the academy. He is an Angellian... and apparently the leader of an Angellian army?"

Marcause rose up to his feet and extended a hand out to

Gavin. For the first time, Caleb noticed the pointy ears that the man had. He stood tall and strong. His skin was pasty white yet not in a gross way but in a smooth and perfect way. He seemed flawless and not at all like the warrior they had just seen him and his army be.

"You are correct," he said to Gavin. "I left the Order to return to my people. My father has risen to the throne of the Angelians and asked me to serve as the commander of his army. I had a duty to him and I have accepted it."

"You came at a good time," Gavin said as he invited his friend from long ago to sit. "I'm surprised you recognized me."

"I did not at first, but the sight of your boys helped me understand the scope of what we had come upon. The rumors have made their way to every end of Carsonia. The Twins of the Prophecy are alive and will soon return to assume their roles. Alas, here they are – and so are you, Old Friend."

"What brings you into the Northern Mountains? In fact, what brings the goblins into the Northern Mountains?"

"Hathian has been moving his forces North through the deserts of the East and along the coastline of the West in order to circle in and surround the last of the Free Lands. He politically controls the Kingdoms to the South – though they are blind to his ways. He is like a puppet master and the men of the South have no idea what he is about to do to them. He will collapse their governments and summon them to himself. Then and only then, will he move in for the final strike to capture the Free Lands and destroy the Knights of Liberty in the Valley of the Fallen."

"The goblins serve him?" Gavin asked as he wiped the blood off his blades in the grass at his feet.

"They have been promised redemption in his new order. A return to prominence – something money cannot buy them. Yes, they serve him."

Gavin seemed to chew on that thought for a bit while Caleb watched members of Marcause's army gather wood and build a series of fires around the area. Others gathered the dead goblin bodies and limbs and tossed them into fires that had been built a ways from the central area where the two friends continued to speak. Still others began to set up tents and build make shift defensive positions in what appeared to be strategic locations.

"What about the Dark Master? Why is Hathian gaining control and not the Dark Master?"

"He is still confined to the shadow world and therefore does not have the power to build his war machine for a final conquest. It seems to me that Hathian is taking advantage of the situation and is asserting his own authority on the land while he has the chance."

Gavin shook his head up and down, acknowledging the logic in that statement. He then changed the subject, "Did the goblins know about the gate that is here or did they just happen to be in the general area at the wrong time?" Gavin asked.

"They knew. They captured this area just days ago from a division of my men. We knew of your pending return and just happened to be returning this night to retake the area."

"Your timing couldn't have been better, Marcause."

"Do you require escort to the Temple?"

"We're not going there. Not yet at least."

Caleb's attention was drawn back into the conversation. He was under the impression that they were going to get Mom and Andrea and then bug out and never return – yet his dad had just implied that they would be going to the temple at some point in time.

"You are looking for your wife and the young girl?" Marcause asked.

"You've seen them?" Caleb jumped in. He drew in close to the two men.

"We have not seen them – though we know through channels that the goblins had entered your world through this gate with a bounty hunter named Mideon. They returned a few days later and are fleeing to the East."

"Into the desert?" Gavin asked.

"Are they alive?" Caleb interrupted.

"They are alive, but I do not believe they will go into the desert. I believe they will go into the Northeastern foothills of the Central Mountain Range. The bounty hunter is a Minotaur. He makes that area his home... as his brothers once did."

"The Minotaur's are not independent beings. They are military machines with a thirst for blood. This one is a bounty hunter?"

"He is unlike his brothers. He has found his own purpose in life and moves along his own path seeking his own gains. He is unlike anything we have ever seen. He serves the highest bidder and his loyalty rests with no one but himself. At this time, he seems to be working for the Dark Master."

"The voices in the woods," Lucas said as he joined the discussion. By this time, a number of Marcause's troops had gathered wood and started a warming fire for the discussion between the two men and the twins.

"What voices in the woods?" Gavin asked.

"When Mom and Andrea were snagged. I heard chuckles and screechy speech… just like the goblins we heard today. I thought it was the Draith but it might have been goblins."

Gavin shook his head up and down as he considered this. Then he turned to Marcause in hopes of a confirmation.

"Mideon may have brought them with him. Many goblins live in the Northeastern foothills with him. He has given them protection from men in exchange for loyalty and service in missions when he needs them. This is probably a factual statement."

"And you are sure he will return to his homeland?"

"Quite sure. We did not pursue him because we did not know if the rumors of your kidnapped wife and the girl were true. We also had a need to secure this gate for your return. But he is moving in that direction."

Gavin stood up and Marcause did likewise. He reached down and grabbed his ruck sack and tossed it over his shoulders and the boys reluctantly did the same. Caleb was in no hurry to begin moving again. He had one too many brushes with death in the last two days and was not eager for another.

"You are leaving?"

"I want to move in the cover of night. If you are already aware of my return to The Kingdom, then chances are that others are watching for us as well. I'm meeting up with Master Voldakov and his apprentice in the village of Tylathion in a few days."

"A homecoming?"

"Sort of like that. I need some supplies and I will need their help in the rescue. I would ask you to come along, but it seems you have more pressing matters to take care of."

Marcause looked over the clothing that the three of them wore and then added, "You also need a change of attire. You will be noticed instantly in this type of material. Is this even natural cloth?"

Gavin shook his head no, "Where we come from, clothes come in all sorts of styles and is made out of crazy things you can't possibly imagine."

The Angellian warrior let a smile grow on his face and

then he nodded his head. He ran his hand through his silky gold hair before saying, "I am afraid we do have to stay back. We must hold this line so that Hathian doesn't discover the other realm and find tools to help his plans of conquest.

"The armies of the North are not well trained and not great in number. It is up to us and the Aquarians to protect this front. I can spare a number of my men to provide security for you in your travels."

Gavin waved off the gesture, "No. We should be safe. We are only a short ways away and the enemy seems to have their hands full with you. I appreciate the offer."

"It is good to see you again, Gavin. The sight of you and your son's has brought hope to myself and my men. An end to the struggles is near. The days of the Dark Master are coming to an end. I will sleep well tonight knowing that the heir to the throne of Carsonia is here." He looked over at both boys with a broad smile on his face.

His remarks seemed to imply that he had no idea of the dark nature that one of the boys was to assume and that the balance of everything seemed to ride on one of the two of them dying. Was it ignorance or something else? Caleb thought about that for a bit and then noticed that his dad and brother were beginning to move out of the makeshift camp.

With one more wave of his hand, Gavin and the boys walked past a stinking pile of burning goblin bodies and disappeared into the woods.

"Does he realize that you're going to get us back to Earth and seal off the gates forever?" Caleb asked.

Gavin didn't answer. He just kept on walking, keeping a short distance in front of the boys.

"Lucas, do you think that Marcause knows that we're not staying?"

"I don't think so. I'm also not sure if he realizes that if we rise to power that one of us is going to join forces with the Dark Master and wreak havoc on the world. Shouldn't he be somewhat scared?"

"Hmm," was all Caleb could muster for a reply. He was wondering why his dad didn't answer his previous question. What was he planning? He hinted at a return to the Temple while implying to the boys that there would be no fulfillment of the prophecy if he had anything to say about it. But the words of Marcause chewed away at Caleb.

Marcause and his men had new hope that the struggles were soon to be over. There was hope and yet there really was no hope at all since they would all be leaving as soon as possible and sealing the gates behind them. Was it right to be part of a grand prophecy and be a light in a dark world and yet have no plans to defend the weak and the helpless but instead turn and run?

Caleb wanted nothing more than to return to his own world and live out his own dreams and yet there was a slim part of him that felt like returning to his former life was all wrong.

Caleb pushed the thoughts out of his mind and scrambled to catch up to his dad and Lucas.

11

They walked for some distance in silence.

Perhaps it was the fear that their voices would travel in the woods and alert other goblins to their presence. Or maybe they were all in a state of shock. Either way, nobody dared to speak for a great while.

The sound of snapping twigs and crunching leaves were the only sounds that came from these three as they hurried through the woods.

Caleb was busy processing everything that had happened in the last few days. Names danced through his head as he tried to connect all the dots of the players that were involved in this game that was quickly changing his life.

There was one name that seemed to have no connection – yet factored into why they were recently attacked. His name was Hathian.

Was he a part of the prophecy? Nobody seemed to mention his name until the Angellian, Marcause had brought it up. How was he a part of all of this.

When his curiosity overrode his desire to keep quiet in the woods, he finally asked, "Dad... Who is Hathian? Is he a part of the prophecy?"

Gavin was quick to answer, "No. He's definitely not part of the prophecy. Back when I was at the academy, the Knights of Liberty began a quest to free the people of the southern part of Carsonia from warlords and slavery. Hathian happened to be one of the most powerful ones in the land. He was also the last one defeated.

"The Knights of Liberty succeeded in freeing the people, but they continued to refuse the protection of the bearers of The Light and so we left the southern region once more."

"Why not stay and force them to accept the protection of the Knights of Liberty?" Lucas asked. "They were free of evil and enemies."

Gavin chuckled. "I know that makes sense, but it's not always in the nature of humans to do what is right. We tend to buck the idea of being held to a different standard than the one we choose. We have a tendency to want to be independent and carve out our own paths... no matter the cost. The Knights of Liberty have always known that people have to choose to be protected by The Light. You can't force it on them or it's just another form of slavery."

"Hmm," was the only reply Lucas had to that.

"Anyways, it looks as if Hathian has changed his ways

and has somehow begun to wrestle power over the people by influencing the political scene. Marcause didn't explain what that looked like… but I can guess."

When the words were exhausted, they all fell into silence once more.

After a short distance, Caleb asked, "What are the Angelians?"

"They are the elves of the sky. They are much like a regular human; except with pointy ears and nearly flawless bodies. To travel, they can take a cloud like form that allows them to fly through the air. There are also elves of the water who are known as the Aquarians. And the goblins that you are becoming very familiar with, were once the elves of the earth."

"What happened to them?" Lucas was the first to ask.

"Many things led to their fall but it mostly had to deal with their lust for power and their jealousy of the majestic nature of the Angelians. The Dark Master promised them a power greater than that of their brothers and they ceased to be the people they were called to be and instead became the cursed race that they now are. Their inheritance went instead to the dwarves, and you can imagine how insulting that was," he looked back at his two sons and realized that they didn't understand why it was embarrassing to be ranked below the dwarves and so he amended his statement with a quick, "well, maybe not yet. You'll understand one day."

"Then what are the Draith?" Caleb asked.

Gavin grew serious, his face twisting as if the very word was sour in his mouth. He drew in a deep breath and began, "The Druids… people who use magic; desired the one thing they couldn't conjure up… immortality. The Dark Master was able to give them an immortal soul by making them Wraiths. Not quite alive, but not quite dead."

"But I saw them die when you, Vladamir and Nathan fought them," Lucas said.

"Their bodies die… but their evil soul lives on. Did you notice their voices?"

"It was like many voices speaking out of one mouth," Lucas answered.

"The demonic souls of every Draith without a body joins those with. When the body dies, the soul joins with another willing body… adding his powers to it. So the body dies, but the soul lives on in unison with many."

They walked on for a bit and finally Caleb asked, "Why did their voices affect me? Why did I hear them and they seemed to take control of me?"

"I heard them too," Lucas said.

"Yea, but you didn't fall into a trance because of them."

Gavin didn't answer but instead quickened his pace. Caleb asked again, "Why did they affect me and not Lucas?"

"I'm not sure yet," he said in a gruff tone.

"Yes you do! Yes you do, Dad! Why?"

Gavin spun around on his heal and came face to face with

Caleb who nearly plowed into him. His finger was in his son's face and spit flew out as he scorned him, "Because you are selfish and desire greatness… just like the Draith. You have many of the qualities that have befallen many men. You need to control your lust and greed or it will control you!" he turned and hurried on.

Caleb was slow to follow. He was shocked by the comparison. Was he really that selfish? Yes, he really was and he knew it.

"But I thought you told Vladamir that we can be taught to block out the voices," Lucas said.

Gavin stopped and turned towards the boys. He nodded his head up and down. His eyes were wild with anger. "I did."

"But I heard you say in the house that you could hear the voices as well."

"I did."

"How?"

He choked back the pain that had balled up in his throat. He tried to calm himself but his red face and fiery eyes betrayed the truth. His voice unleashed with rage, "Because I am selfish as well. Because I am trying to do everything I can to keep you two from falling into the path of this blasted prophecy! I am walking a thin line to destruction because I am ignoring the plans of the Creator to achieve my own ambitions. I am trying to separate you from your destiny because of my love for you two."

Caleb and Lucas stood there – broken. They couldn't speak a single word more as they watched the tears stream down their fathers face.

For so long he had been the backbone of the family. Little did either of them know, but he was holding a secret deep inside. He was battling with his own conscious of doing what he should be doing and doing what his heart desired. This world was waiting for the Twins of the Prophecy and Gavin McGregor was determined to keep them away from it.

Lucas walked up and wrapped his arms around him, squeezing him tight. Caleb watched from a few feet back, contemplating the events of the past few days and the dangerous warnings from his dad.

What if I am the dark one whose life is linked to the Dark Master, he thought. Was his goals and ambitions in life really the seeds to his own destruction?

He refused to be a part of this touchy feely moment and instead walked up and patted them both on the backs as if they were just teammates who he was encouraging to get back in the fight. "We need to get moving, Dad. You wanted to get us out of the foothills by sunrise and I'm guessing we don't have much time before that comes about."

Gavin wiped the stains from his cheeks and pushed the last of the tears out of his eyes as he looked up into the fading night sky and made his own determination. "We probably have another solid hour of darkness and then the daylight is going to sweep in. We'll have to move quickly. We've lost more time than I had planned. Besides, I want to get us into some cover for the day, eat a meal and then I want you to take in the gorgeous Carsonian sunrise. You have never seen a bluer or more pure sky than you're going to see this morning."

The general downward slope of the ground made the going much easier than some of the hilly terrain they had to navigate back home. Caleb was well conditioned and so the quick pace was nothing for him. His major concern was hitting an uneven spot in the ground and tearing up his ankle or knee. He didn't want to return home and miss the rest of the season because of something crazy that happened on this escapade.

They kept up the pace for nearly an hour and a half. The sky to the east was glowing bright and the sun would be rising up over the mountains at any moment. The ground had seemed to level off as they came out of the foothills. Without the momentum of going downhill, Caleb could feel the added work he had to put into each stride and he noticed that Lucas was having a hard time keeping up. He wasn't known for being athletic. His gift was his sense of adventure.

"Dad, we should rest!" Caleb called out.

Gavin came to a halt and then looked around. The vegetation was thick and provided good cover from any eyes that might be looking for them from up in the sky. Without helicopters, Caleb would think that task to be impossible in a world like Carsonia, but after meeting the flying elves, he had something new to be concerned about – though at the moment they seemed to be on their side.

"Can we trust the sky elves?" Caleb asked. He looked over and saw Lucas bent over with his hands on his knees, trying to take deep breaths. "Stand up and put your hands on your head. You'll breather easier."

"You mean the Angelians?" Gavin asked.

"Yea, them."

"Make sure you refer to them as Angelians. They're not fond of being called sky elves. It's a derogatory name to them. Elves is such a general term that just groups everyone with pointy ears together. Each race of elves have distinct..."

"I'm not looking for a history lesson, Dad. I get it."

Gavin nodded his head and then went to work in gathering up brush and building a make shift shelter to keep them hidden from any eyes that might be wandering in the woods. When that was finished, he stowed both ruck sacks inside and then began to check out the orange sky that glowed above. He looked to the West, then back into the mountains from which they had come from and then to the South. The blue skies he had promised were nowhere to be found.

"Something wrong?" Lucas asked as he walked up alongside him and looked up into the sky.

"It's not how I remember it. Something is all wrong."

"You've been gone for a few years," Caleb began, "Things change. Maybe it's a massive forest fire somewhere or pollution…"

"Maybe. But since I rejoined with The Light, I have felt something dark weighing on me. I thought it was just the gravity of the situation; the fear of losing you two. But now I wonder if it has something to do with here. The world feels empty of The Light. Like someone has pulled a heavy sheet over the face of Carsonia and now they are pulling up a heavy blanket to lay over the top and block out the sunlight forever."

"The Dark Master?" Caleb asked.

Gavin nodded his head. He took one last look around and then crawled into the little hut of brush and dug into the ruck sack of food where he prepared a meal for himself and handed out rations to Caleb and Lucas. Together, the three of them ate in silence and then each one took turns staying awake for two hours while the other two slept. They continued this routine until the sun set on that day and then they put the sacks back on their backs and headed out for the next stage of their journey.

The thickness of the woods made it hard to see in the limited night sky now that the moon was concealed under a blanket of clouds. They hurried as best they could and soon found that the canopy of trees above began to lessen until soon they came into a large, open field. In the far distance were glowing lights of a small village and Gavin let out a great sigh of relief.

"Do you know that place?" Caleb asked.

"That is home. Your grandma… my mother, lives there."

Caleb felt his heart miss a beat. A lump found its way into his throat. In all of his life he had heard about the awesome Christmas feasts that the other kids' grandparent would make. He heard about presents.

At football games, some of his teammates would have a huge cheering section made up of uncles, aunts, grandparents and cousins. While Caleb loved having his parents there for each game, he always felt he was missing out.

He didn't have the history of his family to talk about in class. He didn't have the family adventures or stories like the others. Suddenly, he was looking at a series of twinkling lights in the distance and knew that one of them belonged to his very own grandmother – a link to a family history he knew almost nothing about.

"When my dad died, she tried to keep me away from living a life as a Knight of Liberty. She moved us out here. Like any kid though, I followed my own way. I decided to follow in my dad's footsteps."

"Will we meet her?" Lucas asked.

"That is where we're meeting with Vladamir and Nathan. I'm leaving you guys with her while we go out to rescue your mom and Andrea."

"What if she doesn't live there anymore?" Caleb said.

"I hadn't considered that; but I'm sure she will be. When

we left Carsonia, we passed through here. She promised to be right there if I ever decided to come back and I know she will be."

Gavin broke out in a dead run, covering the open area quickly. The running gave Caleb plenty of time to break into deep thought. He was excited to meet his grandma and perhaps that was why he didn't protest the idea of being left behind while his dad and the others went looking for his mom and girlfriend.

Yes, it made him look like a weakling for not being the one to rescue her. But he also was just a kid trying to find his way in the world – plus having to kill wasn't an easy thing to do. Just the quick thought of what he had done to that goblin made him nearly double over. The guilt weighed heavy enough on him.

They were soon to the village. The streets were quiet. Everyone was tucked in their homes for the night. They stayed close to the shadows and worked their way slowly between buildings.

Lights seemed to light up the streets. Caleb looked up at one of them expecting to see a flickering of fire inside the lanterns. Instead he found a round glass ball with bolts of electricity bouncing around inside.

His eyes locked in on that peculiar object and he didn't notice the metal beam that was nailed down in the center of the road until he snagged his shoe on it and toppled to the ground.

He let out a yelp that drew a scolding look from his dad and Lucas. Caleb looked at the single metal track that ran down the middle of the road and off into the vast distance.

"What is this for?"

"The train," his dad answered.

Train? Here? Don't they just ride horses and stroll around in buggies? Don't they just walk here and there and hitch a ride on a stage coach if they have a long way to travel?

"If this is a train track, then where is the other side and the railroad ties?"

"It doesn't ride on the track. It hovers over the metal guide."

"Hovers?" Caleb was dumfounded. "Like in the science fiction movies?"

Gavin didn't answer. He touched his finger to his lips and then turned back to guiding his family through the village side roads until they came to a little cottage that seemed to be on the edge of town.

He ran up to the back side and then brushed away the straw that had been placed on the ground near the foundation of the house. This revealed a trap door that he opened up and he ushered both boys down the ladder. At the bottom, Gavin reached up and touched a glass ball that was attached to the ceiling and a bolt of electricity sprang to life, dancing within the globe and lighting the back part of the basement.

A set of footsteps moved along the wood floor above them. Gavin rushed across the room and quickly climbed up the ladder. A crack of light was exposed as he gently peeked his head up into the above room.

"Mother?" he called out softly.

"Gavin? Is that you?"

The footsteps hurried across the floor and stopped right where their dad sprang up through the floor.

"My lands! My boy! My boy! I knew you would come back here one day."

Caleb and Lucas sat at the bottom, not sure if they were ready to go up. How do you react to a member of your family you have never met? Will she be excited to see them? Will there be an awkwardness to the entire situation? The adventuring side of Lucas wanted to know and so he scaled the ladder as fast as he could. Caleb reluctantly began his climb.

"My goodness! Look at you," Caleb heard her saying to Lucas. As soon as he was through the hatch, she had snagged him away in a great bear hug and now held him out at arm's length. "We need to fatten you up. You are half dead, I think."

Gavin's face glowed with the pride of presenting his sons to his mother after all these years. "He's fine, Mom. They've never missed a meal."

Her eyes fixed on Caleb as he moved away from the cellar

door. She rushed up and grabbed him like a linebacker on the football field. Her arms were stronger than her small figure showed. He could barely breathe as she hugged him tight.

"Now this one... this one has the husky build of a McGregor. Do you steal all of your brother's food?"

"Hardly."

"Give me a minute and I'll whip up something tasty that will put a little meat on your bones."

She rushed over to the stove and went to work even while their dad protested. "You don't need to do that, Mom."

"Sure I do. Sure I do. I haven't cooked for my son in over twenty years... since you ran off to the blasted temple. I'm not going to miss out on that opportunity now. I have just the fixings for a grand homecoming meal and then tomorrow I'll take the train to Florlidia and get some of the finest spices and herbs and cook up something splendid."

"No, Mom. We need to keep a low profile. I don't want to draw any attention to ourselves."

She stopped cooking and turned to him. She had the look of someone who just realized that all of the cards are not adding up to the right number. Something was amiss and amid all the excitement of seeing her son, she realized that not everyone was present.

"What has happened? Where is Catrina?"

And so Gavin told her all that had happened in the past few days as they continued to prepare a meal. The boys set the table with plates, forks and knives and filled the glasses with cold milk from the ice box.

All was in place as she laid out the smoked ham and fresh bread. She added a bowl of greens with a vinaigrette dressing and an assortment of black and green olives stuffed with various herbs and meats. While neither boy were fond of olives, the stuffed ones were an exception and they popped them in their mouths one after another like they were eating popcorn from a bowl.

She seemed pleasantly surprised to hear that Vladamir was still alive and well – he did after all, spend many years serving with Gavin's father. She also felt that the boys would be safer with her and though they protested, they eventually relented when she broke out the fresh apple pie and realized that they were going to have it pretty good. In reality, neither of them were that anxious to eat rations and sleep in the elements every night.

The next morning they woke to new clothes laid out on the kitchen table. "They were your father's when he was your age," she told them. "If you're going to be staying out of harm's way, you better not stand out in a crowd. We'll burn those frail fabrics from your old world. I cannot believe that your father would waste money on this type of inferior material. Is this really considered clothing in your world? It's not even made out of wool or skins is it?"

For the next few hours the three of them had a grand

discussion on the differences between their world and Carsonia. They bonded quickly with her and soon felt like they had known her all of their lives. They learned much about their grandfather and their dad's early years. When Vladamir and Nate arrived and they left with their dad, all seemed calm and fine for them.

Caleb watched as the three men disappeared into the shadows of the night. If not for his mom not being present, he was almost able to forget about how fractured his world had become. By the time a week passed, Caleb and Lucas had molded into this life as if they had always belonged.

Neither one appeared together outdoors. Only one would be with their grandmother at any point in time while the other would stay behind in the cottage. To those that they met on the street, she introduced the boys as her hired servants and often they would be seen doing chores on the small piece of land that she owned.

Caleb was always happy to feed the ducks and chickens. For whatever reason, he enjoyed watching the birds as they moved about the land. The chickens were not particularly interesting, but the ducks were actually amusing. The male and female, who he named Poncho and Lilly, were like two old people waddling around on a typical day with no cares in life.

Lilly would just walk aimlessly around the yard and Poncho would be a few steps behind. They pecked here and there, gathering bugs or whatever else of food value they might find. Their waddle and their interaction between each other almost had some human aspects to it.

At night they huddled together for warmth. During the day they were busy doing whatever thing it was that ducks do. He enjoyed leaving the rushed life that he was living behind and savoring the peace and quiet of a slow life filled with new discoveries.

Lucas took care of the small repair projects that needed to be done on the house. Being that he was the only one of the two who had showed an interest in learning the little handyman techniques that their dad would try and teach them, he was best suited for the tasks that Grandma needed done.

He repaired a leak in the roof, fixed the squeaky hinges on the front door and even mended some holes in the fence where the ducks and chickens would pass through to get into mischief in the village.

They had settled into a routine that seemed like a natural fit for both of them. The worries of their dad, mom, Andrea and the changing world were far from their minds.

12

"Do you have valuable information for me?"

"I do, my Lord. The rumors have been confirmed. The Twins of the Prophecy have entered our world with their father. They are in search of their mother as you predicted. They have rejected the escort of the Angelians – though Master Marcause continues to watch over them from a distance as a favor to the Knights of Liberty. My guess is they will make their way to the village in which his mother resides and set out from there in a few days."

"Very good. It is all unfolding as I have foreseen it. The father is predictable. His actions are those that I would expect from someone whose only interest is to protect their children from harm. It will be easy to predict his future movements. This leads me to my next task for you to carry out."

"Yes, my Master. What is thy bidding?"

"Is your apprentice ready?"

"He is well trained and far advanced for his age. I am confident he can succeed in any assignment you give him."

"What do you know about the gates that connect our two

worlds?"

"I know that they only allow a certain number of people to pass through at any given time. If the allotment is for a hundred to pass through, only a hundred shall. If one or all should die, then new ones may enter to take their place. To seal the gates is thought to be impossible... though King Callam was successful in sealing The Rift to prevent you from executing your grand mission."

"Yes he was. And do you know how he sealed it?"

"By use of a stone, I believe."

"It was a stone. Given to him by an agent of The Creator. Only a McGregor can use this stone to open The Rift... however, any bearer of The Light can use it to seal the small gates permanently."

"But the stone..."

"The Stone of Callam has been lost for centuries. This I am aware of, but no longer."

"You know of its location?"

"I do. The mother wears it around her neck. The seer noticed it over seventeen years ago and reported it to me. Now it is time to put this valuable information to use. I have selected a garrison of my best Draith Knights. They will rendezvous with your apprentice in three days in Kingston. They will go and meet with Mideon, recover the stone and go out and seal all of the gates. Not one shall be left open. The father will attempt to flee with his children once he has *rescued his wife. I cannot allow this. With the gates sealed, he will be forced to accept the fate of the prophecy.*

"Your apprentice has the ability to use the light and the stone to seal these gates. A Draith cannot touch the stone or he will be destroyed. Do you feel he handle this mission?"

"I know he can, my Master."

"Secrecy is of the utmost importance. He must not be discovered by anyone in the Order. Those that they face who protect the gates... all of them must be destroyed. No witnesses can leave the areas and the identity of your apprentice cannot be compromised. He must be able to leave the watchful eyes of the Order and return when the mission is done without being discovered. I have great use for him in the future. Can this be done?"

"I will personally see to it."

"You must not be discovered either. Your standing in the Order is vital to the success of my future plans. Have him on his way by this evening."

"It will be done, my Master."

The face in the communication globe dissipates and becomes a blue cloud swirling in a glass ball. The clouds begin to twist and form into a new face. This face looks like that of a bull with pointed horns.

It's the bounty hunter!

"Mideon, I have a new mission for you."

"I don't work for free. Anything beyond what I have already

done will require further payment."

"I am prepared to offer you a substantial amount of wealth in return for you completing this task."

"I'm listening."

"The father will be leaving the twins in the care of his mother. He believes that they are hidden from my sight and safe if they remain with her. He will soon be in search of the women and will be a long distance from them. While this was an unforeseen change of fate, it is a change that benefits me greatly."

"You want me to go to the village, capture the boys and bring them to you?"

"No. I need them to begin their training at the temple so I have no use for you to bring them to me. Instead, I want a vile of blood from each of them and I want the father eliminated."

"By my count, that is two tasks… not one. I will want a payment for each mark."

"As you wish. Can it be done?"

"Of course it can. I will leave the women in the charge of my assistants and I will personally see to the extraction of the blood of each boy. Where are they now?"

"They will be in a village just north of Florlidia. The Knights of Liberty entrusted an Angellian commander with the task of watching over their protection from a distance… so you will have resistance."

"You call it resistance. I call it a challenge. I am in the

mood for a challenge."

"I am sure you are. So for payment, I will double the amount we paid you for the women in return for the execution of the father. I will triple the amount of payment for the vials of blood from each twin."

"If I get the chance to kill the Angellian commander, I may just owe you a partial refund."

"If you kill the Angellian commander, you will get a bonus. He is dangerous to me and having him eliminated would be agreeable."

"Consider him dead."

"I will have the gold waiting. Before you go, I would like to share one thought with you. You have done very well for me over the years, Mideon. There is a war coming and your brothers are gathering with me once more. You are always welcome to serve in my army."

"My brothers find that their only purpose is to be war machines for rulers such as yourself. I am not like that. I have found my purpose and I have discovered my own pleasures and they are not found in submitting myself to the authority of others.

"I have wealth. I have adventure. Most of all, I have my freedom. My mindless brothers can serve as soldiers in your war. As for me, I will continue to serve the highest bidder. If you want my loyalty… make sure you are always the highest paying."

The face becomes a cloud again.

The conversation is over.

The plan is now in motion.

13

Caleb woke up and threw on the fresh clothes that his grandmother had laid out for him on the kitchen table. Then he grabbed a pail that was sitting by the back door and snuck out to the water pump where he filled it up and poured it into an old rusty wash tub in the back yard that the ducks and chickens liked to drink from and occasionally swim in.

He then grabbed a few scoops of cracked corn and tossed it into a trough before finding a comfortable place to lean up against a fence post and watch the birds do their thing. It had become almost therapeutic to him since arriving.

While he appreciated the opportunity to meet his grandma, he had more pressing things on his mind. His life back home was waiting for him to pick up and move forward, but most of all, he missed Andrea. Not being there to rescue her was beginning to weigh on his mind.

The door to the cottage opened up and Lucas came out. He tucked in the tail of his shirt and then ran his fingers through his hair to give it his patented shaggy look.

"Up early," he said as he joined his brother by the fence.

"Bad dreams."

"Andrea?"

"Kind of. Kind of other things too. I hate just sitting around."

"Me too. We shouldn't have left Dad to do this by himself."

"Hmm," came the grunt of agreement from Caleb. "He wouldn't have let us come anyways. I don't think he ever intended to let us come."

"Maybe if Grandma was dead or didn't live here anymore. He would have had to then."

"Did you ever think that Dad was able to do all those things we saw him do?" Caleb asked.

"Nope. I just thought he was a plain ol' vanilla type dad. Who would have thunk it."

"How did we get here?" Caleb asked as he moved away from the fence and began to look around at his surroundings.

They had become familiar rather quickly – as if he had known them from dreams or had actually lived here at one time many years ago. He didn't feel much like a stranger, yet he didn't have a clue where his dad had traveled off to and other than the few places he had gone with his grandma, he couldn't get anywhere without some sort of guidance. Still, all of this seemed so normal to him. It was that thought that scared him. "What if we are never leaving here?"

"Would it be that bad?" Lucas asked as he put his hands in his pockets and walked over to his brother. "Carsonia needs us."

"Doesn't look like it's in trouble to me."

"But Marcause. Remember what he said about the evil that was taking over the world. Only one of us can save it."

"Yea, only one of us. The other one gets to turn into a blood sucking demon and become the main villain in this fairytale. No, it doesn't need us. It needs to find another set of twins because I'm not doing it."

"Like we're going to get a choice."

"For our sake, I sure hope we do."

"Hmmm," came the grunt of agreement from Lucas.

There was a long, awkward silence as the two of them walked around the small, fenced in yard. The crisp morning air was refreshing and Caleb breathed it in deeply. The cool air filled his lungs and gave him a slight shiver, but he liked the feeling it gave him. It calmed his nerves and gave him a restored hope that in a few days, everything would get back to normal.

"One of us needs to go back inside," Lucas said.

"Yea," Caleb picked up a small rock from the ground and took aim at a stray cat that was making for one of the chickens that had strayed away from the flock. He zeroed in on his target and then unleashed a rocket that slapped into the side of the stalking cat. It jumped straight up into the air, frightened the chicken with its scream and then turned and scampered up and over the fence. Caleb broke into a smile and then made for the front door.

"She's going to be okay," Lucas said. The two of them were able to sense the deepest burdens of each other. Many studies had been done on twin siblings and it was often said that they could sense thoughts, pain and even sensations of their counterparts. For Caleb and Lucas, they shared the ability to read the most pressing thoughts of the other. Lucas had pinned this one right on. While Caleb tried his best to be cool and deny it – it was the worry of Andrea's safety that concerned him the most.

"I hope."

"I know. Did you see Dad's skills with the sword? Heck, he used two swords and he used them like he'd been swinging them for years. He's some sort of Jedi, Bro. With Mr. Voldakov and Nate with him, he'll do just fine."

"Hmm. A lumber salesman, a science teacher and a high school football player… that really gives me hope." The two of them lightly chuckled and then Caleb added, "I feel bad that I'm not as worried about Mom as I am Andrea. She's my… she's our mom."

"Yea, but I already have that covered. I'm worrying about Mom and you can worry about her. But that isn't your greatest concern, is it?"

Caleb sunk his head and took the last few steps to the door. He grabbed onto the metal handle and pressed his thumb down on the latch. It clicked and he began to push it open. Out of the corner of his eye he caught sight of Lucas and then mumbled for only his brother to hear, "I don't want to get stuck here. I want my own life and not this crazy one. The longer Dad is gone, the less hope I have that we'll get to go home."

"I'm not sure we should leave this place, Caleb. Maybe we're supposed to be here."

"Maybe? You do remember what the prophecy says, right? One of us is going to have to die in order for the balance to be restored to the world. Are you willing to kill me? I know I'm not willing to off you."

"Maybe it doesn't have to be that way. Besides, this is our real home. This is where we belong. We have a purpose here."

Caleb spun around to face his brother, stepping up into his face and staring straight through his eyes, "You only feel that way because there is nothing for you back home!" Caleb immediately knew that he crossed a line, but he didn't stop there. "I have a reason to return. I have a future… you've got nothing!"

Lucas drew back from him. His face was blank as the words tore away his spirit and drive.

The door to the cottage opened and their grandma stepped out. With her voice raised, "Boys! What is going on out here! Get in here right now!"

Caleb spun around and stormed back for the door,

147

pushed past his grandma on his way into the living area. He heard her go the rest of the way outside and could hear her say to Lucas, "Come on now. You and I will take a trip into town and give your brother some time to cool off."

"It's okay, Grandma. I'm fine."

"Well, all the same. I think he could use some cooling off time."

He heard the gate at the end of the walk open up and close and he knew he was completely alone. His entire world was spinning out of control and every minute here meant another minute of his real life dying away – never to be recovered. The longer he was away the more the world would move on without him and if he ever wanted to live out the life that he and Andrea had talked about, he would need to get back soon.

Caleb walked over to a rug in the far corner of the room and rolled it back to reveal the trap door underneath. With a squeal, the hinges rotated and opened up to the basement and Caleb made his way back into the dark room where he last felt a glimmer of hope that he would return to his old life.

He touched the glass globe attached to the ceiling and the electrical dance began inside as it lit up the space. Folded nicely on a wood bench were his clothes and tennis shoes that he had worn into Carsonia.

That wasn't what he was looking for though. He had a feeling that this room contained something more. He moved over to the bench and began his search.

He pushed the three ruck sacks away to check that space. A few boxes were concealed behind them. He dug through but didn't find what he was looking for. He then moved the piles of clothes aside and dug through the trinkets of tools that were splayed out on the bench. It was here that he found a metal ring with three key like objects attached to it. He grabbed them because for whatever reason, they seemed to be what he was searching for – though he really had no idea what he was after.

He turned slowly, scanning the room. There were secrets here. He was sure of it. Since arriving, they hadn't talked about this room and they stored the items that they didn't want prying eyes to see down here. The trap door was hidden as well. You don't hide a trap door unless you have something to hide.

The village seemed safe so he was sure this room wasn't meant for hiding people. It was meant for hiding secrets. In the far recess of the stone walled room, he found an old wood door tucked away in the shadows.

He walked over, jingling the keys in his right hand. He was sure that one of these keys would open that door. Behind it, he was guessing he would find whatever his mind told him he needed to find. He pulled on the door handle but it resisted being opened. He looked up and found a latch with a large padlock clamped on it.

One of these keys would open it.

He tried the first with no success. He tried the second and failed. He tried the third and was shocked to find that none of them opened the door.

Caleb threw the keys across the room and let them clank into a wall and disappear into the darkness. Then he ran back to the bench and searched for more keys.

Nothing!

He looked around the room and found not a trace of a key to open the latch. He climbed the ladder and looked upstairs but couldn't find any keys there either, so he skipped the key plan and went to the axe plan.

Running outside, he went to the wood pile out back and found the axe wedged in the log where he had left it the other day. Back inside he went and back into the basement. He walked over to the large wood door and took a hard swing with the axe.

With a thunk, it slammed into the wood. He wedged it loose and wound up for another swing when he saw a glowing light emerge from the cut he had made. The fibers on each side of the wood reached out towards each other and grabbed hold of one another, twisting and pulling until they pulled together tightly, sealing up the mark he had inflicted.

The door had healed itself!

"No way," he said. Defiantly, he attacked the door again. This time he moved at a faster pace but by the time he drove the axe into the door the second time, the first wound was healed. He swung for the third time but the second chop was healed and he knew by the time he delivered the fourth blow, the third one would be patched up as well. The only way in would be through that padlock on the heavy metal latch.

"Try using all three keys at once," a familiar voice startled him from behind.

Caleb spun around with his axe at the ready for attacking purposes. Marcause drew back, his hands in the air to show he was defenseless.

"Why are you here?" Caleb asked.

"The Knights of Liberty asked me to watch over your family. With your father gone, I wasn't sure if I should remain in the shadows any longer while your brother and you seem to be drawing apart."

"What do you care?"

"I care deeply for your dad which means I care deeply for you. He and I were once part of the Order together. I pledged my loyalty to him as a friend and as a subject to the throne of the McGregor family. Either you or your brother will take the throne. It's my duty to protect you both until that time."

Caleb thought about Marcause's challenge to use all three keys. He reached for his pocket and realized that he had tossed them in anger. He hurried over to their landing place, patted around on the floor until he found them and then walked back over to the lock.

He examined the slot where the key was to be inserted but he could tell three keys at once could not possibly fit. "What happens after you find out who the bad blood is of the family? Do you have a duty to then kill them?" Caleb asked.

"I believe that we all have the freedom of choice. I believe we are not condemned to failure and evil unless we choose to embrace that path. I do not wish for either of you to perish and it is my hope that such a fate can be prevented. Or at least turning to evil can be prevented."

"Death is optional?" Caleb snorted.

Marcause did not answer.

Caleb lined the three keys up together and then touched them to the small slit. The metal became fluid like and began to drip down over the key cluster. Caleb could feel the liquid metal pulling the keys inside and suddenly the lock clicked and released. Marcause was correct!

"How did you know?"

"Our world doesn't work the same as yours. You will find many surprises while you are here."

"I don't plan on being around much longer. I'm busting out of this rat hole."

Caleb pulled open the door to reveal a small chamber. Above on the ceiling he found a globe that with one touch, danced to life and revealed glistening metal shields, armor chest plates with an emblem of a lion emerging from the fire. There were gauntlets of gold and a flowing red cape and metal helmets like those worn by knights. Attached to the wall was a metal sword hilt similar to the one his dad had. The room was a mini armory made up of family heirlooms from its days of royalty.

"The lion is your family crest. That flag hasn't flapped in the winds above the castle in thousands of years. It once stood as a symbol of hope. Only through the chosen one can it be raised again and bring peace to the land."

Once again Caleb felt a pang of guilt. He didn't feel any connection to these people and to this land and yet when someone started spouting off words of how the people longed for peace and security that only he or Lucas could bring, he felt guilty for wanting to flee.

"I don't belong here," he protested.

"You do, Caleb. You and your brother are from this world, not the one you are trying to get back to. The Creator formed you here! Fate has returned you to where you belong."

Caleb stepped into the small vault and pulled down a sword hilt from the wall. He flicked it in his hand in an attempt to make it extend out, but to no avail. He tried flicking it harder and then shaking it – hoping that at some point the blade would form.

Still nothing.

"You must will it to life."

"Using magic?"

"No. The majority of magic is evil and I would advise you

to stay away from it. The sword is made of a living ore found in the mountains in the central part of our land. Skilled tradesmen known as Magiths, long ago discovered a way to harness lightning and merge it into the ore to create a material that can be molded and used as anything.

"It is how our trains and other engines run. It is what makes our weapons fire and our lights flicker to life. The sword is an extension of our bodies. Our synaptic activity is channeled into the hilt and activates the ore and brings into being our swords. If you truly want to extend the blade, you must will it to life."

"If I would have known it was going to be that hard to do, I wouldn't have wasted my time," Caleb tossed the hilt onto the floor in the vault and then slammed the door shut. "Where can a kid buy a real sword?"

"And where do you plan to go?"

"Home."

"You are home, Caleb."

"This isn't my home!" Caleb opened the door again and dug through it, searching for something – though he was so confused and angry over Marcause's presence that he couldn't think straight. He finally spun around and faced the man, "Can you leave? I'm trying to do something here and I don't need you interrupting me."

"Never mind me. Just go back to what you are doing and I will remain here and answer any questions you might have."

Marcause leaned back against the workbench and crossed his arms. He became a quiet observer from across the room but the nerves of Caleb were not settled. Caleb waited, hoping that the man would leave and when he was convinced that he was stuck with him, he went back to work.

Digging through the vault, Caleb found a map of the land. Going back to the workbench, he rolled it out next to Marcause who looked at it over his shoulder. Using some of the landmarks that he overheard his dad speak about, Caleb began to flesh out where he was at. He trace his finger along a marking for what he believed to be a railroad system until he came to an unmarked village that he believed to be the one he was in. He rested his finger there and then scanned more of the map.

Where from the North did they come from? Caleb looked up at Marcause, debating if he really wanted to drag the pointy eared elf into his plan and then decided against it as he looked back down at the map.

"You are actually south of that village. We are more around this area," he said as he tapped a place just below where Caleb was marking with his finger. "This village did not exist when this map was drawn up. If you are looking for the gate that brought you here, it is in this area," he moved his finger into the foothills of the mountain range.

"How long would it take for me to get there?"

"Traveling downhill is obviously faster. I would say two

days – but it is no longer worth your trip."

"And why might that be?" Caleb asked with a hint of sarcasm in his voice.

"I received word that it was sealed two nights ago by a force of Draith who overpowered my soldiers and left no survivors."

Caleb stood up in shock. "Sealed!"

Marcause shook his head up and down to indicate yes.

"Can it be reopened?"

"I would think not. Only one source of power can seal the gates and if it is used, you can be sure that no spell can break it."

"How many have been sealed?"

"I only know of this one. Without contacting the Order, I cannot be sure if any others have been sealed up."

"You mean we could be stuck here forever? Where are the other gates?"

"There are no other ones in the North. You will have to travel to distant lands to get to them and most are occupied by the Draith. Fate has brought you here and now it is keeping you here."

"I'm sick of hearing about 'fate' and 'destiny'. It's all garbage! Where is the closest gate?"

"And what will you do when you get there? Will you really leave your mom and dad behind? Will you leave your brother and your lady friend here while you go back to a world that has nobody to support you?"

Caleb stumbled back and fell to his butt. He felt the world collapsing on him. He had to get back! His entire being and self-worth were contained in that world – not this one. He tried to get up but his vision was blackening and suddenly he realized that he had quit breathing. Marcause crouched down next to him and rested a calming hand on his back.

"Breathe," he thought he could hear Marcause saying through the ringing in his ears. He drew in a short breath and then another one. The tunnel of darkness began to open up.

"I have to get out of here," he mumbled.

"Breathe, Caleb. Just breathe."

"I need to go home."

"Breathe. Just focus on breathing right now."

14

Lucas settled into the seat across from his Grandma and looked out the window. The vicious words of his brother were still gnawing at his mind.

Were those words wrong?

No. Lucas didn't have his entire life mapped out like Caleb, but that didn't make him less important. Caleb made it sound as if the world was better off without him and yet, that couldn't be further from the truth.

"Caleb needs time to understand that the path you boys are on is not one of self-interest but one of self-sacrifice. It will be much harder for him to undo the damage that has been done to you boys," she said. Lucas turned from the window and found her gentle eyes looking at him with a slight smile curled on her lips. Her long, gray hair was tied up in a bun on top of her head. "He gets the selfishness from your dad."

"Really?"

"He left Carsonia to protect you two. I can understand that impulsive reaction. The problem with his strategy is that he left a key component out of his decision making process."

"And what's that?"

"He didn't consider the Creator's plan."

"The Creator is some sort of god like being?"

"Oh, he's not some sort of god but is the one true God. He created this world and the one you came from. He is the creator of all the universe. While evil was not of his original design, he still has a grand plan to rid both Carsonia and Earth of all of the evil and restore that which has been lost."

"But you said that Dad didn't consider the Creator's plan. Is that plan the prophecy?"

"It is many things beyond just the prophecy. The entire writings of all of the prophecy have never been found, but we have bits and pieces that have been patched together to form a general idea of what will happen through the ages.

"However, we don't need to know the entire words of the prophecy to know that your mom and dad were in the wrong to sneak into the other world. It was a lack of trust on their parts. They didn't trust that the Creator could bring good from whatever lies ahead for you and Caleb… so they ran. I didn't fight hard to convince your father to say. He is too much like your grandfather in his stubborn ways."

"He was a knight also?"

She smiled as she seemed to recall his memory and her face lit up with the powerful vision. She looked out the window and seemed to return to a distant time where there was a great joy in her life. She reflected in silence for a few heartbeats and then turned back to him and began, "Yes he was. Caleb is very much like him. You are more like your great grandfather... brave, adventurous and not afraid to face the future as it comes to you. As the events of this world move forward, you and your brother will need each other more than you could ever suspect. You balance one another. Your adventurous side will need his calculating side. Your easy going ways will need his cautious skepticism. Together you will be great. But divided, the house of McGregor will fall."

"But one of us has to die. The prophecy says so." Lucas jumped in his seat as the train crackled to life.

He could hear the buzzing of the electrical current as it polarized the slopped bottom of the train. The polarization was the exact opposite as the polarity found in the single track that ran below its massive bulk and so the train lifted up above the track and hovered in place. A new field of electricity was projected from behind and the train began to move forward at a rapid pace and they were on their way.

Grandma continued on, "We are not sure of that part of the prophecy. There is no record of that part of the prophecy being spoken of by a Seer of the Creator..."

"Seer?"

"A prophet like person with the ability to see the future. The prophecy was spoken by the Dark Master Natas in his final days before our ancestor, King Callam, finished him off. Some believe it was a prophetic revelation. Others believe it is a spell that he cast in order to return to life one day. Maybe a seer had a vision of these events and recorded it and maybe not.

"The main thing is we must trust in the Creator. We must understand that the future is in his hands and he will shape it as it must be. We all have some role he has called us to. Some of us have significant parts. Others have very little parts that may go un-noticed by the world or even ourselves. The main thing is, we should always be ready for what comes and we should be leading a sacrificial life so in the event we are called to serve the Creator's wishes, we are able to drop what we are doing and serve in the moment with a faithful heart.

"Your father's heart is divided. I'm not saying it is a bad thing. I am saying that he is so protective of you and your brother that he is blind to the calling that has been placed before this family."

"So I need Caleb?"

"Of course you do. You both need each other if Carsonia has any chance of survival. You balance each other out. You are the best parts of two types of men. You must learn to work together and when one strays away, the other must pull them back in. If there is any hope that neither of you will have to die it will be by working as one and not as two. There will be people who will try to divide you, don't let them. Work as one."

"It won't be easy. Caleb is determined to return back to

Earth."

"That door will be closed to him. You didn't return to Carsonia by foolish luck. The Creator uses the good and the bad things that happen in our worlds to do even greater works. Whatever the Dark Master had planned by brining you back into this world, the Creator will use it to execute his master plan. Be mindful of that."

She reached across and rested her gentle hand on his cheek and then patted it lightly. She smiled and then sat back as her smile dropped down and hurt seemed to fill her face. "Our time was much too short," she said as she dug into her bag that she had been resting on her lap.

"Grandma?" he gave her a confused look – not understanding that she was sensing some sort of danger.

She pulled out the hilt of a sword and with a flick of the wrist, little pieces of metal clanked out and grabbed on to one another as they linked together and formed the blade of a sword. Suddenly, her body began to glow as it was encased in the light and tentacles danced around her.

The train buckled. The people screamed as the vehicle twisted sideways and came off the track. The right side of the train smashed into the car in front of it and then the left side was slammed into by a the trail car – the glass shattering and spraying over the screaming crowd.

Lucas instinctively grabbed onto the bottom of his seat with one hand and braced his other against the wall of the train. He looked over and saw his grandma standing in a ready position with her sword. The tentacles of light had been directed to anchor her in place as the train bounced and spun along the ground until it came to a halt.

"Grandma!"

"I was once a Knight of Liberty," she said with a smile on her face. "How do you think I met your grandpa?"

The door in what was once the front of this rail car, was torn off its hinges as a bulky figure stood on one end. His massive head peered into the car and it immediately found Lucas and Lucas immediately recognized the shape of the creature. It was the one he had seen in the woods back home.

"Give me the boy," it growled.

"Come and take him, Minotaur!"

He stepped back and then his massive hand grabbed on to opposite sides of the door frame and with one large push, the car shook and squealed as the metal broke down the center of the car – breaking open like a fault line in the ground.

One tentacle of light jettisoned towards him and wrapped around the gigantic metal gauntlets around his wrist. With a pull, the beast was shot into the air and then Grandma projected yet another tentacle of light that grabbed on to his other wrist and the two beams of light began to pull him apart in midair. He grunted and steam blew out of his massive nostrils as he resisted the attack and tried to pull his arms back together. She fought hard to command her power but her age seemed to be working against her.

"Grandma, we should get out of here!"

"I didn't realize it until a few minutes ago, but this is where my journey ends, Lucas. I saw this in a dream long ago. I just didn't know that it would end here and now. You need to run. I will hold him off."

"NO! I need to help you!"

"Run!" She cried out as her bands of light broke and the massive beast slammed into the floor of the broken train car. The impact shook both Lucas and his grandma off their feet.

He reached over with his massive hand and grabbed her by the face and picked her up. She quickly swung her sword and took a gash out of his chest, but he didn't flinch. He squeezed hard with his hand and the cracking of skull caused Lucas to collapse to the ground sick and crying uncontrollably as her body went limp and the sword clanked to the ground.

The beast tossed her dead body to the side and took a step towards Lucas and a switch was flipped on inside of him as he jumped to his feet and rushed forward. He slammed into the chest of the beast and his momentum caused it to stumble back a step before its massive foot caught a broken seat from the train car. He fell backwards and Lucas rolled off to the right and caught his balance as the beast fell to his back.

Turning around, Lucas found the sword on the ground and picked it up. He turned and jumped into the air and came down on the thick leg of the minotaur and drove the blade straight into its massive thigh.

"Ahhh! You pesky little rodent!"

He twisted and turned to get away from Lucas and Lucas toppled to the ground. He quickly scrambled to his feet and took off in a dead run. He jumped over broken pieces of the train and rushed for the massive crowd of people who were trying to escape for their lives. If he could get to them, there was a chance he could blend in and disappear.

He chanced a glance back and saw the Minotaur was now standing up. He plucked the sword from his leg and tossed it off to the side. Like a rushing bull, he took a thundering step forward and chased after his prey.

Lucas ran hard, trying to catch up to the group of fleeing people who already had a head start. They cried louder as they rushed for safety and then Lucas realized that even if he did catch up to them, he would be putting them in harm's way. This beast would do to them what it did to his grandma. Lucas let out a whimper of pain as he recalled the sound of her skull being crushed.

He stopped and turned to meet the oncoming beast. He would have to sacrifice himself and trust in the Creator for whatever was coming next – just like she had told him. The Minotaur stopped charging forward and came to a stop. He looked around as if calculating why the boy was no longer running. "Come on and take me!" Lucas called out. He held his arms out to show he had no weapons. "I'm not running. I have nowhere to go! Just leave those people out of it!"

The beast drew back as he studied the situation closer. He was very reluctant to come forward – perhaps sensing a trap.

"What is this boy?" he called out in a gruff tone.

"I'm giving up."

"You are braver than I thought. We met in the woods not long ago... didn't we? You stood your ground with a branch? Perhaps I underestimated your kahunas."

Lucas didn't say anything. He took a step towards the beast and the beast took a reluctant step backwards. He seemed timid. Lucas took another step and while the beast seemed to want to hold his ground, he took yet another step back.

"Stay where you are at, boy!"

"I'm surrendering. It's what you wanted." Lucas felt in charge and he was suddenly feeling bold. He took a few more steps towards the beast and it took a few more steps back before he let out a steamy blast from his nostrils and his foot kicked the dirt and he took a hard stance.

"I will not be cornered. Step back or I will not hesitate to kill you. I don't care what the bounty is on your head!"

Lucas stopped. It had taken a strong stance and he didn't doubt its intention. He took a quick look around, trying to calculate how he could get out of this situation. He was certain that the Minotaur was not going to back down any further. He knew he couldn't outrun the beast because it had a massive stride. He didn't stand a chance in fighting it hand to hand but he couldn't just stand here and surrender himself willingly – could he?

Lucas took a second to study the beast. It had pistols strapped to its chest with extra round tucked in the bandolier. There was heavy chest plating covering its vital organs and the metal gauntlets seemed more like battering rams than a form of protection. Perhaps he used them for both.

"Lay down on your stomach, boy. Put your hands behind your head and don't move an inch."

Lucas did as he was told, not certain that he had any other choice. The beast came forward and then knelt down, driving his bulky knee into the small of his back. Anymore pressure and Lucas was worried his spine would snap in two. The beast pulled Lucas' arms down to the middle of his back and tied them together at the wrist. Then he stood up and pulled Lucas into the air and tossed him over his shoulder.

Perhaps Lucas was hoping for a miracle and that some massive ball of light would encase him and give him the powers and ability to defeat the Minotaur – but instead he was tied up and dangling over the shoulder of the beast. It broke into a run and started towards the West.

"Where are we going?" Lucas asked.

"I need the two of you to complete this bounty. Luckily for your sake, you both are to walk out of this alive. I only need your blood."

"You're a servant of the Dark Master?"

"I serve nobody! While there are many that quiver under his rule… I am not one of them. I work for my own gain and I work for the highest bidder."

"What's he paying you? We can double it."

"You haven't the gold to pay for my service, boy. You haven't the means to outbid the Dark Master."

"Try me. I'm the future king of this land."

"You have no future, boy. I know who you and your brother are. The throne of the McGregor's has long been vacant and the wealth is long gone. You have nothing to barter with and therefore have no power over me. If by chance you do come across a small fortune one day, then feel free to hire my services. Until that day, be silent. I hate talking to those I am charged with capturing."

And with that, the conversation was over. His grandma had died to save his life and yet he was on the shoulder of a bounty hunter with no idea what was coming next. If this was part of the plan of the Creator, Lucas was lost to find any possible good that could come from it.

15

When Caleb finished the short climb up the ladder and back into the main living area of the cottage, he looked over to find Marcause fixing a sandwich from the ham that Grandma had cooked the other night. He sliced off two thick pieces of bread and then tossed a thick cut of meat between the two pieces and took a large bite out of it.

With his mouth full he said, "She cooks the meat in such a way that it keeps its juices for days. She is a master cook," a piece of chewed food rolled out of the corner of his mouth and fell on the counter. He reached down, picked it up and tossed it into his mouth.

Caleb turned back to his work at hand. He added the map and the hilt of the sword to his sack of provisions and then heaved them up onto his shoulder and made his way for the front door.

"Leaving Carsonia?"

"I'm heading south. I need to get to the nearest gate before they close it."

"And leave your lady friend here to fend for herself? That

is rather selfish. Are you sure about this decision?"

Caleb threw his pack on the ground and then fell into the chair nearby. He dropped his face into his hands and sobbed. It wasn't a crying with tears but more of a whimpering as his mind raced with so many scenarios and none of them seemed like the right path to follow. He really had no choice but to remain where he was and follow this fate – and that revelation was scaring him to death.

"You have the potential to be the greatest Knight of Liberty that has ever walked the face of Carsonia. But it comes with a great price. You must sacrifice what you hold dear and embrace the path the Creator is placing before you."

"I have a lot going for me back home. None of it requires the world being placed on my shoulders! None of it requires me sacrificing the things I like to do!"

Marcause walked over and placed both of his hands on Caleb's shoulders. He gently pushed the boy back so that their eyes could meet. "Those who live for selfish gain can live a fabulous life… but in their dying breath they will all tell you that it was empty to them. They lacked that feeling of true closure and accomplishment.

"The people of Carsonia have been shrouded in darkness for thousands of years. They waited for the one who would bring peace back into the land and now he has arrived. Is it you? Is it your brother? Does it really matter? Just you being here has given me great hope. Imagine the hope that can be restored to this world when it learns that the Twins of the Prophecy are here. Imagine what joy and possibilities your presence will bring to the people of this land."

"And what if I'm the evil one? I have these..." Caleb trailed off. He didn't want to reveal too much about himself and instead chose to keep the unfinished thought to himself. "What if I am the chosen one to rule and I have to kill my brother to bring that balance and peace? What if it's me who is evil and he has to kill me. One of us walks away a murderer of his own brother. One of us walks away with that scar."

"Perhaps. Perhaps not. I told you before, I believe the Creator gives us the freedom of choice. I believe that you only have to become evil if that is the path you choose to obtain your power. You can never gain the powers of the Light if you continue on your current path. However, you can tap into the powers of dark magic if you so choose. You have that ability. We all have that ability. It falls on our decisions.

"Will you rise up and follow your destiny or will you run like your father? Will you choose to sacrifice your own desires and be a bringer of peace in a land with no hope or will you pursue the riches and gains of your heart and become a servant of the Dark Master? Only you can make those choices."

Caleb's eyes drifted away from the bright blue eyes of the Angellian. They were powerful and somewhat familiar eyes and he was certain that the elf could use them to make him do anything he chose. Andrea always seemed to have that same power over him. He had always figured it was her natural power of being a woman. But now, looking into the eyes of this Angellian who had almost the same eyes as her, he realized that there was some sort of mystic power contained there.

His heart told him to run but his gut told him to stay put and follow the guidance of Marcause. "How do I tap into the power of the Light?"

Marcause smiled and then patted him on the cheek. "Purge the selfish desires and you will see the way. Everyone gets there in a different manner but the key to taking the first step is to get rid of the obstacles that block your path. For you, it is your ambitions. Choose instead to follow the path that the Creator has placed before you. Learn to sacrifice and follow and it will all become clear."

Caleb reached down to the pack at his feet and opened it up. Inside he found the sword hilt and the map and he took them out. He tucked the rolled up map in his belt at the small of his back and then fumbled with the handle. He flicked it a few times in hopes of getting it to transform, but to no avail.

"Will it, Caleb. You need to will it to life. Feel your mind command it to come to life. Close your eyes and feel the connection between your mind and the sword. See the electricity inside the handle and stir it to life. Touch it like when your fingers touched the glass ball and caused it to dance and light up."

"But turning on the light is simple. It's just a matter of touching it."

"Yes, but your mind told you that by touching it the light would come on. And so it did. Your mind must tell the sword to come to life. Right now, your mind is working against you as it says it is not possible. You must get rid of what you know and just believe. Touch the sword with your mind like your fingers touched the light. The two work together as one."

"Are you trying to sound like a riddle?"

"Put the doubt away. Believe that it can happen."

Caleb closed his eyes and searched for that doubt. He could clearly see his mind telling him that a sword blade doesn't appear from nowhere. The rules of physics in the world he grew up in cannot be applied in the same way here – at least not in all circumstances – NO! That is doubt. He had to cast that doubt out. The laws of physics have no power here at all. He had to convince his mind of that. He willed his mind to believe that the impossible could be possible. He willed his mind to see the blade click out of the handle.

With a flick of his wrist, he tried again. He heard a metallic clink. Then another clink. Then he heard what sounded like little metal pellets raining down on a tin roof and he looked down to find the balls of metal coming out of the handle and forming together into a blade. They continued to roll out until the full sword blade extended out from the handle. His eyes grew big and his heart beat became rapid. He turned to look at Marcause and found the elf with a wide smile and dancing blue eyes.

"You have done it, Caleb. You have done well."

Caleb raised the sword up and held the blade before his face. He reached out and gently slid his finger along the flat side, careful not to accidently run it along the razor sharp edge. "This is incredible," he said.

"It is only a small step, Caleb. You and your brother have much more to learn. Which reminds me, they have been gone for a long while and should be returning soon. You cannot tell your grandmother I was here. My presence is only for security purposes and I don't want her thinking the Knights of Liberty are spying on her. She is rather paranoid about them."

"But you are a family friend and you're not one of them."

"Your grandma was a spy in the Order. Her job was to infiltrate and disseminate information from warring kingdoms many years ago. She does not take ones words at face value but looks for hidden meanings – which are good traits for a spy I guess. While I can tell her I am no longer with the Order, I highly doubt she would believe me. When your father returns, I will reveal myself and then we can speak again."

"Why did you come here?"

"To encourage you to see the gift that is before you and not the curse that you perceive," he turned to leave but stopped just short of opening the door. He turned and smiled back at Caleb, "And to tell you to make up with your brother. You only have one you know."

Caleb smiled and watched as the Angellian walked out the door and closed it tight behind him. Caleb turned his attention back to the sword. He didn't ask how to retract the blade and so he practiced that exercise until he accidently figured it out. Then he flicked it to life again and then retracted it once more. He did this for a while until he realized that night was falling and his family had not returned.

Caleb tucked the sword hilt in his belt by his side, grabbed a cloak from the rack on the wall and threw it around himself and then stepped out. Pulling up the hood, he began to make his way to the train station. The boys had been careful to conceal the presence of two of them in the village and so he tried his best to be inconspicuous since Lucas had gone out with Grandma that morning.

How could they be gone for this amount of time?

As he neared the station he picked up chatter from people. There were murmurs of an accident and a rampaging Minotaur that was on the loose. He heard one lady crying and saying that there were deaths at the scene and that the people fled for their lives and that the beast murdered them all. The discussions varied greatly and to Caleb they seemed more like a game of telephone where one person began a conversation and by the time it was passed on to the last person in the line, the conversation was completely different.

He approached a young girl that was around his age. She was leaning against a post, watching down the track for any sign of a hopeful return of the train.

"Excuse me," he said to her. She turned to look at him and noticed her eyes were filled with tears. "I'm sorry. What's going on here?" he asked.

"Did you have a loved one on the train?"

"Did something happen?"

"It did not return at the proper time. There are rumors of an accident and even rumors of an attack. There was a time here in the North that nothing bad ever happened. Now we hear of goblins in the foothills – striking the villages on the edges. We hear of armies surrounding our land. Now we hear that those who left this morning may all be dead. It could be by accident or it could be by an attack like what we are hearing right now. There is no way to tell."

She broke into a deep sob as the tears streamed down her cheeks. Caleb reached out and pulled her close. Her head rested on his shoulder and for the first time he felt his sadness for the pain of someone else. He could feel her worry and pain and it reminded him of his own. His wrestling with the loss of being in control of his own destiny. His longing to hold Andrea. A tear ran down his cheek as well.

"It's okay," he whispered.

"Carsonia is falling into great darkness. The skies grow orange from the fires that rage to the South. Evil has flooded the mountains to the North. My father came from the Southern Kingdoms many years ago and spoke of the great sadness there. The people here are starting to feel that same hopelessness. We pray for deliverance, but there is none to be found. The world grows darker and the Creator remains silent."

"There's something coming!" someone called out.

"What is it?" another cried out.

Panic engulfed the train station and everyone ran for cover, scooping up the young children and rushing down the streets for the cover of home. The girl in his arms didn't make a move, she only clung to him tighter.

"You should go," he said to her as he pushed her towards the exit. "Get back home."

"I have no home without my dad. He is all I have left."

"I'll find him," Caleb said for no obvious reason. He had problems of his own and yet he was suddenly willing to go searching for her missing dad?

She looked at him, the tears still rolling down her cheeks. She studied him in detail and then looked down at his waist and caught a glimpse of the sword hilt. "Are you a Knight of Liberty?"

Caleb wished that he was because he suddenly was finding a new found urgency to protect these people and yet he wasn't even equipped for such a task. "No... maybe... it's kind of complicated." He pushed her out the door and shooed her away with a gesture of his left hand while his right hand went for the sword. "Get home. I'll take care of this and then go and find your dad."

Reluctantly, she backed away from the station and then turned to run for the safety of her home – wherever that was. Caleb stepped back inside and then flicked his wrist with the sword handle. Nothing happened.

"Crap. I need to do this exercise again?" he was feeling taxed as he heard the thundering steps of the large beast approaching. He could now make out a body that was thrown over his shoulder. With the fading night sky, Caleb was hard pressed to make out who was on the beasts shoulder, but he had a strong hunch that it was Lucas – and how his brother got there was a complete mystery to him.

He closed his eyes to concentrate. He cleared the doubt from his mind and then went through the motion of flicking his wrist and suddenly the sword was back to life in his hand. He stepped off the platform and into the train track and looked at the oncoming creature. He took a deep breath to calm his nerves but he was lost for what he could possibly do. He was one kid with no training and about to go face to face with some bulky creature that looked like a bull with a human body.

How do you stand up to that?

He felt a whoosh of the air move around him. He jumped to the side and caught the sight of a glowing, fuzzy object landing on the ground next to him. The particles of light merged together and formed the body of Marcause.

He threw back his long flowing blond hair like some movie star and then pulled a bow and arrow off of his back. He looked down to load the first arrow and without looking up, said to Caleb, "You took my pep talk a little farther than I would have liked. This isn't a goblin in case the oversized object rushing towards us fooled you. This is a Minotaur and a very dangerous one at that. His name is Mideon. He is one of the best bounty hunters and mercenaries in Carsonia. Not someone I recommend you taking on during your first bout."

"I don't know how I got here. I was minding my own business and all of a sudden I got…"

"The feeling that you are called to protect these people?"

Caleb didn't answer, but it was the feeling that had washed over him. It was a feeling he didn't have just hours ago. To go from fleeing to standing in the path of danger was not something new to him. He did it all the time on the football field, but this was different. He was standing in the path not for personal glory but because of some sense of duty.

Maybe it was the pep talk. Maybe it was the compassion he felt for the girl who reminded him of Andrea. Either way, here he was. He felt much better with the Angellian standing next to him.

"I think he has Lucas."

"I know he has Lucas. I'll take care of Mideon. You and your brother need to make a run for it. Take the map in my back pouch."

Caleb brushed aside the Angelians flowing cape and reached into the pouch to find a map folded into a tight square. He looked it over and then to Marcause who was taking aim and soon released his first shot. The arrow deflected off the chest plate of Mideon.

"I marked off the route your father took. I will hold off Mideon and you and your brother must follow the path on there. Stay off the main roads. Conceal yourself in the cover of the woods and vegetation. Mideon will follow and he will find you if you slow down. You must move quickly. You are seven days journey away from where he is going."

"What about you?"

"I will hold off Mideon and try to wound him enough to keep him off your trail for a few days. Hopefully you can meet up with Vladamir, Nathan and Gavin before he catches up."

Caleb wanted to argue, but the Angellian was firing arrow after arrow at the beast and it was now within a few yards of them. Marcause pulled out his sword and charged forward, slashing down with a hard attacking chop.

Mideon dumped Lucas to the ground and met the challenge with his right hand. He raised it up and the blade of the sword slammed into his gigantic gauntlet. He then came around with a hard left handed punch that slammed into the ribs of Marcause and threw him into the side of the platform.

He turned to grab Caleb who was rushing over to his

fallen brother. Caleb slashed his sword with a wild movement and Mideon grabbed the blade with his bare hand. With a twist of his wrist, he snapped half the blade off and tossed it aside like a twig. He then reached out to grab Caleb but Marcause fired an arrow into the beasts left arm.

"Ahh!" he cried as he turned his attention back to the Angellian. "I will rip you in three parts!" He threw a hard fist at the head of Marcause who ducked under the blow and then lunged forward with his sword, aiming for an unprotected part of the Minotaur's mid-section. He connected with something because Mideon reared up with a roar and backhanded Marcause to the ground.

Caleb knelt down to cut the ropes from Lucas only to turn and find the bounty hunter coming towards him again. Caleb reared back with his broken sword and threw it straight at the head of Mideon. The blade tore into the flesh on the left side of his face and he snarled with even more rage as the blood sprayed from the wound.

Marcause returned to his feet and then surrounded himself in The Light. Reaching out with a tentacle, he lifted Mideon up into the air and tossed him into a group of rocks over fifty yards away. He turned to Caleb and reminded him one last time, "Take the route on the map. Stick to it. Stay out of open areas and move quickly. Break no longer than an hour at a time and find your dad."

Caleb had a sinking feeling as he looked at Marcause

whose perfect hair was now greasy and gnarled from battle. He trusted the Angellian and wanted to stand by his side to fight off the bounty hunter – and yet he knew he had to obey.

"Will you come find us?"

Marcause didn't look confident that he would survive this battle, but he mustered up enough of a smile to give Caleb some hope that they would meet again. "Go kid. Follow your path."

Caleb grabbed Lucas by the arm and guided him in the general direction that Marcause indicated for him to go. He could hear the din of battle behind him and his heart ached at having to leave a friend behind. What would happen to him? Did he even stand a chance against such a warrior?

He left those thoughts behind and focused on the escape. They ran across an open field and discovered a dirt road that moved through the woods. Caleb chose to stay on the road against Marcause's orders for at least a few miles, so they could get a better head start. When he felt confident that they had a safe lead, Caleb darted into the woods and Lucas followed him.

By moonlight they traveled as safely as they could. They dodged fallen trees and took slaps to the face by stinging branches. They ran through small streams and crossed over a couple of fields. Caleb wasn't sure how long they traveled but he made sure to keep the road just to his left as a way to guide them on the path the Angellian had mapped out.

It wasn't long until Caleb regretted not taking the pack of provisions he had put together back at the cottage. His stomach growled and his mouth was dry. He stopped and waited for Lucas to catch up. Panting, Lucas bent over and caught his breath.

"Put your hands on your head," he told Lucas. "You'll get deeper breaths and recover faster."

"I don't care... I really don't."

"Where's Grandma?"

"Dead."

That word hung in the air for a bit. Caleb felt like he had been slapped across the face and he stumbled back to a nearby tree and reached out and used it to keep himself from falling to the ground. "How?"

"The Minotaur."

"But how?"

"I don't want to talk about it. Where are we going?"

"Marcause gave me a map that will lead us to Dad."

"Does it take us to a Walmart or McDonalds? Because we've got nothing."

Caleb smiled and regained his composure. Stress from battle was something he was used to from the football field. While this was an entirely different situation, he saw a common thread and used it to draw confidence and leadership.

"I'm sorry, Lucas. For what I said this morning."

"It's over. I don't want to talk about it anymore. I just want to get out of here," Lucas said. "You were right. We don't belong here."

Caleb almost broke into laughter about the irony. Suddenly Lucas was in his shoes and he was in Lucas'. The roles were switched. "I'm glad you're finally seeing things my way, but it's a bit too late. I don't think we're ever going back," Caleb said with a snort. "Marcause told me that the gates are being sealed up. By the time we find Dad, we'll be lucky if any of them are open to get out of."

"This just keeps getting better all the time."

Caleb pulled the map out and positioned it so that it caught a bit of the moonlight that glowed overhead. He could read it enough to see that they only had to follow this road for a few more miles and then it would fork to the North and to the Southeast. They would follow to the Southeast. Both ways had villages marked off and it looked as if Marcause had written a note at each one. Caleb tried hard to read it.

"What does it say?" Lucas asked as he stood next to his brother.

The howl of a wolf startled the two of them. It sounded fairly close.

"Think its hunting us?" Caleb asked.

"I don't want to find out."

Caleb quickly folded the map and tucked it back into his belt and the two of them hustled on for the rest of the night.

When day broke, they found a cool stream to drink from and a bush filled with berries. They looked much like raspberries so the boys took a chance and ate them with hopes of not killing themselves. Both seemed to survive and so they moved on with somewhat full belly's and hydrated.

By midday they had come to the outskirts of a small village. Caleb pulled out his map and read the note that Marcause had written for them. It read:

I have taken the liberty to leave provisions

for you at the hut of an old friend. Tell him

I sent you and he will take care of your needs.

Caleb looked over to Lucas as if hoping that he had the answer to the obvious question. Who was the old friend? Where in the village did he live? Lucas took the map from his brother and looked it over.

"He forgot some key details here," he said.

"Hmm," Caleb grunted in agreement. He took the map back from his brother and the two of them were about to move on when they heard the cracking of branches behind them. Both froze still and then slowly sank back to the ground.

The sound of a grunt made Caleb immediately worried. It was similar to the sound that Mideon had made during the battle. Had he caught up already? The grunt came again as something large continued to move towards them.

Caleb raised his head just a bit, hoping to get a look at whatever was coming, but Lucas pulled him back down. He motioned for his brother to be patient and wait – perhaps hoping that they wouldn't be seen and Mideon would move on.

It let out another grunt and came to a stop. They could hear him sniffing the air and then it began to move quicker, crashing through the woods. The ground shook with each step and Caleb looked over to Lucas who shared the same expression.

It was coming straight for them.

16

Andrea was startled awake.

Yet another dream about Caleb. She kept seeing him in every dream as she slept. Her sudden jolt must have waken Catrina because she could hear her stirring.

"Are you okay?" Catrina asked.

She shook the thoughts of Caleb holding another girl in his arms from her mind. He didn't seem to love her – only care about her situation. Still, it wasn't the type of dream she felt like having right now.

"Are you okay?" Andrea turned the question around.

"We're going to be just fine."

"I'm asking about you. Are you okay?"

She was slow to answer. They were tied up back to back against a pole and so she was able to feel Catrina's head move up and down as she answered with a silent "yes."

Just days ago, a wicked man in a dark cloak had come to the camp with a small force of Draith knights. While she couldn't see his face, his voice and movements were familiar. He looked intimidating from the outside, but his words were calm and controlled. He reminded her of one of those mad men in a Bond film as he methodically walked into the camp and did what he set out to do. Andrea was sure that he had come to dispose of them. Yet he didn't even attempt to lay a hand on them.

What he did come for was a necklace that Catrina wore around her neck. It was a necklace that as Andrea thought more about it, had always been around her neck. With all that she had learned over the past week, she was sure that necklace had some sort of meaning in Carsonia and so she drew up the courage to at last ask about it.

"What special power does that locket have?"

"You remember the gate we came through?"

Andrea shook her head up and down. She remembered it well. Something from that gate had changed her inside. She knew it. Suddenly she was having dreams and her ears were burning. Her skin even seemed to be growing pale. There was this feeling that the effects of passing through the portal were slowly killing her – some sort of toxic radiation.

But she didn't want to alarm Catrina and so she kept those dreadful feelings to herself.

"Yes, I remember," was her simple reply.

"The stone in the necklace has the power to close those gates."

It hit her with brute force. "They're locking us in this land!"

"They are."

With her right hand that was given enough length of chain to move, she ran her hand through her long hair. It was a calming technique that she had used since being a small girl. It brushed through one time, two times and a third time. She saw a glimpse of being stuck in this world forever and it frightened her.

What would her grandparents think? Would they have to go the rest of their lives not knowing what happened to their granddaughter? Would they have to bear that pain and never have any answers?

What about her life with Caleb? What about the treatment she was receiving from these beastly goblins? Would she have to continue to endure these constant slaps across the face and intimidation of being raped?

She breathed harder. Deep inside she wanted her heart to explode and free her from this chaos.

"It's going to be okay, Andrea. Calm yourself. I'm here," she heard from behind her.

She felt the gentle touch as Catrina reached behind and laid her palm on top of her head. She stroked what part of her hair that she could touch and it sent a ripple of hope through her. As she closed her eyes, she could see her mom holding her close during a thunderstorm and stroking her hair to calm her and assure her that the sun would shine in the morning.

"Gavin, Lucas and Caleb will rescue us. You'll see. Everything's going to be just fine."

Andrea closed her eyes and drifted off to sleep. For the first time in many days, nightmares did not wake her.

She only hoped that they would arrive before the poisoning from the portal, killed her.

17

The unseen beast stopped moving towards them and seemed to stand in place for a few seconds. It then took a thundering step forward.

Caleb jumped at the sound and came out of the deep thought he was just having. Lucas remained still, as if he were in the woods and trying to avoid detection by a deer that had become alert to his presence. Another step slammed into the ground. It was moving closer. Finally, Caleb couldn't take any more of the waiting. He refused to just be trampled on by the monster.

He grabbed a fallen branch that was near him, jumped to his feet and hurled the chunk of wood at it. With a clank, the wood hit the metal body of the fifteen foot robotic looking thing and fell harmlessly to the ground. Caleb took a step back, not sure what to make of the metallic hulk he was facing. It was definitely not the bounty hunter he had seen back in the village.

"Hi Ho there!" came a squeaky voice from inside the robot like creature. It looked like an overgrown, metallic troll. The body was made out of poorly pounded metal that was shaped to look like muscular arms and legs with a torso. The head was almost the same size of the massive chest and had no features to it except one single pane of glass that was stained a dark color so Caleb couldn't see inside. There seemed to be two screen like vents where the nostrils of a real life creature might be.

"Wait a tick. I'll be right down!" came the voice again.

By this time, Lucas was back on his feet and standing alongside his brother. The fear they had both felt was now replaced with curiosity as obviously, this thing didn't pose a direct threat to their safety.

They both examined the metallic beast from a safe distant and then jumped when the chest of the monster sprung open to reveal a slide. Suddenly, a set of little legs shot into view and were followed by the entire, short and stout little body of a tiny man who slid down and plopped onto the ground before the boys.

He dusted off his black tunic and straightened his pointy green hat and then lumbered forward to the boys, extending his hand out as a gesture of welcome. He wasn't more than waist high to the twins. His little pointy beard was thick with gray.

"I am Bombadore! I assume you are the Twins of the Prophecy? Marcause told me I could expect you and should be looking for you. You would be in need of my services... he was certain of that."

"Are you an... inventor?" Caleb's eyes darted back and forth between Bombadore and the metallic creation.

"No, no my dear boy. I am a Magith. A metal smith who has mastered the art of using electricity to enhance the metal ores found in the mountains. Some people call us magicians... but I assure you there is no magic involved in what we do. We are masters of our craft and sometimes that appears magical to others. But, that is the price you pay for being as great at this craft as I am.

"Did I mention that my name is Bombadore? Oh dear me. I do get a little wordy and speak a little more than the average dwarf. I sometimes get off track and completely lose sight of the original question. Which was..." he trailed off as he looked to the boys for prompting.

Caleb and Lucas exchanged confused glances at one another.

"Which was?" Bombadore asked again.

"I have no idea what you are asking us about," Lucas said.

"What were we talking about, indeed? I can't remember your original question."

"You answered our original question," Caleb said.

"I did?" his face lit up and he did a little hop into the air and snapped his fingers, "Jolly good! I often never get around to answering questions. I am very happy that I answered yours. Shall we get on with it now?"

"Get on with what?" Caleb asked.

"Well, with what you want from me, of course. Why have you come looking for me?"

"We didn't. We didn't even know we were supposed to meet with you," Caleb said.

"The map! I almost forgot about the map. Did you read over your map? If you will take note, the first stop on your journey was marked here. You were supposed to find me."

"The provisions in the notes," Lucas reminded his brother. "Marcause told us that he left provisions for us at the hut of an old friend. You must be his old friend."

"Indeed. Marcause got his first sword from me. Often, many Knights of Liberty purchase their swords from me. I am after all the greatest Magith in all of the land. Did you know that my swords and only my swords can morph into battle axes and a powerful mace? Quite the feat if I do say so myself. Do you realize how much manipulation it takes to give the metallic ore that much memory? To remember those three forms? To train it. In many ways, our technology is based off teaching the metal to do what we want it to do from magnetic impulses. But that is an entire new discussion all together. Which reminds me, who are you two?"

"The Twins of Prophecy," Lucas said.

"Well of course you are the Twins of Prophecy, but what are your names, Silly head? We all have names."

Lucas opened his mouth to introduce himself but

Bombadore interrupted, "Speaking of names... I haven't given this contraption a name but it is my prototype battle suit. One day I hope to equip every Knight of Liberty with one. With this, can you imagine what the armies could accomplish? We could wipe out the Draith once and for all. Push darkness out of Carsonia forever. I thought I should bring it out on a test run while I wait for you two to arrive. I cannot even imagine having someone else test run this suit. It has been known to crush itself. I would hate to watch someone inside be crushed if it were to go crazy and do such a thing. I would assume you would hate to see such a thing as well.

"Speaking of which, what are your names?" Caleb almost answered before the little guy continued on, "The woods can be a dangerous place for a little dwarf like me. There are beasts like no others in these here woods. I'm actually surprised you haven't been eaten yet, but that is a conversation for a different time. Come along now, we need to get back to my hut so I can get you two on your way."

With a little twirl, Bombadore hobbled over to his battle suit prototype and reached inside to grab hold of a little rope. He hopped up and climbed back into the head part, closed the chest plate and began to lumber back through the woods and towards the village. Both Caleb and Lucas needed to jog to keep up with the long stride of the robotic like creation.

"If we're not careful, this guy's going to bore us to death with his drawn out, one way discussions," Caleb said.

"I kind of like the little fella. He seems nice."

"He's also small. I don't want us to be anywhere near this village when the bounty hunter arrives. I don't want someone else to die for us. First Grandma was killed, then Marcause. Something tells me that the bounty hunter won't pass through here nicely. Let's get what we need and then get the heck out of here."

Lucas hung his head low as the thoughts of his grandma returned for the first time since she was killed. Things had been happening so quickly that he didn't really have time to dwell on the events of the past day – and it had only been a day. So much had happened.

"She was a Knight of Liberty. Did you know that?"

"Grandma?" Caleb asked.

"Yea. She and Grandpa both served in the Order. I suppose it really runs in our blood."

"I guess. I almost feel like we should become Knights of Liberty... but my heart just isn't in it. I just want to get home – away from all of this craziness."

"I'm starting to agree with you."

The two continued to follow along behind Bombadore and his beast of a machine. Surprisingly, he walked right down the middle of the village and straight to his hut where he stopped alongside of it as if he were parking a car. None of the dwarfs who were outside working paid any attention to Bombadore's creation. Perhaps they were used to seeing him and his inventions out on the street. The chest plate popped open and Bombadore slid back out and escorted the boys into his home.

"Righty-then. Welcome to my humble home. I have cookies on the table, goat milk in the cooling box and I probably have some fried potato flakes in the cupboard."

"Chips," Lucas commented.

"Chips?" Bombadore asked.

"Your potato flakes. We call them chips from where we come from. Grandma had some in her cupboard also."

"Interesting. Feel free to take a jar or two with you. I made too many to eat all by myself. I do not suppose you two will be staying long. In fact, if I might be saying, I think you two should be on the move very soon. I have a feeling that Mideon will not be far behind."

"The bounty hunter?" Caleb asked. "His name is Mideon? How do you know this?"

"News travels faster than one might think, my boy. Speaking of which, you two still haven't told me your names." Caleb was about to answer when the little guy continued on, "Ah! Here are the two sacks that Marcause has prepared for you. Both are packed with extra clothing, food rations, a few essential tools that you will need as you navigate the terrain and who knows what else."

He tossed the sacks at each boy who in turn caught them and threw them over their shoulders.

"It is a very dangerous world out there. You will both need

weapons… and not some of those poorly made garden tools that the other Magiths try to pawn off as 'weapons' mind you. I am talking about the perfectly crafted weapons of beauty that I make by hand."

Bombadore walked over to the far side of his hut and slapped a metal plate that looked like a mirror that was hastily hung on the wall. A bolt of electricity shot along the wall and struck a book case which then began to slide along the edge of the wall, revealing a hidden compartment that lit up as the bookshelf finished moving out of the way.

Caleb and Lucas looked up at the gleaming, shiny objects that were clipped to the inside wall. There were magnificent sword hilts, gauntlets, helmets and what looked to be grenades. He had a variety of pistols that didn't seem to require bullets because there were no cylinders for the rounds to sit in and no hammer to draw back and fire them off. They did have a trigger, but it didn't look as if it were designed to move.

"Can I get one of those?" Lucas asked, pointing at one of the guns.

"I think not. But I will give you two of these," and he handed the boys two grenades each.

"You won't give us a gun but you'll give us grenades?" Caleb asked as he cautiously handled them as if they were fragile eggs.

"Grenades? I have no idea what a grenade is, but what

you have here is teleporting explosive devices."

"Sounds like a grenade to me."

"You pull the pin, toss it and wait for it to explode. It will open a portal hole that you can leap into. Once inside the portal, you pull the pin and toss your next grenade wherever you wish and it opens up the exit for you to leave the teleporting tube. It really is complicated to explain but very much self-explanatory once you are inside. Just make sure you have a second TED so you can get out... or you might get stuck in the tube forever."

"TED?" Lucas asked.

"Teleporting-Explosive-Device. T-E-D. Are you not listening?"

"I'm listening, but you are going so fast," Lucas complained.

"Just keep up with me, my boy. We do not have much time for conversation. I am a very busy dwarf and you need to get on your way before Mideon catches up to you two. By the way, you still haven't told me your names." He didn't give them time to answer, "Both of you need to pick a sword. As I told you before, you can transform your sword into an axe, a mace or of course, the weapon of choice for all Knights of Liberty – and a bit cliché if you ask me – a sword."

"Thank you, Mr. Bombadore. You are very generous," Lucas said as he selected his weapon and Caleb chose his. The boys clipped them on the thick leather belt with many pouches that they had found tied onto their travel packs and then tucked the grenades into the pockets of the pouches. "Do we have to worry about these things blowing up in our belts?"

"No, no. You need to pull the pin first. Then the lever on top will pop off because it is spring loaded. Once those two mechanisms have been released, then and only then will it blow up. But you get a few seconds to throw it of course. The pins might be able to wiggle out inside your pouches, but the chances of the lever popping off are doubtful. They seem quite snug in your utility pouch. You should be safe. Worst case, one blows up and half your body gets transported. I have not seen it happen all that much. Normally under extreme cases only. Now, we need to get you two on your way."

He ushered them out the back door and then took them between rows of huts as they made their way in an easterly direction. It didn't take long to reach the edge of the village and then they stopped. He looked over each boy and then patted them both on their elbows. His eyes seemed to be flooding with tears.

"I am going to miss you boys. I haven't had this much fun in so long. I wish you both a safe journey. May the Creator light your way," He quickly hugged both boys and then pushed them on their way. "Now get going you crazy kids. You still haven't given me your names. What are your names?" Caleb opened his mouth but Bombadore continued on, "Stay safe and follow the trail that Marcause has marked out for you.

Look out for strange beasts. They may seem cute and cuddly, but they often bite and are sometimes known to tear off body parts."

"Tear off body parts?" Caleb asked.

Bombadore ignored the question and moved them along, "Now go!"

Caleb and Lucas took off in a light jog as they made their way for the woods and were soon on their way again. Both felt as if they had suffered whiplash. Bombadore seemed to be a very pleasant dwarf, but he didn't stay put for very long. It was really hard to get a word in edge wise, and while he seemed to bond with the boys, they barely had a chance to get to know him.

"After hearing those stories about little beasts that tear off body parts, I think I'd rather take my chance in his prototype battle suit. I'd rather have it crush me then to get ripped apart," Caleb said.

"You don't think he was serious, do you?"

"Let's not find out. I don't feel like tangling with some crazy bunny rabbit with twenty inch fangs."

Night had settled in on the land. The boys ran along the edge of the road, careful not to get too close to the center and expose themselves. Instead, they stayed tight to the woods. They were able to move faster by not going all the way into the forest, but still able to blend in with the darkness that the shadows of the trees provided.

While they weren't following Marcause's directions completely, it was a good compromise they believed. The most important thing was to find their dad and if possible, get the heck out of Carsonia. Neither Caleb nor Lucas wanted to be a part of it any longer. If what Marcause said was true, every day that passed was another day that the Draith had to close up more portals.

It was a race against time if they ever wanted a chance to return home.

18

They traveled through the night and as the daylight began to break over the horizon, both of them realized that their strength was fading.

"How did we make it through the entire night without eating?" Caleb wondered out loud.

"Adrenaline, man. Pure adrenaline. Nothing makes you move with a purpose than the idea that you could be the prey of some wild animals hunt. At least, that's what worked for me."

"Hmmm," Caleb agreed with a grunt.

Lucas stopped and began to take in his surroundings. "We need to find some place to bed down for the day. We could build a make shift brush pile and hunker down inside like we did with Dad."

Caleb gave Lucas a queer look and then asked, "Do you really feel like going through all that work? Can't we just find a cave or a fallen tree?"

"Just saying. I really don't care what we do. I just want to eat and close my eyes for a bit. I'm feeling it now. I need some shut eye."

They both moved into the woods and scanned the area. The vegetation wasn't very thick. The woods had age to them as the trees reached high into the sky and blocked most of the sunlight. There wasn't a tangle of shrubs and tons of fallen trees. Instead it was a soft, clean forest floor. Finding shelter wouldn't be as easy as they had once thought.

They walked in farther and continued to look around. A large rock formation caught Caleb's eyes. "Hey, over here! I think I found something."

The two walked over and found a hill of rock not far from the road. There were many outcroppings of rock and nooks and crannies that provided a small amount of protection and concealment. This had strong potential to work for their first rest stop. The two of them continued to examine it closer until they came upon a large hole that went deep into the hill.

A cave!

"Well lookie here," Caleb said in a southern drawl.

"Vicious animals, Caleb. This entrance is just screaming, vicious animals."

"You're the mighty hunter. Look," he said as he pointed to the ground around the entrance, "none of the ground is disturbed. Nothing has been going in or out of here in days. Look at the dirt inside. I don't see even one paw print."

"That's what scares me. This is the perfect place to live in and nothing is using it? What's inside that keeps the critters out?"

Caleb gave it a quick thought and then decided to take a chance. He stuck his head into the shadows, looked around and then went into the darkness, leaving Lucas outside. "Come on! It's nice and cool in here and the ground is soft. This should work out just fine."

Lucas cast a quick glance around the woods and decided that he didn't have any other choice. They needed a good days rest before they began the next stretch of their journey and his stomach was gnawing away inside. He was fearful it might begin to eat its way out. He took a leary step into the cave, turned back and crouched down and used his hand to wipe away their footprints from the sand and then joined his brother in the darkness.

"Caleb?"

"Right here. Give me a second," came the voice in the darkness. Lucas could not see anything but he could tell that his brother was right. The ground was definitely soft and should provide a nice bedding place.

Suddenly there was a pop and a crackle of electricity and Lucas jumped back, instinctively reaching to his side and grabbing the hilt of his sword. The cavern lit up in a light blue glow and Lucas realized it was his brother holding a glass glow rod.

"I found it in my ruck sack at our last stop while you were looking at the map. I wasn't sure if it would light up, but I couldn't figure out what other use it would have. Thought I would give it a try."

"Nice. Now we have a source of light. We might need it tonight. I noticed the clouds rolling in from the west. I'm thinking we're going to have some rain."

"Then I say, let's take the night off. I'm not feeling up to a wet walk."

"We need to keep going, Caleb. We need to find Mom and Dad and get out of here."

"Andrea too," he reminded him. "She's stuck here too. You seem to be singing a different tune."

Caleb began to walk deeper into the cave. The light wasn't powerful, but it still gave off enough glow that it could possibly be seen if someone got close enough to the entrance. He felt safer by moving farther back.

"What do you mean?" Lucas asked of the last statement.

"Just that you seem more eager to get out of here than you did before. You're sounding more like me when we first got here."

"Hmm," came his reply.

They came to slight bend in the cave and both of them seemed to feel that this had given them enough buffer space to protect them from being found by any passerby. Caleb dropped his ruck sack along the curved wall on one side and Lucas did the same across from him along the other curved wall. Caleb dropped his light stick in between them so they both got some light and then he flopped down and let out a deep sigh.

"I'm so eating a whole pizza when we get home. I'd give anything for a large, deep dish pizza from *Pizza Hut* right now," Caleb said.

"What are you willing to give up?" It was the beginning of an old game the two of them had played for as long as they could have conversations.

"I would give you my car if you could magically turn my ruck sack into a pizza. Heck, you can have my car and my cell phone. What about you?"

"I'm not craving a pizza. I think I'd rather have a half pound cheeseburger from the bar and grill on Main Street. Dad and I get those every year when we go into town to register our deer. I don't know what they season that thing with, but it leaves me drooling for another one. I honestly could sit there all day and keep eating those dang things!"

"So what would you give to have one?" Caleb asked as he dug out a ration meal from his pack and began to tear off the wrapping. It was some sort of hard bread or cracker – though he couldn't tell which it resembled more as he took a bite.

"I'd give up my gun and stop hunting just to get one."

"Wow! Now that's some serious sacrifice, Bro. A car I could replace but to give up hunting? You live for that."

"I live for those burgers, man. That's the only reason I

hunt," he said with a smile as he bit into his crumbly bread thing.

Caleb grabbed his canteen and took a long drink from it to wash down the dust like remains of the bread that was in his mouth. He swirled some water to clean out what was wedged in his teeth and then spit it off to the side.

"I'm going to grab some shut eye," he said as he laid his ruck down flat and then rested his head on the pack and sprawled out on the soft ground. He noticed that it was a little damp and had begun to give his clothes a moist feeling, but he was too tired to care. Once they were up and moving later on, his clothes would be wet from the rain – if Lucas' amateur weather report could be trusted. Right now, his body was screaming for sleep.

"You think Mom, Dad and Andrea are okay?" Lucas asked as he pulled out his sword and began to play with it.

"Yea. Between him and Vladamir and Nate, I would say they have a pretty good shot of getting out of there in one piece. Better odds at living than we probably have."

"We're scrappy. We'll make it."

"Sure. Now be quiet. I need some z's."

Lucas held the hilt up in front of him and concentrated on bringing it to life. Bombadore had given them a brief lesson on how to use the swords, but to this point, he hadn't had a need to use it.

He concentrated on what he wanted the hilt to do. He

could visually see the little blocks coming up and out and clicking together to form a long blade – yet nothing happened.

"How did you get your sword to come to life?" he asked Caleb.

"Dude, go to sleep! I'll teach you later."

"I'm not tired yet. Just tell me and I'll leave you alone."

"I willed it to life."

"What does that mean?"

Caleb let out a long sigh before saying, "I just did what they told me to do and the blade came out. Just imagine it coming out, give the handle a flick and... bam! You have a sword. Now let me get some sleep."

Lucas didn't flick it. Maybe that's what he was missing. He went through the cycle again but added the flick at the end. The first tiny piece of metal rolled out and clicked into place, followed by an army of other pieces and they joined together and worked their way up into the air until Lucas held a full length sword in his hand. "Awesome! I did it!"

"Good. Now go to sleep!" Caleb let his annoyance be well known in his tone.

With a clumsy swing, Lucas slapped the sword into the side of the cave. He expected a clank, but instead it was more of a slurp sound followed by a rumble as the entire cave shook. A gentle breeze filled with a horrible stench rolled up from the darkness and washed over the boys, bringing Caleb to a sitting up position.

"What the heck is going on?" he asked.

Lucas scrambled to his feet and Caleb jumped up as well. The walls began to twist and the floor rolled up, tossing both boys back to the ground.

Something was seriously wrong!

The rolling floor of the cave became more constant and suddenly they realized that the rolls were pulling them deeper into the cavern.

"Something isn't right here," Lucas said.

"What was your first clue?" Caleb pulled out his hilt and extended his sword. He reached down and grabbed his ruck sack, tossed it over his shoulder and then lunged for his glow rod that was quickly being pulled in. There was more rumblings from the cave and then both of them realized a horrible truth...

"This isn't a cave, Caleb!"

"Seriously? Is this even possible?"

"Run!"

Both of them stumbled over the oncoming waves of fleshy ground that struck them and knocked them both to the ground. They scrambled back up and fought their way forward. The waves were like a hard ocean current slapping them and attempting to push them to the shore – except these waves seemed to be trying to pull them in.

Caleb began to understand the pattern of when the waves would strike and was able to leap over them and move forward quicker than Lucas. "Follow my lead!" Caleb called out. "Jump when I jump!"

Lucas had his feet swept out from under him and he was pulled back and out of the light of Caleb's glow stick. He scrambled back to his feet and lumbered forward, jumping just in time to miss the next wave but stumbling forward and being taken out by the next. Back on his belly, he went deeper into the cave.

"Lucas!" he heard his brother call out. Lucas was quickly tiring. He struggled to get back onto his feet but was taken out by the next wave and deeper he went. He could no longer see the blue hue of his brothers glow rod. He was a goner for sure.

He tried to get back up but the fleshy wave grabbed him and slammed him back to the ground and pulled him deeper and now he was too tired to fight on. He simply laid his head down on the slimy surface as it inched him deeper into the cave. Each wave lifted him up and pulled him further in. He closed his eyes and just enjoyed the ride.

In many ways, as each wave lifted him up, he had flashbacks to the times when his parents would take the two of them to Wisconsin Dells and they would swim in the large wave pool at Noah's Ark. It was a great memory and one he convinced himself he was living out.

He no longer felt the fear of dying but instead felt the joy of those summer days. Those happy moments with his family. Togetherness. Laughter. Loving embraces. It made his coming death so much more bearable.

Suddenly he was jolted from his restful state when he felt something grab onto his wrist. His eyes jolted open and he looked up into the glowing blue light that Caleb had clutched in his hand. "Get up! What are you doing?"

The next wave took out Caleb and he fell on top of his brother and the two of them were pushed forward until they ran into a slimy wall. The waves continued to slap into them and the wall gave way just a little bit with each push. Caleb struggled as he tried to get up, but the growing intensity of the waves kept pulling him back down. Suddenly, both boys were encased in the slimy membrane and then they rolled out the other side of the slime wall and landed in bubbling water.

The stench rose up and pierced their noses and both gagged at the same time. Lucas quickly got to his feet and shook the water off of his hands. He felt a slight tingling sensation and he almost feared to look down at his skin. "I think we're in its stomach."

"You think?"

"What could possibly be this big?"

"Who cares? We need to get out of here before we get digested."

"It must not be that acidic. Our clothes aren't burning off."

"Way to be positive, Lucas." Caleb waved his blue glow light around the vast stomach of the beast. He found the skeletal remains of some poor animal that had wandered in here at one point in time. How long did it take to get to that state? The stench continued to rise up and both of them took turns puking up what they had eaten for lunch as the smell of acid and rotting flesh, nipped at their noses.

"The grenades!" Lucas cried out. "We can use the grenades to get out of here!"

"We don't even know how to use them properly! What if we screw something up and half our body is on one side of Carsonia and the other just stays here?"

Lucas opened one of the pouches on his belt and pulled out two round grenades. "He said we pull the pin, throw it and then a portal opens up when it explodes. We jump into the portal, toss another grenade and it will create an exit for us."

"An exit where?"

Lucas shrugged his shoulders. "At this point, does it matter?"

"I could cut away at that stomach membrane."

"And we can try to hop over all those convulsions? It will pull us right back in and I don't have the energy to fight against those again." He waved the grenade in Caleb's face and grit his teeth as he said, "This is our best option. Trust me."

Caleb drew out his sword and then took a poke at the stomach wall. The room shuddered and both of the boys stumbled, nearly falling into the stomach juices. "I could try cutting my way out of the stomach, finding the heart and killing it."

"Knock yourself out," Lucas said as he pulled the pin on the grenade and tossed it a safe distance away, "but I'm going this way."

The boom of the grenade shook the entire stomach cavity and tossed both of them back against the membrane wall that kept them locked inside. Stomach juices were tossed about and both boys gagged as the stench intensified by stirring up the layer that had settled on the bottom. With water pouring out of his eyes, Lucas ran forward to the glowing ball of light that had been created in the aftermath of the explosion. Caleb was right behind him.

Just as he was about to go in, Lucas shouted, "I lost the other grenade! I must had dropped it when the beast started moving!" He turned to go back and look for it. The beast had started to move and thrash from the pain that was coming from its stomach area, making the footing of both boys uneven. The juices sloshed up and licked at the flesh of both boys and they both knew they couldn't risk wandering away from the portal.

Caleb dug into one of his pouches and produced a grenade. "We'll use this one!"

They both leaped into the portal and the violent world of a stomach disappeared and they were now in a world of swirling lights and clouds. It was a calm place with only the whooshing sound of a gentle breeze tickling their ears. Caleb turned and could see the dark area where the stomach of the beast was.

He looked to the front and there was only a great expanse of white nothingness. It was such a calming feeling to look into the sea of white. His anxiety was washed away. His heart had slowed down to a normal pace and he felt at peace for the first time in weeks.

"Pull the pin and throw the other grenade!" Lucas shouted, "The portal is closing up!"

Caleb looked back and he could see that the chaotic world they had left behind was now growing big and seemed to be overcoming the world of light they were standing in. He pulled the pin and tossed the grenade into the white space in front of them and after another powerful explosion, an expanse of woods could be seen. It was as if a large, white drape had been torn down the middle and exposed what was on the other side.

"GO!" Lucas shouted as he jumped through the new opening.

Caleb took a running jump also and both of them fell to the ground and rolled to a stop at the base of a large tree. He looked back at the portal they had just come through and could see the calming sea of white, shrink up and then disappear altogether.

"Can we go back into that world of light?" Caleb asked as he longingly looked at the space where the portal had once been.

"Hmm," Lucas grunted in agreement.

The two of them got up and quickly looked around at their surroundings. Caleb tossed his back pack on the ground and laid his sword down on top of it while he grabbed a canteen of water and began to wash the stomach acid off of his skin and clothes.

"Not a bad idea," Lucas said as he went through the same motions. "Where do you think the portal took us to?"

Caleb splashed some water on his face and rubbed hard at one spot on his cheek that was tingling a great deal. He looked around, searching for the rock pile where they had found the cave entrance, but couldn't find it. The terrain looked different. The woods were thicker. The trees were lower to the ground and there were more patches of grass and thorn bushes growing in this area. If he truly had an internal compass like his dad had always said he had, Caleb felt that his compass was telling him that they were a very long way from where they had started the day. "None of this looks right to me."

"What did I tell you?" Lucas asked. He seemingly was changing the conversation.

"What are you talking about?"

"What did you say to me? 'You're the mighty hunter' and what did I tell you?"

Caleb threw his hands up in the air and said, "Are we going back to that?"

"Didn't I warn you that something didn't seem right?

Didn't I say that there was probably a good reason why animals weren't using the cave for shelter? Didn't I say that?"

Caleb brushed Lucas aside and began to look around the area. Which way would the road be if they happened to emerge from the portal near the cave? Did they teleport to the other side of the road? Were they still in the general area?

"Well?" Lucas was still waiting for an answer.

"Well, we're not going to get un-lost until you forget about the past and worry about our current situation."

"Un-lost isn't even a word you dipstick."

"I'm fairly certain you can throw 'un' at the beginning of any word and make it a new word, so get over it. Now where are we?"

"We're lost. We are truly, utterly lost and we have no clue on where to begin."

Caleb rushed over and grabbed the map. He spread it out on the ground and began to frantically search it for answers. "We were about here," he said as he jabbed a finger just off of the road. He looked up and scanned the area as Lucas came over and looked down on the map.

"What are you trying to do? Compare your surrounding with what is on that map? There's no contour lines on there. No interlacing county roads and highways to cross reference. It's just a piece of parchment with a few features drawn on them with black ink. I swear it looks like the same one I drew in first grade!"

"Lucas Land?"

"Yea, Lucas Land!" he shouted. He threw his hands on his hips and looked off into the distance with a pouty look on his face.

Caleb looked up at his brother. He couldn't help but smile at him while he had a temper tantrum. That was perhaps one of the biggest features that separated them. Under pressure, Caleb could control his fear and keep a calm head while Lucas often over exaggerated and became easily flustered. "Didn't Lucas Land have rainbows and unicorns in it?"

A smile grew on Lucas' face and suddenly he spit out a deep laugh. Both of them laughed harder than they had in a long time. "I hate you," Lucas said through a rolling fit of giggles.

"I'm pretty sure you had colored in a pink unicorn that guarded the gate to the rainbow."

"It was an important job. He was the right horse for the job."

"Yea, because pink horses can scare the pants off of any troll that might come up from under one of the bridges."

Lucas chuckled as he dropped cross legged next to Caleb and looked over the map. "Where do you think we're at on here?" he said as his face became serious.

"I have no idea. There are some key land features drawn in, but from down here I can't tell where they are. If we could get to some higher ground, maybe I can start to piece together an idea." He traced his fingers along the mountain range in the middle of the map. "These were to the south of the road we were traveling." He then pointed to the mountains in the north that cover the top line of the map and curved down and into the desert area in the east. "These were to the north of us quite a distance off. If we can get high enough…"

"From the road we were traveling, those mountains would be three to four days walk from here. There's no way we would be able to see them no matter how high we climbed. We need to find a village. We need to pick a direction and walk it until we hit a village, and then we will know where we are at."

"Unless we stumble into an unfriendly village. Then we're screwed."

"Hmm" Lucas grumbled an agreement. "Do you think Bombadore knew that the grenades would send us off in a different direction but forgot to warn us?"

"I think the purpose of the grenades are to get us out of a dangerous situation in a timely fashion. Most people probably could care less with where the grenades dump them as long as it gets them out of harm's way."

"Hmm" grunted Lucas in agreement. "Well, if we have no idea where we're at, then we might as well get walking and hope for the best. We can't get 'un-lost' if we just sit around here."

"I agree. Let's assume this… We walked into the cave going in a south direction. The cave…"

"We walked into the mouth of a beast, man. Let's call it what it is. We didn't walk into a cave, we walked into a beast."

"Whatever. We walked into the cave… er… beast in a south direction and it curved slightly to the left or east. Once we were in the stomach, you tossed a grenade to what would probably be the south east direction… right?"

Lucas shook his head up and down in agreement.

"Then logic says, when I threw the second grenade in the same south east direction, it would open somewhere over here," he pointed south east of the spot where they once were. It put them near the foothills of the mountains in the middle of the map – if his logical idea was correct.

"You're assuming that the grenade works like a tunnel that catapults you a safe distance from where you once were?"

"Do you have a better idea?"

Lucas looked down on the map and then traced his finger along the line that Caleb had traced his. It did make sense. The grenade would create a portal opening in a direction of travel – in essence, creating a highway of some sort. "Nope. I think you're reasoning works well. Let's start here and move north and we'll make any adjustments from there."

Caleb folded up the map and then got to his feet. He

tucked it away in his ruck sack and then tossed the equipment on his back. Lucas did the same and the two of them began to walk in a northern direction.

"Its daylight you know," Caleb said.

"We're off track. I don't think the rules apply anymore. This woods is thicker and we are probably better off moving during the day or we'll get eaten alive by the thorns. Besides, if Dad is going to come looking for us on the path that Marcause sketched out for us, we better be on it by the time he makes his journey back to Grandma's or he'll pass right on by and we'll never find him."

"I bet you he's got Mom and Andrea right now and is trucking back to the village."

"Then let's move faster so we are where we are supposed to be when he gets there!"

19

Gavin was tired and frustrated.

The goblins always seemed to be one step ahead of him and Vladamir. When they closed in on a suspected camp, they would discover that they had packed up and moved on just days before they arrived. They had to have scouts somewhere, but to this point, they had been undetectable.

The locals had been very cooperative in helping the two knights in their search. They were eager to get the riff raff off of their land. They noted that the goblins were often following a Minotaur bounty hunter by the name of Mideon — the very bounty hunter they were after. Not only did they follow this bounty hunter, they also were joined by other shady beings who seemed to have dangerous and dark agendas. The people all agreed that the sooner these two knights could clear these goblins out, the better life would be in this region.

Gavin was shocked at how protective the people were of this area. The terrain was rocky with rolling hills of jagged boulders that made navigation very hard. It was the constant climbing up and down on these rocks that tired him out so much and made him resent his return to Carsonia. He only wanted to get Catrina and Andrea back and then find the boys and get the heck out of Dodge.

Vladamir had sent Nathan back to the Temple to give the Knights of Liberty High Council a full report on how the boys had "escaped" their grasp – while in truth, Vladamir was going to help Gavin find his wife and the kids and then smuggle them back into their own world and then help Gavin seal up the remaining portals.

Vladamir had proven to be a very loyal partner on this mission. Vladamir had shared a bond with Gavin's father and pledged an oath to protect the twin boys if they should be born in his lifetime. To this point in their journey, he had obeyed that oath to the letter – even if lying to the Council could cost him his position in the Order.

They had been walking in silence for quite a while when Gavin decided that he owed Vladamir a lot of gratitude. "You have sacrificed a lot for us these past few weeks. I don't know if I have thanked you for it."

Vladamir turned and looked at Gavin with a straight, hard and chiseled face, "You never have to. Your father was a dear friend of mine. I pledged my true loyalty to the House of McGregor – while the Knights of Liberty are my family, my life is forever in your families service."

"Even if you don't agree with my decision to hide the boys?"

Vladamir didn't say anything at first. He scaled up a jagged rock and then reached down to lend Gavin a helping hand. Once they were up on a somewhat level area, they began moving and he began talking again, "I don't know if your decision is completely wrong. If the Creator truly wishes to use your boys to restore peace to this land, then it is safe to say that our actions here will have no lasting effect. He will find a way to put the boys in the position he has chosen them to be in. If however, we have read the prophecy wrong all of these years, then perhaps it is best for you to hide the boys so they cannot be negatively impacted by false teachings – if that is what they truly are."

"In other words, one way or the other, His will shall be done," Gavin commented.

"Exactly."

They walked on in silence for quite a while. The village they had passed through two days ago had complained about a camp of goblins that had disturbed a herd of grazing goats just a few days before their arrival. Apparently the goblins wanted some fresh meat and ten to twelve of the farmers goats had disappeared. Upon further investigation, he discovered the camp. The villagers didn't have the means to fight off the enemy and so they rounded up the remaining herd and took them to safer ground.

"Why haven't the Knights of Liberty been protecting the people here in the North?"

"The Council has resigned to living quietly in the valley and preparing for the final war."

"While the Dark Master slowly takes over the land?"

"The people rejected our divine appointment by the Creator. What else can we do?"

"Fight for them in secret. You don't have to rule over them. You could simply be protecting them, guiding them and keeping them from the evil that is consuming this land. By doing nothing, Carsonia is collapsing and the forces of evil are growing stronger and surrounding the Knights of Liberty. The final kill will be much easier if the Order resigns itself to being trapped in the valley.

Vladamir turned back and looked at him with an actual grin. It was the first time that this gruff man had smiled since they first met. "You are sounding much like your father. I happen to agree with your assessment. If only you would have stayed here. The title of Grand Master would have eventually been yours. A McGregor has long sat in the post as the overseer of the Order. Your grandfather was the last to sit there. Your father would have been there today if he hadn't died."

They continued on in silence. Gavin quietly reflected on the day that a member of the High Council had come to their chamber to inform them of the death of his dad. His parents had been together forever, meeting as children, attending the academy together and becoming Knights of Liberty at the same time. For years they had served together – and then he was born. His mom left her post in the Order and stayed home to raise him while his dad continued on in his service to the Knights of Liberty.

She had no immediate reaction when the Knights told her of his death. She stood there with a stern look – almost a look of defiance. She refused to cry in front of him and instead put on a brave face. She kept Gavin busy as if nothing had happened and was the rock that he needed now that his dad would not be returning. She gave him strength even though late at night, he could hear her silently cry to herself in the dark. Whatever pain she had, she contained it in front of him and released it at night.

She moved Gavin out of the valley and into the small cottage in the north. She didn't want to see him follow in his dad's footsteps, but as a teenager, Gavin knew that was exactly what he wanted to do and she was not going to stop him. Reluctantly, she watched him leave on that fateful day and Gavin began his training with the Knights of Liberty.

The McGregor blood ran deep within him and he quickly excelled at using the powers of Light. The members of the Order would often look on in the courtyard as he and the other students practiced their skills. There were rumblings of how a McGregor would soon sit on the High Council once more. There was actually an energy of anticipation in the air by the very notion that Gavin would fulfil the role that his dad never had the chance to do. And then Catrina became pregnant. They fled the valley and the rest was history.

Vladamir was right. The Knights of Liberty would be actively protecting the people of this land if he were sitting on the throne. The lack of regard to doing what they were called to do, angered him. His father had given his life for the Order and now they chose to sit back in the comforts of the valley and do nothing. It wasn't right!

But it was also his fault.

If he had followed his path and put his trust and faith in the Creator, he would never have run away from the Order or the destiny that awaited his two boys. But love was a powerful motivator and right now it was motivating him to run and protect them from whatever uncertainty lay ahead.

"We're nearly there. I believe we would be wise to split up and search for the patrol that continues to give away our location. If this is the group we are looking for, we know that they are wise to our travels. We need to get a step ahead of them this time."

"I agree," Gavin said.

Vladamir reached into his pouch and pulled out a small orb about the size of a golf ball. He handed it to Gavin who immediately recognized it as being a communication globe. He peered into the glowing blue glass and could see the smoke that rolled around inside of the ball. When they wished to speak with one another, they simply concentrated on the person they wished to reach and waited for them to reply.

As both communication globes linked up, the smoke would form into the face of the speaker on the other side. So when Gavin would call Vladamir, the smoke would form into the shape of Vladamir and likewise, when Vladamir held his globe and looked into it, he would see Gavin's face looking back at him. It was Carsonia's version of a cell phone.

"If you find them, you call me. Do not do anything until we are together. If we can catch them before they find us, we have a chance to get the girls and get you out of here. If you find them and go in alone and can't take them all out, then one could get away, the goblins will move their camp and we will still stuck at the beginning. I for one am getting tired of hiking through this land."

Gavin nodded his head up and down and then tucked the globe into his belt pouch. His body was worn out from sleeping on the hard ground, navigating the rocky terrain and stressing about the ones he loved.

Leaving the boys behind with his mother had been a mistake. He could see that now. He worried about them constantly. By having thoughts of them pulling on one part of his mind, and worrying about his wife and Andrea with the other, he found his nerves and heart being pulled apart in two directions. He had become the rope in a game of tug of war.

How long could he mentally and physically hold out?

As he reflected on these thoughts, he ran his fingers

through his beard that had grown in during their time here. He wasn't used to having facial hair, but he had noticed that he instinctively had begun to do this as a measure of thinking and calming. Vladamir had apparently caught on to this trait as well and asked, "What are your concerns?"

Gavin shook the fog from his mind and focused in on the elder knight. "None. Your plan is sound. My thoughts trailed off for a second."

"Stay focused. We have lost a lot of time on this hunt. We can no longer afford any more mistakes."

With that, both men split up and began their hunt. Gavin pushed the thoughts of his boys out of his mind. Though they fought to return and cloud his focus, he managed to push them away and found security in the fact that he had sent his trusted friend, Marcause to retrieve them. If anyone could protect them from the dangers of this world, it was the Angellian warrior and trained Knight of Liberty.

Gavin tapped into his hunting skills as he began to comb the ground and his surroundings for any signs that could tip him off to the movement of the goblins or the location of a scout team. He moved slowly, making very little noise. What noise did escape his movements could be easily mistaken for the snapping of a tree branch or the scurrying of a busy animal. It wouldn't be enough to give away his location. He kept a low profile to avoid being easily detectable with the eyes. If he could stay low enough, he should be camouflaged by the piles of rock and small clumps of growth that was scattered here and there.

After venturing on quite a ways, Gavin discovered a small wall of rocks that did not have a natural look to it. Someone had taken the time to stack the rocks up to form a blind; taking great care to build something that wouldn't accidently collapse on them while they sleep. It stood about three feet high and had two openings for spying out on the land.

There were a few branches and twigs that were hastily thrown on the front of it to give it a sort of natural look – though the builder had failed miserably at building something believable. The real question was, could anyone still be in there or did they bug out? Was this the right time to call in Vladamir or should he wait and investigate closer?

The best course was to hunker down and monitor the bunker for a while. He wanted to see if anyone came out of it on their own, thus keeping his presence secret.

But how long should he wait?

What if he was spending his time watching over something that had been abandoned for months or years? It looked fairly new, but he couldn't be certain. If he called Vladamir now and it turned out to be empty, he might set back their journey even that much more.

He decided he couldn't wait. Time was precious and Gavin didn't want to waste any more of it. Creeping slowly towards the blind – and against Vladamir's wishes – he decided to move on without him and hope for the best.

He moved forward a few steps, came to a stop, crouched low and listened. The wind blew lightly and the small flecks of grass that grew between the rocks sang a quite song as they swayed. He caught the sound of something moving in the distance, but it came from behind him. Probably a small field mouse. The bunker was quiet. He moved forward again.

He continued the process, slowly navigating to the side of the blind where he found another viewing port built into the rock. He studied it hard, searching for any signs of movement or beady eyes staring back at him.

Nothing. He continued on.

He was now within arm's reach of it. His sword was drawn and he kept it just off the ground, being sure not to let it scrape against rock. He needed the element of surprise. He listened and could hear a rumbling.

Snoring! Had he caught all of them asleep?

He came up alongside of the wall and slowly stood up, his eyes slowly rising above the rock and looking for anything to alert him to danger. He could see the edge of the wall on the other side and as he rose up higher he began to see the base of the floor and then a set of bloodshot eyes popped up in front of his face. The scaly green skin of the goblin set off alarms in his head and it screamed in terror as he had caught it off guard.

It stumbled back as it searched for a sword. Gavin reached out with a tentacle of light and picked the goblin up and slammed him into the ground, pinning him down as he jumped over the wall and landed into the den of angry goblins. The four who had been asleep, scurried for weapons.

"Run! Warn the others!" one of them yelled. The smallest of the four leaped over the wall and took off across the rocky plain.

"NO!" Gavin cursed as he was forced to deal with the three who remained. Their swords were drawn and quickly engaging Gavin who moved with a fluid motion. He blocked and slashed before successfully taking the head off of one goblin. He used a tentacle of light to grab a discarded sword and bring it back to his other hand and now as he wielded two swords, he became a lethal flurry of attacks in the small confine.

The first goblin that he had slammed into the ground, slowly shook the cobwebs from his head. He was about to get up when Gavin took his right foot and slammed it into his head and knocked him back out. He would need someone to interrogate when this was over.

Gavin lunged forward and drove his sword into the chest of one of the two remaining goblins. The final goblin swung for Gavin's head. Gavin blocked it, forced the sword of the attacker up and then drove his other sword into its chest. With three dead and one out cold, Gavin leaped over the wall and ran after the one who escaped.

It was very far off and in a dead sprint. To catch him seemed impossible but Gavin didn't want to just give up. Yet he had one to interrogate back in the blind. If that one woke up, then he would have two roaming free through the rocks. He could try and use the Light to grab the fleeing goblin, but it was too far away. Nobody possessed enough power to create and control a beam of light that far from the body. He would have to let it go.

Turning back, he knew he was now pressed for time. Gavin hurried back to the bunker to find the goblin just coming to his senses. He leaped in, rolled it on its back and clutched it by the throat.

"Where is your camp? Where are the human women?"

"I ams not a betrayer of my clan. I will tell you nothing," it hissed. Gavin clamped down harder on its throat. He squealed and squirmed under his might.

"You have taken people that I love dearly. I want them back!"

"They are not yours. They belong to ours Master. They belong to ours Protector."

Gavin pulled the goblin to its feet and then dropped it back to the ground with a boot to the face. It tried to crawl away but Gavin drove his booted foot into its rib. "Tell me where they are!" His rage was becoming unbridled.

"I wills not speak. Kills me if you must!"

Gavin drove his boot into its face and then took his sword and drove it into the arm of the goblin, pinning it to the ground. It screamed and howled like nothing he had heard before. He twisted the blade to see what other response he could get from it. "Tell me where your camp is!"

"Ahhh!"

"Stop it!" Gavin heard the strong accented voice of Vladamir call out. "He's going to alert all of Carsonia of our location."

Gavin's head shot up and he saw the blood smeared across Vladamir's tunic. "Did you get the other one?"

"Luckily for you, he ran straight to where I was. Almost took me by surprise, but I got him."

Gavin looked down at the goblin pinned to the rock with his sword. He wanted to punish this beast for all the trouble it had caused him and his family – to blame it for the collective actions of its clan. He decided he would make it speak before he killed it and twisted the sword some more.

"Stops it!" it screamed.

Vladamir's hand rested on Gavin's shoulder and then he said, "You will get nothing of value from this goblin. But based on the direction of the one I intercepted, we should be able to find the camp without him. Just kill it and let's move on."

"I want him to suffer," Gavin said as his eyes danced with anger.

"That is not the way of the Knights of Liberty. Torture is not our way. Kill it and let us move on. No prisoners, but no torture either."

Gavin looked down at the beady, blood shot eyes of the pointy eared creature. It glared its jagged teeth at him and he had to draw in some deep and calming breaths to keep from inflicting more pain. He pulled the sword out and with a swift backhanded motion, decapitated the goblin. "How is killing it anymore merciful?" he asked with a snarl.

"It is not. Ideally, we would take it as a prisoner or set him free. But he will alert his clan and ruin our only chance at surprise. It is their way. This was the only logical option. It is the only option that keeps you from losing your own way."

Gavin took a few more calming breaths and let the anger and hatred be washed away by the crisp, cool air. "Let's move on."

Vladamir extended a hand and helped Gavin leap up and over the wall. Once on the other side, they set out in the direction in which the goblin had fled. After a short distance, they came upon the fallen body of the goblin and found Nathan hunched over it, examining the corpse.

"You have returned," Vladamir said to his young student.

Nathan stood up and handed Vladamir's communication globe back to him. "I have kept the Order busy and out of our way. We should be clear to complete our work but I cannot guarantee that we can get the McGregor family out. The Draith have been busy closing up the portals around Carsonia. There is no longer any to escape through."

"How is that possible?" Vladamir asked.

"Someone would have to get their hands on the 'Stone of Callam' which only I know where it is," Gavin answered. "Perhaps the goblins or the bounty hunter figured out what they had in their possession and took an initiative to trap us here."

"You know where the stone is?" Vladamir asked.

"It's contained in a necklace that I gave to my wife on the day we married. To almost every observer, it was just another beautiful jewel – hidden in plain view. It has been safe with my family for generations. It figures that during my watch it would be used for the purposes of the Dark Master."

"We do not have the time to reflect on this event. We need to move on. The day is still young and we have much to do." Vladamir began jogging in the direction in which the goblin had once been traveling.

Nate gestured for Gavin to go next and he then took up the rear, watching carefully for any eyes that might be watching their movement. Gavin called back to the young knight, "Any word from Marcause?"

"None. My time was spent convincing the Order that you and your family had already escaped Carsonia and that dispatching more knights was not necessary. If he contacted the council, I am not aware of it."

"I don't like it," Gavin mumbled to himself. His thoughts were now squarely on the boys. He was certain that Marcause would have returned with them by now. Perhaps something unforeseeable had waylaid them or maybe Marcause decided it was safer to stay put – he had given his friend that option. Of course there were the thoughts that the boys had been captured or killed – no, they were too valuable to be killed. But they could definitely be captured and on their way to an appointment with the Dark Master.

While finally having an opportunity to rescue Catrina and Andrea should have been lifting his spirits, his instincts told him he should be worried about the boys. The Dark Master had obviously orchestrated the entire kidnapping and now the closing of the portals – which dumfounded him as to how they figured out where the stone was. That would also mean that the Draith had paid a visit to Catrina, which created another unsettling feeling.

Natas and the bounty hunter were way ahead of everything Gavin and Vladamir were trying to do. The forces of evil had formulated a solid plan that was keeping them on the defensive and now, there was a good chance that the three of them were walking into a trap.

There was a reason Gavin tried to leave Carsonia and this life behind him forever. The very things he feared might one day happen were now playing out and he had no way of making it all stop.

20

Both of the boys could feel it.

Maybe it was the lack of a good night's sleep on a warm, comfortable bed. Maybe it was the lack of a tasty meal cooked with care by their mom. Or maybe it was the fact that they seemed to be climbing upwards and not gaining much ground as they tried to journey back on course.

Whatever it was, their spirits were being sapped of energy at a rapid pace. They were tired, cranky and sick of walking with no end in sight.

It had been three days since the cave worm ate them and they escaped using Bombadore's Teleporting Explosive Devices. Three days since they speculated that they only needed to walk north for a bit to get back on track. Three days since they last saw the sunlight, because the rain had been pouring with unrelenting strength. Three days had taken both of the boys to the breaking point.

How much worse could this all get?

"We need to find some shelter," Caleb said.

"I'm not taking any more chances on being eaten by some

gigantic worm or anything else that might live in one of these caves. I'd rather freeze to death."

They continued on in silence, still climbing upwards. The ground had been level just days before. Since jumping through the portal created by the grenades, everything seemed so much harder. The smart thing to do would be to stop moving and reassess where they might be. The map didn't offer much in the way of landmarks and terrain features to help them orientate themselves to where they were at, so it would have all been a guessing game anyways. They just had to continue on walking. At least by keeping their legs moving, they would be able to stay warmer than if they just sat down and rested on the cold, wet ground.

"What if we actually ended up on the other side of the mountain range? What if we are in the southern part of Carsonia?" Lucas asked.

"Then we are in for one hell of a long walk."

They moved on through the rain. The leaves of the trees laughed at them as they shook the water off and rained down on the boys harder. The birds seemed to be jumping from tree to tree, watching them as they worked their way through the woods. Perhaps they knew an easy meal when they saw one. The entire world seemed to be against them as they ventured forward.

"I miss home," Lucas said. "I'd probably be sitting in the deer stand right now. I don't mind the rain when I'm in the deer stand because I know that whenever I'm ready, I can climb out and go back to the warm house and Mom's chocolate chip cookies."

Caleb smiled with that thought. That actually sent a warm feeling through his tired body. "I'd probably be coming home from football practice. We'd be gearing up for the state tournament. Some cookies and milk would definitely be in order."

"You think we'll get back to that life again?"

Caleb didn't answer right away. He wanted to say yes, but what chance did they truly have? Two teenage boys in a world where things were much different and even more dangerous? How long could they really last out here without some sort of help?

"Caleb?"

"We need to keep moving. We don't give up and we keep on moving. At some point we will get out of this."

The two of them put their heads down and charged on. The terrain continued to bend upwards and soon they realized a clearing was forming up ahead. Could it be the road?

"Do you see it?" Caleb asked.

"I see it!" Lucas darted off ahead of Caleb and charged up. Whatever energy he had left deep inside was now being used to move him up to the top of the hill with great speed. He was excited to see if their gamble had paid off.

Caleb picked up the pace. He wasn't in a hurry to stumble

through the wet woods and kill himself on a mossy covered rock or half rotten log lying on the forest floor. He took careful and calculated steps as he moved towards the clearing with a growing sense of peace washing over him. At last they would be on the right path and they could afford stopping for a real rest.

Lucas burst into the clearing and came to a dead stop, looking off into the vast area beyond. Caleb wasn't sure if that was a good sign or not. He quickened his pace and then watched in horror as Lucas fell to his knees, still staring off into whatever the clearing was showing him. "Lucas!" he shouted, worried that something had happened to his brother.

Caleb stumbled over a low branch and nearly did a full plunge into the ground but he reached out just in time and caught himself from falling and straightened back up. He raced to the top of the hill and then collapsed next to his brother. His eyes were fixated into the distant landscape just like his brother. He couldn't catch his breath as the cold rain washed over his face and poured into his mouth like a rushing river. The sky seemed to be trying to drown him with its onslaught.

Caleb felt the last bit of resolve drain out of him and tears mixed in with the water running off his face and he threw his arm over his brother's shoulder and pulled him in tight. Before them were mountains that rose up into the clouds. Peaks and valleys were found in every direction that they could see. They had absolutely no idea where they were anymore. No idea on how to get out. No idea if they would ever see their mom and dad again.

"There," Lucas said as he slowly pointed at an orange glowing light in the distance. It seemed to be perched on a mountain with streams of orange pouring down. "A volcano?"

Caleb closed his eyes and concentrated on the map in his pocket. They had looked at it so much the past few days that he often dreamt about it when he slept. He searched it for any sign of a volcano that might have been drawn on it. "Yea, there was a volcano on the map."

"In the north? Do we need to turn around and go back?"

"No. It was in that mountain range in the middle of the map… off to the Far East. We are on the other side of the mountain range. We are way farther south than we ever thought!"

Lucas flopped down on his butt. Any hope of getting home had left him at that very moment. He was lost for words and his spirit was crushed. His heart seemed to slow down to a very slow pace and he could almost feel the blood in his veins growing colder as if they were about to freeze inside his body. "I'm done, Caleb. I'm not going on anymore."

"We have to go on. I'm not dying like this."

"Look at those mountains! How long do you think it would take just to get to that volcano? A month? Maybe more? And that is only halfway through the mountain range."

"We can do it. We're McGregor's. We live for this type of adventure. You especially."

"Not like this, Caleb. This is impossible. This adventure will kill us."

Caleb looked around. He needed to find some place dry. Some place to hunker down until the rain stopped. Some place to start a fire and warm them back up. He had no intention of dying in this land.

He dug deep in his collective thoughts and found a dream that he wanted to fulfill. It was a dream of him and Andrea, married with kids and living out their lives together. This memory warmed him and gave him new hope. It was enough hope to make him want to keep moving and fight on longer. He grabbed onto that dream and squeezed it tightly.

"We're not done yet. We have the prophecy on our side. Do you think we'll really die before the prophecy is fulfilled?"

Lucas let out a chuckle, a slight grin coming across his lips. "Really? The one thing we are running from and you're going to use as motivation to keep me moving?"

"You're smiling. That's something."

"I should just lay back down and die… save you the hassle of having to kill me later."

Caleb stood up and reached out a hand to his brother. Lucas took it and together they got back on their feet and began moving into the woods. "Worm or no worm, we're finding a cave and hunkering down for a few days. We need rest."

"At this point, I wish we would have just stayed in our last worm. At least we would have died warm."

"That's the spirit," Caleb said. They were back to talking – even though it was just childish banter, it was the talking that reassured both of them that they could still survive. Together, anything was possible. For now they would take things one step at a time.

Their first priority was to find some shelter, eat some food, dry off and get some good rest. If they could accomplish all of that, then they could focus on the more important task of getting through the mountains and back on track.

Through the woods they went. The rain continued to pour. The elements continued to laugh at them, but their new sense of urgency helped them move forward and ignore their current predicament.

The already gray skies began to grow darker and Caleb knew the day was about over. As they traveled through the woods, keeping a close eye on the rock formations around them in an effort to find some sort of shelter, he had also been gathering items to start a fire.

Bombadore had supplied them with fire starters, but they still needed kindling and fuel. When he found rabbit burrows, he would stop Lucas and then chance a reach into the hole and dig out the dry nesting that he found inside. He tucked this material into the pouches on his belt that for the most part, were still dry.

Lucas caught on to what Caleb had been doing and started to follow suit. While Caleb would dig out dry nesting, Lucas would search for another burrow and dig out his own. Both of them agreed that they wouldn't waste time and energy carrying firewood through the forest. They would take their chances that once they found some shelter, they would find ample wood nearby to use.

"I think I see something up ahead!" Lucas shouted and began moving towards a large rock formation. Caleb followed close behind.

As they approached the massive wall of earth, they found a divide in the rock that had a covering and had kept the ground below dry. It wasn't a cave, so both of them were sure they wouldn't be eaten this time. With rising spirits, they charged up to the area and found that someone had used it as a camp once as well. To their surprise, there was a small pile of wood waiting for them.

"What did I tell you?" Caleb began, "We can't die yet because we are the Twins of the Prophecy."

Both boys laughed as they threw down their ruck sacks against the far wall and went right to work on making a fire. Caleb and Lucas dug out the dry bedding they had collected and laid it down in the charred area that was used as a fire pit by the last person. They then grabbed one of the chunks of wood.

"Too big. We need small pieces," Lucas said. He reached into his ruck sack and drew out his sword hilt. He remembered Bombadore saying that his weapons could take on three different forms. It could be a sword, a mace or a battle axe. While a battle axe might be a little over the top for splitting wood, it was what they had available and he fully intended to use it.

He envisioned the axe and snapped his wrist and watched as the little pieces of metal rolled out and extended to the full length of his sword. He waited – expecting the sword to reform into a battle axe, but nothing happened.

"Try it again," Caleb said as he set up a log to be split. "Retract the blade and concentrate harder."

"Yea, yea. I was going to do that." He retracted the blade and then focused on what a battle axe would look like. He could see it in his mind, a clear image of something he had seen in a Google search one day. There was a large variety of axes dancing in his mind. It was a lot of confusion but he hoped his weapon would understand what he wanted and just do it. He snapped his wrist and again, the sword blade came out. "I think Bombadore gave me a bad one."

"He wouldn't do that. What are you focusing on?"

"I have a bunch of images in my head of different battle axes. My mind is focused on a battle axe."

"Maybe your mind is focused on too many. Zero in on one image only. Push out the other images and just focus on one. Maybe you're confusing your weapon."

Lucas rolled his eyes and let out a snort. He hated it when Caleb made sense. If this worked, he would have to be stuck knowing that his brother solved yet another of his problems. How he wanted to reverse the roles and be the one that was sharp in high pressure situations.

Lucas brought up the images of battle axes in his mind. It was a confusing, swirling cloud of images and it was hard to grab just one. He created a mental image of his hand entering the cloud. He drew in a deep breath and used his imaginary hand to reach out and grab one of the many pictures. He liked how this axe looked. It had a good feel to it. It had broad blades on both sides and the handle was well cut with a nice gripping area. This was the one he wanted.

"You did it!" Caleb disturbed Lucas' concentration.

He opened his eyes and looked over to his brother. "I almost had it!"

"No," Caleb said. He nodded his head towards Lucas' weapon, "You do have it… you did it."

Lucas looked down at his hilt and saw the very battle axe he had imagined, extending from the handle. The sensations he had felt as he concentrated were the actual feelings he was experiencing in his hand as it obeyed his commands and formed.

"You're going to have to get quicker with that, though. If you take that long to form a weapon, the enemy is going to be celebrating your death before you finish your task."

"Shut up. Why don't you make yourself useful and hold the wood steady for me while I chop it."

Caleb did a soft laugh and then backed away. He didn't want to be in the path of the huge battle axe his brother was now wielding. Lucas raised it up, concentrated on his aim and then swung down. With one perfect slice, the wood broke into two pieces.

Caleb jumped in, stood one piece up and Lucas took another swing and split the wood again. Soon, the chunks of wood were stacked up in the fire pit and with one flick of the wrist, the fire starter ignited the dry bedding and the wood crackled to life.

It wasn't long before they had a full, rip roaring fire going. The rain continued to pour down outside their shelter, but as their bodies warmed and their clothes dried, their spirits began to rise. Lucas took the first fire watch. He would watch out for enemy and make sure the fire kept burning while Caleb shut his eyes for a bit. At some point they would switch roles, but Lucas actually felt more alive than he had in days.

He munched on one of the dried bread cakes in his ruck. While he was sick of the blandness, his stomach was happy to have something dropping down inside and filling the void. He actually found himself savoring every bite – imagining it to be a piece of steak or a slice of pizza. He threw some more wood on the fire and the heat intensified. His spirits went higher. For the first time in days, Lucas felt confident that everything would work itself out. He just had to have faith...

But at some point in the night, his head fell forward and he went into a deep sleep. He hadn't woke Caleb.

Something stirred outside their shelter.

Lucas' eyes shot open. The rain had stopped. The fire was out. A hazy light was illuminating the woods. How long had they been asleep? Did he even wake Caleb for his shift?

A soft hacking noise caused his head to snap to the left and Lucas jolted to full awake mode as he scrambled over to Caleb, igniting his sword on his way over.

Caleb snorted and shoved his brother off of him before taking in the scene. He shot up to his feet and scurried to the back wall, grabbing his sword and making it come to life as well.

With their backs to the walls, the two of them looked in disbelief. Barring their only means of escape stood a line of thirteen goblins.

All of them had their crooked smiles exposing their pointy teeth.

The odds were not in their favor.

21

He was startled. Like a bolt of energy suddenly surging through his body, Caleb jolted upright and the world hidden behind his eyelids was exposed in an instant. His gaze darted back and forth, taking in the beastly creatures that were known as goblins. His heart beat fast, thumping loudly and overpowering his ability to think.

He scrambled back, his hand reaching for the hilt of his sword. His back slammed up against the hard rock of the wall behind him. Lucas drew close. He had his sword at the ready as well. Then one of the goblins took a step forward, his sword in position for battle...

Andrea's eyes jolted open as her body violently shuttered.

"Are you okay?" she heard Catrina ask from behind her. Their hands were bound together around the center pole of the tent.

"Just a nightmare... I think," she could feel the sweat beading up under her hairline. Her heart was pounding heavy – as heavy as the thumping she had heard in her dreams. Her breathing was at a faster pace than normal also.

"Was it about Caleb again?"

Andrea tried to shake the thoughts out of her head. She had a similar experience not long ago. She had seen the Minotaur creature charging at him while he stood in the open. It was as if he were challenging the beast. Before that, he was embracing another girl. Soothing her and promising to bring back her father.

Of course it had to be a dream, but it seemed as if she were in that space with him. As if she were sharing his thoughts, his sense of feeling, even his sense of smell. She was seeing through his eyes and the images were as vivid as if she were awake and living in his skin.

Maybe it was all just one grand hallucination.

Her face was numb now. Every day, the beastly creatures would come in and slap them around yet never demand anything from them. Their tactics seemed straight from a spy thriller where the villain is trying to get intelligence from an operative – except no questions. None in the least. Just daily beatings and occasionally an unwanted touch. Nothing sexual, but just enough to stir up strong surges of panic – as if this might be the time they go beyond just this sadistic game.

She enjoyed the nighttime when she was assured they were asleep and wouldn't be coming in to administer more pain. When she heard the stirs from outside, her muscles would tense in fear that her time of solitude and peace was soon to be over. But now these dreams were coming to her. Dreams that gave her just as much emotional pangs. She didn't know what to make of them.

Real or not real?

She wanted to push them out of her mind and forget that she had the dreams, but Catrina was so curious about them. She wanted to know every detail and it troubled her having to relive the thoughts.

"What did you see this time?" Catrina asked as always. The grilling was about to begin. Then it would be followed shortly by more torture from the goblins.

"It was nothing. None of it means anything."

"It might. Was he okay? Did you see Lucas?" her questions came out with force. She was concerned about her dreams. Why?

"It doesn't matter. It's just dreams... right?"

Catrina was eerily quiet. Andrea had been in the McGregor house long enough to recognize when something was off limits to speak about. A new rage began to build up behind Andrea's cool exterior. "Right?" she asked again.

"You're probably right..." she trailed off. She seemed to be considering divulging something else. "Were they in any danger?"

Andrea looked around the tent. Daylight was illuminating the thick walls that were made up of stitched together flesh, and her stomach told her that the goblins would be bringing some sort of slop to eat at any moment. But the words left unsaid by Catrina were eating at her. She felt that there was a new twist to this story.

Catrina had already told her the entire story of who the family was and how they were tied to this world. During her telling of the story she seemed to be leaving holes – avoiding bits of information that left her feeling as if there was more to say. Did her dreams of seeing through the eyes of Caleb have anything to do with it?

What about her skin turning pale? Catrina assured her that she wasn't dying. It wasn't some crazy side effect from the portal.

And her ears!

Andrea had felt a burning sensation a few days ago – or was it weeks? – and now she had a crazy feeling that they were disfigured. Did her ears get hurt during the kidnapping? Everything from that night was such a blur.

They sat in silence for a long while. The food was late in coming. Finally, Andrea cleared her throat and put force into her words, "These aren't dreams, are they."

She could almost hear Catrina's eyes roll back in her head. She could sense the woman tilting her head back and resting it against the wood pole. She was in agony. She was keeping yet one more secret.

Andrea waited for an answer. In her mind, she chased around ideas that were zipping here and there. A story was emerging slowly. She continued to wait for an answer. Catrina continued to hold on to the answers.

The food still hadn't come. Andrea's stomach reminded her with a growl that it needed something – even that slimy garbage that they served for meals – to keep her going. She listened for footsteps, wanting to know what was taking their captives so long to deliver one stinking meal.

Then she heard it.

It wasn't the footsteps. It was a sob. A soft sob that Catrina couldn't contain. She let it slip and then more came out. Soon, Andrea could envision the tears streaming down the woman's face. Her heart ached to be able to take her in her arms and comfort her. With her own parents gone, Caleb's parents had become as close as her own family. She cared for them as much as her own.

"I'm sorry," Andrea at last said. "I didn't mean to push so hard."

Catrina whispered lightly, "Gavin and I almost died in the mountains... on the night we escaped. We were wet and on the run. We had lost most of our supplies and other than his sword..." she drew in a deep breath and exhaled it slowly. Her voice grew in strength. "We were destined to die out there. We should have died out there. Ironically, the entire prophecy would have been derailed because of our young stupidity. But the Creator always provides when we are in need. On that night, he provided."

"How did you make it?"

"Four weary travelers were sent to find us. A seer had informed them that their lives and their family destiny were tied to a young couple. They didn't know who they were searching for. They were not even sure if they had gone to the right place. They just ventured out on faith and stumbled across two dying people."

Andrea felt something grow in her throat. Her vision was now distorted by the wild seas that had grown in her eyes. "My family..." she mumbled as her lips became wet by the tears that were streaming down her face. The bits and pieces of information that had been held back were the pieces that contained the parts of her parents and grandparents.

Catrina spoke bolder now, the weight she carried had been removed. "You and Caleb are meant to be together. Your destiny is intertwined. Always has been. You were born two months before we met your parents in the mountains. Your grandparents were encouraged to come along because the seer couldn't see past a dark moment in your families' future. Turns out that she saw their deaths.

"I am from Carsonia?"

"It's why you can see into Caleb's mind. Your mother was the seer who informed me that I was pregnant with twins. At the time she was just passing through the valley, but little did she know, I was the one they would eventually be aiding. You have her gifts. You can't focus them yet, but you do have them. For whatever reason, you seem to be developing them by seeing through the eyes of the one person you are most close too."

"I can't believe it. I mean, I did think it was strange that nobody came to my parents' funeral except Grandma and Grandpa and you guys. I just never thought…"

Catrina interrupted, "By coming back into this world, your body is discovering its true roots and you are gaining the characteristics of your true form. It's why your ears burn. They are returning to their biological shape. Your skin is paling because that is the natural skin color of your people."

"My people? I'm different from you?"

"Yes… and no. But before I get into that, I need to ask you again, what did you see when you saw through Caleb's eyes?"

"He was startled. He had been sleeping but when he woke up, the two of them were cornered by goblins."

"Was Gavin there? Vladamir or Nathan?"

"Nobody. Just like last time, except Lucas is with him now."

"What about that girl?"

Andrea shuddered at the thought of that girl. Now that she knew she was experiencing the thoughts and feelings of Caleb, she felt a pang of jealousy flood over her. She shook her head no and then realized that Catrina couldn't see her reaction so she answered with, "No. I think they've traveled away from that last location. They seemed to be deep in the woods."

"Are they lost?"

Andrea searched through the feelings she had experienced when she last saw through Caleb's eyes. He was sound asleep. A deep sleep in fact. "I don't know. He was jolted awake by the goblins. I can't tell what his feelings were before that moment except that he was sound asleep. They seemed to be okay."

Catrina didn't say anything. She struggled with the bindings on her wrists for a few moments and then let out a long sigh. "I'm going to let you in on a little secret about me."

"What's that?"

"I may seem like a classic, 'Suzie Homemaker', truth is, I'm anything but. I'm not a patient person and I'm getting a little tired of waiting to be rescued."

"Based on some of the stories Caleb shared with me, I always figured you to be more about 'I am woman, hear me roar' than the damsel in distress." Andrea worked at her own bindings. She slid her slim hands back and forth, trying to find any bit of wiggle room in which to begin working free from them.

Nothing.

"We're not going to get that lucky. Goblins are a stupid lot, but they do have warrior instincts. I think instead that our best hope is for you to use one of your abilities."

"Besides seeing what Caleb is seeing, I'm not sure what abilities I have."

The pattering of feet could be heard outside. The clanking of bone utensils against metal pots indicated that food was about to be prepared. Slowly, grumbles and wails of goblin chatter became more noticeable. The camp was waking up and beginning to go about their business. The window of opportunity for escape was nearly closed and Andrea could tell that Catrina's mindset had suddenly changed.

Since being captured, she had stressed that the most important thing to do was obey their captors and stay alive. Carsonia was too big to be wandering around. She knew Gavin would be coming to rescue them and so being patient and waiting for his arrival was the smartest thing to do. Yet this morning, Andrea noticed the change in Catrina's demeanor.

"Caleb and Lucas are the fulfillment of a prophecy that encompasses all of Carsonia. You, my dear are the fulfillment of another prophecy."

Bombshell.

Andrea's mind raced. What did that all mean? Before she could ask, Catrina continued, "I'm not the one to answer all of those types of questions. Nor is this the time to discuss them. The most important thing for us is to get out of here right now."

Andrea wanted answers to Catrina's statement, yet at the same time she also wanted to be free of this camp and get back home to her grandparents. Her face was puffy and she was tired of tasting the iron of her blood from busted lips. She wanted the things that had always comforted her most. All of this was quickly becoming too much. She stammered a response, "Okay. I'm with you."

"Good. You are an Angellian. I know you have no idea what they are, but you need to trust me. Angellian's have the ability to fly. It's a strange thing in many ways…"

"People don't fly," she put bluntly. Her mind was racing and a part of her was beginning to reject all of this nonsense.

"Yes, they do," Catrina countered. "In this realm, they do. You do also. You have grown up in a place where there are limitations on what can be done. Back home, you have only known limitations. Here, those are gone. We have greater freedom. We have the ability to defy logic and laws of gravity and all of the other theologies that mankind has put in place. I need you to put away those feelings. I need you to forget what you know and embrace what I am telling you. I need you to accept all of this with the heart and mind of a child. Can you do that?"

"I don't know."

"I need you to do it, Andrea. If we are going to escape, I need you to sell out to what I am telling you. Put away what you know and trust in what I say."

"This is all crazy. Put yourself in my shoes…"

"I am in your shoes. We are in this together. We are one. Neither of us will walk out of here unless we can develop a greater trust. I need you to do that. Can you do that?"

Andrea nodded her head up and down. Everything inside her said to say no and just give up, but her head nodded in agreement.

"Andrea?"

She had forgotten that Catrina couldn't see her gestures because they were back to back against a pole. "Yes. I will try." If for no other reason, in hopes that she wouldn't have to endure another beating.

"Angellian's are very majestic when they fly. It seems to be something they will to happen. Their bodies begin to glow and then it breaks up from a solid form to almost a collection of little balls of light. You remember before televisions went digital that sometimes you would get fuzzy pictures?"

"Static?"

"Yes. Static. That's the form that Angellian's take on when they are flying. It's as if they break into particles and then just float with the wind. It's very graceful and beautiful. I'm not sure how it's done, but I have seen Angellian children. Often, they learn to fly before they learn to walk. Everything that we learn is done by mimicking what we have seen. If I had to guess, learning to break into particles of light and flying is done the same way."

"This is crazy."

"Back home, yes. If I hadn't seen it done with my own eyes, I'd probably doubt it as well."

"I never saw Mom or Dad do it. If Grandma and Grandpa are Angellian's, I haven't seen them do it either."

"There are limitations in what can be brought over from this realm and into the Earth realm that we know. The light can be used in both places. Most forms of sorcery can be used in both places. Flying as an Angellian, cannot."

"How am I supposed to mimic something I have never seen?"

"Picture it. Focus it. Free your mind and just imagine your body dissolving into little particles. Imagine the breeze gathering you up and lifting you into the sky."

Andrea closed her eyes. She tried to picture what Catrina was talking about. She could smell the odor of rotting flesh. It had filled her nostrils since being brought into captivity by the goblins. She tried to shut out that sensation.

The air was still inside the tent. Floating on the breeze was not a sensation she could call on. She again tried to focus on the concept of being swept away with the wind, but the scream of a distant goblin jolted her eyes open. "This is hopeless!"

Footsteps could now be heard outside. There were noises of rattling chains and the movement of goblins that had purpose. They would be coming very soon to check on their prisoners and bring food. That horrible, mushy garbage that they called food. Andrea was tired of that slop. She tried harder, but it was out of fear now. She wasn't focused as much as she was panicked.

"Stop," Catrina ordered. "You're getting frantic. Stop and focus."

"I can't."

"You can."

"I'm not going to pick this up in one lesson, Catrina. I don't even believe I can do it."

"I know. I know. You're too frustrated to continue right now. Just close your eyes and focus on breathing. Calm yourself down and we'll try again later."

"I don't want to stay here. I want to go home."

"I know. We will. Let's eat a good meal, get some rest and we'll try again tonight. Having the cover of darkness would be better anyways. In this light we would be spotted before we could get out of the camp."

A single tear rolled down Andrea's face. This was becoming too much for her. This was the nightmare that she couldn't force herself to wake up from. Her calm, life loving demeanor was slowly being broken down. The majestic beings that Catrina had described sounded nothing like how she was feeling right now. Slowly, she was falling into a pit of desperation.

Catrina seemed to still have hope.

As the thought of taking more backhands to the face washed over her, Andrea had none.

22

The rocky plains of this region provided little cover for Vladamir, Nathan and Gavin as they worked their way closer to the camp. Occasionally, a large pile of rocks or a dried shrub would provide a little bit of concealment. Otherwise, they were hopelessly out in the open. If they hadn't given their approach away to a goblin scout, Gavin would have been surprised.

"I will follow you to the end of this mission," Vladamir said as he trotted up alongside Gavin, "but perhaps it is time to consider calling in reinforcements. We may need to inform the council of our situation."

Gavin snorted.

Nathan offered his view as he moved in line with the other two men, "I would actually prefer we didn't, Master. You just had me back at the temple lying to the Council on the whereabouts of the boys. If they find out that I lied to them… are you trying to get us exiled?"

Vladamir looked over at Nathan with furrowed eyebrows and a stern expression that warned him to stay out of this conversation. Knowing his place, like all good apprentices, he dropped back behind the two men as they continued their swift movement across the terrain.

"I thought you were here to honor your vow to my father," Gavin spoke. It had been a while since he last said anything to either of his companions.

Since killing the goblin, he had become very quiet. He felt a part of himself being lost since beginning this journey. While he didn't consider goblins worthy of respect, he was surprised that he so easily justified the torture he had inflicted on the one he had captured the other day. That was out of his nature. He knew he had it in him, but since leaving the ways of the Knights of Liberty behind, he had also successfully found a way to contain that part of his savage personality.

"I will honor the vow. But I also know that we are seriously outnumbered. Have you given any thought as to how we will rescue them when we find this elusive camp?"

"A solution will present itself. I'm sure of it."

"Is that how it always works? In the din of battle, how often does one succeed when he has no plan of attack to fall back on? You spent time in the academy…"

Gavin cut him off, "This isn't about my training. I don't care about the teachings of the Knight of Liberty. If I thought I could trust the Order to let me take my family back to the World and live peacefully as I choose, do you really think I wouldn't have called on them already? I won't allow my kids to get roped into the trappings of this prophecy and loose themselves."

"They are from the bloodline of the McGregor's. Their fate has been decided by The Creator. How long do you believe you will really be able to run? Besides, the gates are closed. There is no hope of returning to your realm… unless you have a secret to share?"

Gavin didn't answer. He continued to move forward. Vladamir had a solid point. It's not like he hadn't thought of the very same thing since escaping Carsonia with his pregnant wife all those years ago. He was running from the Creator of the Universe. How far could he go, really?

"Gavin…"

"We stick to the plan. We rescue my wife and Andrea. We then go back for the boys. Then I get them home and close the gate."

"Gate? Do you know of another gate?"

"Not here. Not now. We need to keep moving."

After a short jaunt, Gavin said, "I thought you didn't believe in the prophecy?"

"I believe that the boys have been called by The Creator to execute his grand plan, but I don't agree that one of them has to serve at the right hand of the Dark Master. We all have choices. I cannot imagine a world where The Creator would strip us of our ability to choose whom we will follow. Either way, I do still believe strongly that the boys must remain here and follow the path that has been laid out for them. I promised your father to protect them and guide them. I never promised to hide them."

Gavin slowed down to a brisk walk and then crouched down behind a pile of dried branches and bushes that were lying on the ground. Hopelessness was sinking in. Nathan and Vladamir took cover with him. Gavin looked into the old eyes of Vladamir. The face staring back at him was the last one to ever see his father. He couldn't help but feel that the only person who knew the wishes of his dad the best, were Vladamir. "Was this the wish of my father?"

Vladamir nodded his head up and down. "We both saw the darkness that was slowly sweeping over this land. He knew, like I know now, that only your boys could bring freedom and restore the hope of the people. Only they can defeat the Dark Master. They alone hold that power to bring Natas to an end. That part of the prophecy I have no doubt about."

"But I can't let go. They are my children."

"As they are also the children of The Creator. As you are also his creation as well. We are all children of the Most High and therefore must serve his purpose before our own."

Gavin lowered his head and thought about that for a while. They were words of wisdom, but words he refused to take heed of. Gavin turned back to his task at hand and surveyed the expanse. He could see that the terrain seemed to drop out of sight just ahead. Perhaps a valley was coming up. If so, there was a good chance that they might come across the goblin camp. There appeared to be a pile of rocks that they could take cover behind and would possibly provide a view of what was down below.

"We drive on," Gavin said at last. "Without help. I trust that Marcause will come to our aid and help us complete this mission. Perhaps you are right and no matter what I do, the wishes of The Creator will trump my own selfish ambition. But I won't stop trying to protect my sons. I won't leave them to make decisions of life and death. I won't leave them to have to make choices of allegiance. Go with me or not, but I will finish this as I see fit."

"And I will honor my vows to a dear friend. I will follow you to the end, Gavin. To the death if that may be, but you can count on my sword and my strength. I leave you to make your own choice, Nathan. I will not force you to betray your allegiance to the Order."

Nathan rested his hand on Vladamir's shoulder and said with a smile, "To the end, Master. I am with you both to the end."

Gavin nodded his head in approval of the alliance and then rolled out from behind the cover. He got in a low crouch and sprinted forward to the pile of rocks. It was a long haul and his eyes continued to scan the area for any signs of scouts who might be on the lookout.

He prayed that this would be the last leg of the journey. He was tiring of the constant running, hiding, scouting, formulate plans and doubting his prior decisions. He wanted to reunite his family and get out of Carsonia. He desired to leave this world behind once and for all. If only he had sealed the portals all those years ago. Perhaps none of this would be happening right now.

Or maybe it would. What if he really couldn't escape the plans of The Creator? What if everything he was doing was in vein?

As they drew closer to the rock pile, Gavin was alarmed at the silence that seemed to be surrounding them. He could hear the distinct sounds of boots slamming into the ground and the clank and chatter of equipment as it bounced around, but he wasn't hearing the sounds of a bustling camp. If they were drawing near the goblin's camp, where was the sound of beings going about their daily chores?

Gavin ignored the pile of rocks and continued to move forward. He moved up to the lip of the valley and fell to his knees as his heart stopped beating and the oxygen was sucked out of his lungs. He felt a veil of death wash over him as he looked upon a large expanse of nothingness. More miles and miles of rock to forge across and no signs of a goblin camp to be seen.

He wanted to cry. He wanted to just quit going forward. He felt the hand of Vladamir rest on his shoulder and he shrugged it away. He didn't want sympathy. He wanted this nightmare to be over.

How much longer would he have to endure this torture?

23

One of the goblins shot forward with his sword at the ready. Caleb prepared to counter the attack but instead was shocked when it lowered its sword and fell to its knees before the boys. The other goblins did the same. Caleb wasn't sure if he should take the moment and strike them all dead or to take off in a dead run. He looked back at Lucas who answered him with a shoulder shrug.

"The Masters of our redemption," wailed the goblin who fell before them.

"What?" Caleb asked.

The others repeated the same thing as the first goblin had. In many ways, it was a disturbing chant.

"Do we kill them?" Lucas asked.

"We don't want punishment. We want redemption."

"You're goblins," Caleb said, still reluctant to lower his sword or even move a step towards the seemingly helpless creatures. "Since we got here, you've only wanted to kill us or capture us."

"Maybe our brothers, but not us. We would never kill you."

The lead goblin began to climb to his feet. "We are from the clan of the River Bottom. The men of the South hunt us. The Knights of Liberty pay no attention to us. The other goblin clans reject us. We are not fighters. We wish only to be redeemed. As we were told we would one day be, by the Twins of the Prophecy."

Caleb was tired of hearing this type of talk. With every being they came in contact with here in Carsonia, he felt more and more pressure to take up this mantle and play out his role in the prophecy. He looked over to Lucas who wore a smirk on his face. For him, this was just more reaffirmation that he belonged here and not back home.

"Don't even think about it, Bro," Caleb said. "We're going to find Mom, Dad and Andrea and get the heck out of here."

"No! You mustn't! Our fate depends on you."

Caleb retracted his blade and tucked the hilt of the sword into his belt. "Get up. You look pathetic."

"Be nice," Lucas said. He walked over to the lead goblin and extended a hand to him. The goblin reached out and took a hold and together, they got him back to his feet. The other goblins slowly rose, but kept a safe distance away.

"You are lost. The Angellian warned us to watch for you."

Caleb's mind instantly thought of Marcause. Perhaps they would be found?

"You met an Angellian?" Lucas asked.

"Yes. He came to us just two days ago. Says he tracked

the Twins of the Prophecy into a cave. He lost their trail and suspects they became lost. He doubled back to recheck his trail but he asked us to search for you. Just in case."

"You're friends with an Angellian?" Caleb asked. He wasn't ready to accept their help yet. With all the trouble they had found up to this point, he wasn't ready to accept the hand of a goblin. Especially not after the greeting they received by their first goblin encounter.

"They are the few who accept us. They understand our desire to be redeemed."

"And who are you?" Lucas asked.

"I am Greactus and these," he gestured back to the crew behind him, "are my brothers."

"We were trying to find our parents when we accidently traveled here..." Lucas paused as Caleb shot him a look. Caleb was not ready to divulge information to these beasties, but Lucas was loose with his lips as always. "We need to get back to the North," he continued against the stern warning of his brother's glance.

"We can get you there. But we must be very cautious. You have been spotted by the eyes of Hathian."

Caleb's shoulders slumped down as he felt more of his life flow out of him. Everywhere he turned there seemed to be someone looking for them and none of them were his parents. He was quickly tiring of being hunted. He waited for Lucas to ask the question that was now occupying his own mind.

"Who is Hathian?" he asked.

"He is the leader of the New Order. Secretly, he has turned the twelve kingdoms against each other. He works behind the scenes to weaken the governments and turn the people against one another. He supplies weapons, drugs and has been putting dangerous people into leadership positions within the governments. His ultimate goal is to ride in as the hero of the people, overthrow the corrupt and install his New Order. He will assume the mantle of the Carsonian Emperor and unite this world under his power. But he has one enemy that he must outwit and defeat..."

"The Dark Master Natas," Caleb finished for Greactus. "If Natas is to regain his powerful form, Hathian can never accomplish his goals."

"And the easiest way to defeat Natas is to kill us," Lucas said.

Greactus nodded his head up and down.

"So what are these 'Eyes of Hathian'?" Caleb asked.

"The trees of this region are in allegiance with him. They have seen you pass and they have sent word to him. He knows you are here. There have been rumors for weeks that you two have come to Carsonia to fulfill your destiny. Everyone is watching for signs of you."

"Two things," Caleb began with a cold tone in his voice, "We haven't come to fulfill anything. Once we find our parents, we're out of here. Number two, you're basically telling me that if we hadn't gotten stuck in the belly of a worm and detonated two portal grenades, this Hathian wouldn't have a clue we are here?"

Greactus shook his head up and down and then said, "Yessem. That's basically it. However, you must fulfill your destiny. You cannot escape it."

"Watch me."

"Watch you what?"

Lucas shook his head in disgust and then said to Greactus, "Never mind him. He's got his undies in a twist."

"And what does that mean? 'Undies in a Twist'?"

Lucas pushed Caleb behind him and took on the role as official spokesmen of the McGregor's. "You were saying that we have been spotted… by trees?"

"The trees. Enchanted by the dark wizard who serves Hathian. The trees and the birds in this region are his watchful eyes. They hear our words and betray our secrets. With Hathian, there are no secrets. He gathers information and knows all… just as he knows you are here."

"If that's the case, we should be moving on as quickly as possible."

"Yessem. I agree."

"And you did say you could get us back to the North?"

"Yessem. We can do that. We actually know a very quick path that will take us into the caverns of the deep where we can take a train into the village of Naechester. We cannot emerge to the surface with you, but we can travel with you that far and offer you protection."

"We would appreciate that. Thank you for your kindness."

"But first, we should take you back to our camp and feed you. You need rest and food before we go on such a journey."

"We don't have time for that," Caleb said. "If Hathian knows we're here, then we need to get moving right now. Straight on for the train. We don't have time to travel out of the way to your camp."

"Our camp is on the way. We will pass right through it."

"Oh," Caleb said. He was embarrassed for speaking too quickly without knowing all of the facts. He felt foolish now. "Then… yea. Let's get going. I want to get out of Carsonia as quick as possible." He looked at Lucas out of the corner of his eyes and mumbled just for him to hear, "I feel like the walls are closing in on me. Maybe because I don't know who I can trust anymore."

"What's that supposed to mean?" Lucas said loud enough for everyone to hear.

"If I didn't know better, you're not concerned if we ever get home. You'd be quite happy if we got trapped here forever."

"Get off yourself," Lucas said as he pushed pass his brother, grabbed his ruck and threw it over his shoulder. With purposeful steps, he moved up to the small detail of goblins from the River Bottom Clan and motioned with his head for them to lead the way.

"We should wait for your brother," Greactus said.

"If he wants to live, he'll catch up."

"Yessem," the goblin said as he motioned for his men to begin moving and the crew got on their way.

Caleb cast an angry glare at the group as he tossed his ruck sack on his back and scrambled to catch up. A good meal did sound good. He just hoped it actually tasted good.

Everything else in this world was leaving a sour taste in his mouth.

24

The shuffling of goblin feet along the rocky surface outside the tent, bit at the nerves of Andrea. She could already feel the slaps across the face. The fist to the stomach that would push the air right out of her lungs and make her feel as if she would never be able to draw in another breath again. The touches meant to intimidate her and give her a glimpse into the sadistic minds of these beasts. Then there were the screams of Catrina behind her. To hear her painful cries only heightened the fear and panic inside – and perhaps that was why the goblins did this daily ritual. They enjoyed the smell and taste of fear that filled the tent each time they entered and executed their bouts of torture.

She was tired of it.

In desperation, she continued to work on doing the things that Catrina told her she could do. She imagined her body breaking into pieces of light and escaping into the sky above – but nothing happened. She imagined a spell she could cast with her mind that would free her from the bindings – yet nothing happened. At this point, she wished she could just ignite the tent into a ball of fire and burn to death, just so she wouldn't have to look into the beady eyes of her torturer and have to see the wicked grin of mangled teeth that looked to have been sharpened to points with a jagged stone.

The footsteps stopped outside the tent flap. Time was up.

The flap was pulled back and in walked a goblin guard – the goblin guard who came to them each day. He had with him the same two bowls of garbage. He did cast his gnarled smile in her direction like he did everyday – but this time he drew back. His eyes grew big. He smelled something different in the tent. His head tilted like that of a puppy who was investigating a new sound. He seemed to sense something was different.

Andrea wasn't sure what to make of it. What was he seeing? What was he sensing? He took a step back. He set the bowls down on the rocky surface and then moved a step towards her.

"What are you?" he asked as he took another step forward.

What could that possibly mean?

"What's going on, Andrea?" Catrina asked. She could feel her trying to crank her neck around to see what was going on.

Andrea's blood began to run cold inside her. With each step he took towards her, the hair on the back of her neck seemed to rise up and she could almost feel sparks of electricity snapping along her body. Was she transforming into the ball of light that Catrina had described to her? She allowed the fear to grow stronger. She imagined the horrible things he was going to do to her and then she saw it – one single bolt of electricity curled around her leg like a snake. It worked its way down her thigh, across her shin and then exploded from her foot. It slammed into the side of the tent and blasted a large hole into it.

The goblin dropped to the ground. He covered his head with his hands. He was afraid to look at her. Through barely parted fingers, he cast a glance at her.

He trembled.

She liked it.

Smoke began to rise up from the ground around her and then she heard Catrina call out, "Andrea, are you okay? What's going on? You're burning up!"

More electrical bolts shot down her legs. Some fired off and slammed into the bowls of slop, causing them to explode. Other bolts just wrapped around and rushed back up her body. Suddenly she could see her entire body was turning into a ball of electricity. It wasn't the gentle flecks of light that Catrina had described, but she was glowing – or surging with energy.

The bindings around her wrists fell off and she quickly jumped to her feet. The goblin scrambled to his feet but she quickly caught him in her grasp. Her right hand wrapped around his thin neck and she squeezed. His eyes leaped out of their sockets and he choked on something he desperately wanted to say.

She couldn't help herself.

She allowed every speck of hatred to be poured into this defenseless creature and all the energy that was inside her rushed into him. His skin began to smolder as the smell of burning flesh reached her nostrils and she inhaled deeply.

She enjoyed it!

His eyes began to turn red and then they seemed to turn to goo as the eyeballs slid out of their sockets and ran down his charring cheekbones. She poured more anger into him. His body shook violently as all the electricity rushed into him. His skin boiled and blackened and soon, dried chunks began to break off and fall to the ground.

He was as good as dead, but she held on longer.

The flap to the tent opened up. A goblin rushed in to rescue his comrade. Andrea raised up her free hand and a blast of electricity tore through the air and slammed through the chest of the rescuer. He dropped dead to the ground.

She could hear crying and screams. She could smell a new type of fear. She could taste the terror that the goblins had been tasting all this time and she liked it. She desired more and so she dropped the dead creature who shattered into pieces of charred flesh and bone when he hit the ground.

She bent over, summoned more power and then she stood straight up, her arms stretched up high into the sky. A pulse of power exploded from her and the tent vaporized. Like a cloud of destruction, the wave of power went out for quite a distance around her and ignited all of the other tents in the area into balls of fire. Goblins scrambled out of their burning homes. Some dropped to the ground and rolled around to put out the fires on their bodies. Others were caught by the bolts of electricity that she was firing into all of the directions.

She could see herself doing all of this – yet none of it seemed real. Part of her wanted to stop; yet the other part said that she must continue if she wanted to live. With that new thought planted in her mind, she took a step forward.

Three goblin warriors charged towards her with their bone axes at the ready. She pointed a finger at them and unleashed strong bolts of electricity that tore through their bodies and dropped them to the ground dead. Small goblin children stood in the open, screaming for their parents. Andrea unleashed her anger on them as well. The gentle soul she had been in the Earth realm was seemingly gone in this one. Here, she was a killing machine.

She continued to hurl balls of electricity in every direction. Tents that had been spared in the first wave were now dancing with flames. The smell of burning ozone and flesh filled her nostrils. Deep inside it was very nauseating, yet this persona that seemed to capsulate her body – fed off the destruction. She unleashed more havoc until nothing – and no one – was left standing.

The electricity stopped flowing. Her hair fell gently on

her shoulders and Andrea collapsed to her knees in utter exhaustion. She was thirsty, her lips chapped and her skin flaky from being so dry.

Catrina!

She turned and found the pole they had been bound together on for so many days. It was gone. She frantically got to her feet. She looked around and then saw in the distance a pole with a charred figure trapped underneath it.

"No!" she cried out as she ran in that direction. She stumbled and fell onto the rocky surface. The sharp rock tore into her palms and ripped up her knees. She crawled the rest of the way and took Catrina into her arms. She cradled the head of the woman that had been a mother to her for so long. A single tear rolled out of Catrina's eye.

"Catrina – you're going to be okay."

The woman opened her mouth to speak, but nothing came out. Her tongue ran over her lips as she attempted to moisten them and then she tried again.

"I'm here, Catrina. I'm here. Please be okay. Please don't leave me…"

"And…rea…."

She brushed the crinkled hair of Catrina, out of her face and held her tighter. Her own tears were gushing from her eyes and she couldn't hardly see the mother of Caleb that she was cradling in her arms.

"Protect… my sons…." She said.

"You can do that. You're not going to die. Not here... not like this..."

"Protect... my sons..."

"I don't want to do it without you. I need you. Don't die!"

"No... protect my sons..."

Andrea gasped for air. She was fighting against the urge to pass out from all the emotions that were racking her body.

"I'll protect them. I promise."

"No... protect them... from you..."

And with that, she exhaled her last breath.

Andrea was alone.

And in shock.

25

The smoke was now rising, thicker than before and a strong odor of burning flesh was wafting towards them as they ran into the unknown.

Gavin was confident that this was the goblin camp they had been searching for. It was just over two miles from where they had suspected it to be. He was closer to his wife now than he had ever been since returning to Carsonia. He could almost smell her hair and feel the soft touch of her hand as it brushed over his cheek.

But the smoke! The stench! He was now concerned of what destruction they might find in the camp.

Had a faction attacked the camp? If so, was Catrina and Andrea safe?

The thought only made him lengthen his stride. His heart was beating hard to keep up with the blood that was required to flow through him to keep him going. Even if it had blown up, the adrenaline that was now coursing through his body was more than enough to get him where he needed to be. He wanted to call out her name. He wanted to hear her call back to him.

Nathan was in top shape and was able to match stride for stride with Gavin. If he wanted, he was sure the young man could outrun him. As for Vladamir, it was clear he had lost a step or two. He wasn't far behind and maybe being a little ways back, he would be able to provide support in the form of a sneak attack if the two of them ran into more than they could handle.

The rocky terrain began to give way to lush trees. The ground was beginning to slope upwards as they had reached the foothills of the Central Mountain Range. Smoke had settled in the area like a dense fog. In some places he couldn't see anything. In other places, the smoke had cleared out and he could make his way through the vegetation with ease and at a quick pace. He could see a clearing just ahead.

He reached in for more strength, calling on the light to surround him and prepare him for battle. He pulled the hilt of his sword off his belt and snapped it to life. Just a few more maneuvers to get around some fallen brush and he emerged from the woods and found a landscape of charred death.

The remains of tents and wooden furniture were scattered about the area. Blackened bodies of adult goblins and even children goblins were lying on the ground. Smoke still rose from many of the bodies, and in the center of it all, he saw the sight he dreaded most.

Andrea was cradling the head of his beloved in her

arms.

He rushed forward and then fell to his knees, tears already streaming down his face. He looked into Andrea's eyes and saw the pain and turmoil of a girl who had witnessed too much and was now broken. He knew he should console her, but his attention went to Catrina.

His hands cupped her face and he pressed his forehead to hers, his tears washing the dirt from her delicate features. His body shook as the pain escaped through every pour of his body and through it all, Andrea continued to hold her in her arms and stroke her singed hair. The two of them wept while Vladamir and Nathan kept back.

"What... how..." he tried to ask. He looked up and saw Andrea biting her lip very hard, tears streaming and her eyes puffy red from the anguish.

She shook her head and he took it as she was at a loss as to what had happened. It had to be some sort of enemy of the goblins – perhaps some of the homesteaders in the area that had been chased off their land by the massive clan of goblins that had moved in under the protection of Mideon.

He felt rage towards the farmers – though they only fought for what was theirs. He couldn't blame them, however, didn't they know about his pursuit of his wife and his son's girlfriend. Didn't they know to be careful of two innocent prisoners? How could they be so reckless?

He could hear the heavy footsteps of Vladamir as he

approached from behind. He could almost see the hand reaching down before resting on his shoulder. He could feel the squeeze, but he received no comfort from it.

"We cannot stay here long. I caught a glimpse of a massive beast along the wood line. I believe Mideon has returned."

"He is to blame," Gavin said as a new fire ignited in his blood and he rose to his feet with his sword at the ready. "He brought her here to her death. His blood for hers!" he shouted in hopes that the Minotaur would hear him and answer the call.

"Calm your emotions…" Vladamir started to say before Gavin pulled away.

He knelt back down and took his dead wife from the arms of Andrea. Andrea's head fell into her hands and she collapsed in heaving sobs of pain. Gavin walked slowly across the camp, his eyes scanning the ground before he found a large piece of canvas that had survived the attack.

He laid her down on it and then slowly wrapped her body tight inside of the fabric. As he pulled the last piece up over her face, he knelt forward and placed a soft kiss on her forehead.

Her skin was just as soft now as it was just weeks ago when he last held her. Oh, to have that moment back again. To laugh with her. To hold her. To kiss her and feel the warmth of her touch right now. He had missed it all the while he searched for her. He never realized that those moments would be the last he would share with her. His life was no longer complete.

"We'll be together again, Love. My heart will always belong to you and only you…" he broke into a soft cry as he laid the cloth over her face and patted the area where her cheek would be. "I don't even know what to do next…"

"We get the boys and then we get you all home," Vladamir said. This time he had snuck up without Gavin knowing he was there.

Gavin tried to focus on Caleb and Lucas. He knew they still needed him, but he didn't have a clue how he would explain the death of their mother or how he would raise two boys on his own. She was the calming voice in the house when they had successfully pushed him over the edge with their antics. She was the one who cooked meals from scratch that provided nutrients and sparked the conversations that drew them all closer together at the dinner table.

The family would never be complete again. There would always be one seat at the table with nobody to sit in it. One voice of reason, compassion, and love that would never be heard again. He lowered his head and rested it on her chest and cried harder. He could no longer catch his breath and he shook with each wail, letting it all flow out of him. He had to force the pain out of his body so he could recapture enough sense and strength to do what still had to be done.

As he continued to be lost in himself, he could hear the voices of everyone talking behind him. But then he stopped sobbing. Something didn't seem right. It wasn't the voices of two men and a girl that he heard – it was the collection of many voices.

He raised his head and looked back. Nathan was escorting Andrea up to Vladamir's side and then he felt a cool air blow over his body. A darkness seemed to be settling into the area. He looked at the trees on the edge of the clearing and saw the cloaked figures ahead.

It wasn't the voices of his companions he heard, but the voices of the Draith, speaking into his head. He pushed them out with sheer rage and the light encompassed his body. The rushing surge of blood and anger throbbing in his ears drowned out the warnings of Vladamir to move cautiously. He charged forward and launched a full, one man attack against the powerful Draith squad that had come to destroy them.

He hurled five tentacles of light at the line of Draith and slapped them into the air and out of his way as he drove into the middle of them and began to swing his sword in every direction. His sword clashed with the swords of his attackers. He spun around and brought his sword across his body and through the neck of another Draith. He used a tentacle of light to scoop up one warrior and then threw him through the air and into a tree where a branch pierced through his chest.

He projected another tentacle of light, picked up a

Draith and pulled him towards him. As it flew through the air towards him, he reared back and then drove his sword through its chest and then ran it up and through his head. He let the limp body fall to the ground.

He was a wrecking ball; tearing through the wall of Draith and racking up a body count in a quick manner. From a distance, he could hear the chattering and screams of goblins. He could feel the Draith circling around him and so he naturally summoned all of the arms of light to close in tight around him for protection and then he unleashed it back out in every direction, unleashing a surge of power that threw all of his enemies back fifty yards and giving him breathing room.

He looked up and saw that a new band of goblins had come to claim vengeance on the death of the members of their clan. They would probably assume that Gavin and his party were responsible and that was fine with him. He was feeling renewed and powerful and the death of his love was now far from his mind.

He was all about getting vengeance for her death. He would exact that vengeance on the goblins who worked with Mideon to capture her and then he would hunt down the mastermind himself. There was going to be a lot of blood spilled on this day and that was the one thing that was making the pain go away.

The goblins were many, completely surrounding Gavin, Vladamir, Nathan and Andrea. He reached down and picked up a sword and then walked it over to Andrea. "You will probably need this."

She took it in her hand and looked it over as if she had no idea how it worked. Gavin didn't have time to worry about her. He should take the time to protect her, but he was more entertained by the thought of killing goblins and then killing the bounty hunter. If she made it, that was great. If not, chances were none of them would. For this one moment, it was every person for themselves.

Vladamir, Nathan and Gavin wrapped themselves in the light as the goblin forces joined up with the Draith and they all charged in for the kill.

Off in the distance, Gavin could see Mideon watching the proceedings. He felt the rage building up – wanting to break through the wall of goblins and Draith and tear into the bounty hunter. But then his stomach sank when he watched the Minotaur get up on a very large horse and ride off into the mountains with a handful of his remaining followers.

Gavin shook off those negative feelings by reassuring himself that Mideon wouldn't be able to hide from him for long. He would hunt him like a wild boar and drive his sword deep into his chest in the name of vengeance. In the meantime, he had to fight out of this situation in order to get that opportunity.

Outnumbered, the four Carsonian's dug in and prepared to spill blood.

26

"I am so sick of walking," Caleb mumbled as he tripped over the branch of a fallen tree. It was concealed under the foliage of the forest floor – just one of the millions of obstacles that had nearly killed him that morning.

He didn't see the beauty of Carsonia that his dad had bragged about. As the days went by excruciatingly slow, he began to find a deeper resentment to this place.

Lucas seemed to be taking it all in stride, which also irritated him. He had been socializing with the goblins – whom Caleb was not as ready to embrace as allies like Lucas did. He would stop every so often and point out something that reminded him "of back home" or scenery that "you could never see back home."

For the love of all that was holy, Caleb wanted Lucas to stop talking about home. He wanted to be there. Reminding him of what he desired most had never been a strong motivational tool. It typically served to lower the dark cloud over his head.

They had been working their way out of the high points of

the mountains and into a low valley known simply as the River Bottoms. This clan of the goblins had chosen this as their home because nobody wanted to live in this land. It was much too hard to get to and it was prone to flash flooding from heavy rain storms. The river didn't empty into any great body of water and there were absolutely no villages of any importance along it. There were no places of interest or trade. No way to sell goods or purchase goods.

If you lived along this river, the only thing it could supply was fresh fish, water and the occasional flood which would wipe out your home in a matter of hours. Granted, the fresh food and water were keys to life and for that, the river served its purpose. But all the headaches that came along with it and the isolation – why would anyone choose it for a home?

Greactus was proud of his home. He spoke fondly of it. His clan had been rejected by the other goblins, hunted to near extinction by men. The Knights of Liberty offered his people no protection, so perhaps this place was the best place in the world for these goblins. That was probably the best reason to choose this as a home.

"Can you lighten up?" he heard Lucas say to him. With all the befuddled thoughts running through his head, he hadn't realized that his brother had come up alongside of him.

"I'm fine."

"You look like someone stuffed a dirty wet sock in your mouth. We are going to get some much needed rest and a good bite to eat. I think you could at least lighten up a bit."

"I don't trust them," he said in a voice for just the two of them.

"If they wanted us dead, we'd be dead. If they were taking us to the bounty hunter, they would have tied us up. They told us their testimony. We are the ones who are called to redeem them from the atrocities of their forefathers. We give them hope!"

"They give me the creeps."

Lucas didn't answer with a reply. He gave a stern look.

"They are too eager to help us out," Caleb continued in protest. "You watch. They'll poison us with bad fish and then at some point we'll find ourselves tied up over a fire pit. They'll fatten us up tonight and eat us tomorrow."

"Knock it off!" Lucas stormed away from his brother and went up to join Greactus in the lead.

Maybe his brother was right, but with all that had happened in the past few days... or was it weeks? Could it have really been over a month since they came to Carsonia? He didn't know anymore. And before he could answer that thought, up in the trees, along the crisp, fast moving water of the river, a gigantic network of huts were inviting them in to shelter.

The aroma of cooking meat filled the air. There was a faint sound of music coming from the distance and suddenly, all of Caleb's issues with the goblins of the River Bottoms drifted away.

The homes were built around the trees. Some extended quite a distance away, many of them hanging over the river itself. They looked well built, as if crafted over a long period of time. In the windows he could see glowing lights. From time to time, a goblin adult or child would pass by, busy with the day's activities. The huts were linked together by massive bridges that would branch off in different directions, sometimes connecting four of five huts on one line. It was amazing!

"Somebody is quiet," one of the goblins hissed in his ear. Caleb turned to look at him and found a wide smile of jagged teeth. He was quickly reminded of the real danger they could be in and his mood shifted back.

They climbed the rope ladder that was at the base of one of the larger trees and all grouped up on a large platform high in the trees. Greactus held out his arms like he was about to offer a giant hug and then said through a huge smile, "This is our home. This is Treefore… home of the River Bottoms Clan. Come," he said with a gesture, "we have a meal preparing for you. We shall eat well tonight. Yessem."

They weaved through the network of huts. Many of the goblins were excited to see them. They would bow to the guests, the children rushed up to him and Lucas and offered little trinkets that Lucas gladly took and Caleb tried to shrug off. When he realized how rude it was to dash the hopes of children, he would accept the offer with a forced smile and then tuck the trinket into a pouch on his belt.

Greactus informed him that for the kids, this was equivalent to meeting a mighty king or a famous warrior. In their customs, the kids would create a personal item and give it to the famous guest as a token of having the honor to be a part of that person's life. Caleb thought of it to be equivalent to getting an autograph from a favorite ball player. That gave the handmade gifts a sudden high value in his mind and he felt bad for those he rejected earlier as they entered the village.

"How did they know we were coming?" Caleb asked. "Each child has made two gifts."

"Marcause was here, remember?" Greactus said. "Word travels fast when it concerns those who will bring our clan redemption. You have restored hope in us. Our children see a day when we will no longer be feared or hunted but will instead be considered equal with man and free to roam Carsonia without persecution. The sins of our fathers will be forgiven and we will have life again. You are a very good thing for us."

Caleb allowed those words to settle on his heart. There was such a genuine tone in Greactus' voice. He truly felt honored to be escorting two twin boys into his village. Perhaps his earlier judgment was incorrect.

The spicy food smell continued to travel through the air and it tickled Caleb's stomach with delight. He hadn't had a well cooked meal since the morning that his Grandma was killed and this crazy adventure had really begun.

They continued weaving through the network of bridges that connected the round platforms that encircled the trees and gave birth to massive huts that were busy with goblins doing their normal routines. From time to time, Caleb would peek into a window as they passed by and he was amazed at how their lives seemed very similar to that of his own race.

The idea of a single creator for two worlds made sense to him. It seemed like everyone was hardwired with the same internal programing that created the same outcomes in his own world and here in Carsonia. Love, peace, happiness, passion, hobbies, cooking, families, greed, lust, the desire for power – as he caught snap shots of the lives of the River Bottom Clan, he discovered that maybe these goblins weren't the beasts he had labeled them to be, but were in fact, just as much capable of being human as he was.

Actually, maybe they were just as much human as he was, only with different characteristics.

Their path began to wind back to the North and he could hear the rushing sound of the river. It was coming up and soon he realized that the dining area of the goblins was a large platform that had been built up over the river.

A band was in full swing playing what sounded like guitars and flutes. It was a soothing tune that seemed to be written to mimic and enhance the sounds of the river flowing below them. Eight long tables were evenly spaced on the platform, each one filled with food and wine and goblins who were busy talking about whatever goblins talked about.

On the far side of the platform was a single, small table turned to face the eight rows of other tables. Seated in the center was one goblin decked out with a crown, purple clothes and a flowing cape of gold. Caleb didn't need Greactus to tell him that this was the king of their clan.

As they approached the table, Greactus and his men bowed low for their majesty. Caleb saw Lucas do the same to his right and decided it probably wasn't a bad thing for him to follow suit – though it did feel uncomfortable to bow to someone he didn't know.

"The Twins of the Prophecy bow to me?" the gruff voice of the king said. "Ha! We shall all bow to you I think."

With that, he rose from his seat. The other goblins around the platform did as well and all of them, including the king, bowed low to Caleb and Lucas. This was an even more uncomfortable feeling as suddenly they had become the center of attention.

The king stood upright again and then gestured for the boys to take a seat at his table. As they sat down, two female servants laid plates heaping with cooked meat and veggies on the table before them. Then a cup of wine was set down for them to drink.

Caleb hated the taste of wine and so he asked the

servant, "Could I possibly have a glass of water?"

"Ha!" the King shouted, "Wine is the best tasting water in the land!"

The platform erupted into a roar of laughter. Caleb smiled, but not getting the joke, he had to force it to form on his face in order to be polite.

"Drink!" said the King as he raised his cup high and then tipped it back. The red fluid rushed out and straight down and into his mouth, much of it splashing out and running down his face and splattering over his clothes and plate of food. His lips never touched the rim of the cup.

"It's going to be one of those types of parties," Caleb whispered to Lucas.

Lucas looked over to him with a big smile. Grabbing his cup, Lucas said, "Hey, when in Rome..."

He raised it up, tipped it back and poured it down. The first tip sent a river of wine flowing down on his shoulder. He made a quick adjustment and the next attempt splashed down the side of his face and then with an adjustment, he found his intended target, his mouth.

The platform erupted into cheers again.

As Lucas finished up, he slammed his cup down on the table and turned to Caleb, "Come on, Bro. You owe it to these people. They saved our lives. Don't be rude."

Caleb picked up his cup and took a sip. Boos filled the area, drowning out the sound of the river below. He noticed that the band had quit playing and all eyes were on him. Against his better judgment, Caleb decided to follow suit.

He raised it high, tipped it back and got most of it down the front of his tunic before finding his mouth and glugging the remaining wine down. The platform exploded into celebration as the music started up again and the King looked over at the boys and gave a curious wink.

Caleb smacked his lips, savoring the flavor. It didn't have the strong, fermented taste that he had remembered from the wine back home. Not that he drank much, but he remembered a strong taste that just never settled with his taste buds. He hated it. The single taste he had drank at a New Year's Eve celebration with his parents was enough to give him a negative opinion of wine and almost all alcoholic beverages. Yet, this didn't have that impact on him. In fact, he wanted more and almost had an unquenchable desire for more.

"You like?" the King asked.

"I like!" Caleb said as he slammed his cup down on the table and then let out a large belch. "I'll take more of that!"

"Wow," Lucas said, "I know I told you to loosen up, but man, you're taking that advice to a whole new level."

"It's like drinking Kool-Aid. Goes down smooth and gives me a hankering for more."

The King gave a toothy grin and said, "I don't know what this Kool-Aid is, but if that's what you think it tastes like – that is what it tastes like."

He got up from the table and the entire platform went silent as he held up his cup that had just been filled by the servant and proclaimed, "We shall call this, Kool-Aid!"

"*Kool-Aid!*" everyone shouted in unison. They all tipped their cups back and drank it down. Caleb and Lucas took their newly filled cups and did the same thing. Like one big thundering explosion, everyone in the dining area slammed their cups hard into the tables and everyone that could, let out a large, sickening belch. The cheers exploded and the band went back to work providing entertainment and all seemed well for the first time in a long time.

Perhaps it was the alcohol in the wine and the fact that he didn't drink that often. Or maybe it was because for over a month his nerves had been on edge during their travels and tribulations. But whatever the reason, Caleb was suddenly feeling the impact of restless nights because he was suddenly becoming very tired. He was ready for a deep sleep – something he hadn't had in quite a while.

He smiled over at Lucas as the platter of meat before him, called out his name. He dug in and began to eat quickly, washing it down with the new glass of wine that was placed before him. "I could live like this forever," Caleb said to his brother.

Lucas didn't reply back. Caleb stuffed more meat into his mouth and then looked up to find his brother face down in his mashed potatoes. His heart jumped. He looked up and

Greactus also looked startled.

Both of them sprang from their seats as Greactus quickly got to Lucas and began to shake him. Caleb stumbled back. The world took off in a spin and he fell backwards on his back. He tried to get up again, but blackness began to cloud his vision.

He looked over and saw Greactus coming to his aid, trying to help him up, but his legs wouldn't work. A ringing began to drown out his hearing.

"Are you okay?" Greactus asked. He then turned to the King, "What have you done? I've seen this look before. You poisoned them!"

"Poison!" Caleb mouthed with his lips but no sound came out. "Why?" he mouthed again, even though nobody could hear him.

"Why would you do this?" he could barely hear Greactus say over the increased ringing.

"You've made a deal with Hathian?" Greactus cried out.

Darkness overcame Caleb and he fell into a deep sleep.

27

The tears built up in her eyes and then flowed over her bottom eyelids, mixing with the soot on her cheeks and sending black streaks down her face. She was tired of all the pain, all of the battles and all of the death. Since the night when they were kidnapped in the woods, her life had been on an uncontrolled spin and Andrea was tired of it.

She missed her grandparents. She missed her Caleb. She missed her friends back at the school and her dog back home. This place may have been where she was born – it may even be where destiny calls her to be, but she didn't want any part of it.

In her one moment of control – where she had the power to escape the grasps of the goblins, she ended up killing a wonderful woman who had been as much as a mom to her as her own. Now the battle unfolded before her.

Vladamir and Nate were surrounded by Draith and bloodthirsty goblins. Gavin was just a few feet from her, fighting off the enemy and doing his all to protect her. But he wouldn't last long. None of them would last long. And once they were dead, she would be next. They would probably continue to torture her and break her down mentally. She didn't want to do those things again. She didn't want to be a part of Carsonia any longer.

Gavin blocked a bolt of lightning that was fired from one of the cloaked demon like beings. His sword was jolted from his hand and it crashed at her feet. He couldn't turn to retrieve it. Instead, he picked up the Draith with a tentacle of light and hurled him as far as he could, but he couldn't let his attention drift far from the battle at hand. She could see the Draith regain his composure and rise back up. He was about to return to the battle again — just like all of the other Draith had been doing.

With all of the attacks going on, none of them could use their powers to effectively battle against the onslaught of Draith and goblins. They could only cast their attention on directing a tentacle or two of light for a little bit before they turned their attention back to defending themselves using their swords.

Did they even realize how close they were to dying?

Andrea was growing tired of being weak. She was tired of having to wait to be rescued. She was tired of having her life balance in the actions of others.

She bent over and picked up the sword.

Gavin gave her a quick glance and then reached out his hand to take back his sword. Andrea looked down at the cold steel that she had in her grasp. She slowly looked at him and made eye contact. He gestured for her to hand it over and instead she shook her head no.

She was done being helpless.

She closed her eyes and took a deep breath. She felt a rush of power gather inside her and then suddenly it pulsed through her veins. She could almost feel herself growing large and becoming bigger than all of the world – though she was still the five foot ten inches that she always was. She could hear the din of battle and all of it came into focus.

She could feel the battle playing out before her. Vladamir was spinning around, deflecting attacks high and low while hurling tentacles out like fists of light, slamming into goblins and crushing their faces with a single blow. She could see Nate doing the same thing as he ducked under a mighty swing and then spun around with an outstretched leg to sweep the legs out from under a Draith knight. He stood up and then drove a sword into its chest.

Gavin was suddenly on his knees, being overwhelmed by a flurry of goblin and Draith attackers and she could hear a sword hissing through the air as it prepared to pierce his chest.

Her eyes opened.

The world seemed to stand still.

Andrea unleashed the beast inside.

Lunging forward, she swept her sword in an upwards

motion and deflected the killing blow. Pushing the enemies sword up, she spun around and jabbed her foot into his gut and then came around with her sword and cut him off at the neck.

She pointed her hand to a Draith behind Gavin and hurled a ball of glowing light straight at it. The ball slammed into its chest and he fired back into a crowd, taking out an entire troop of goblins and disappearing into the woods beyond.

She turned back to swinging her sword in motions and directions she didn't even realize she had the ability to do. Heads were severed and falling to the ground. Goblin blood was spraying all about, covering her face and clothes and yet she continued to move around the area, slaying goblins and Draith with ease.

She could feel the shock flowing from Gavin's life force but chose to ignore it. She didn't care what he was thinking. She only cared about killing these beasts who had stolen her life.

Like a tornado, she twisted and spun, hurled spells and slashed her sword and blew through the area – laying waste to anything that got in her path. Vladamir ducked out of her way when she approached the area where he was making a valiant stand. More bodies fell to the ground.

She was soon coming to the rescue of Nate and likewise, she unleashed an assault that an overwhelming group of highly trained knights could not defend. They all fell by the sword of Andrea. She could sense new players coming into the battle. These figures didn't feel like darkness, but they were charging in with great speed. She didn't know if they could be trusted so she dove in to attack.

Her sword met the sword of one of the new soldiers and then she heard a soft voice say, "It is over. Stop."

All at once, the energy that was moving her, switched off. She was trapped and suddenly unable to move.

Her eyes met his and she became instantly lost in the wave of crystal blue that stared back at her. They were powerful eyes with a calming effect – like watching the waves of the ocean slide up on the beach and then roll back to the sea. His hair was long and golden, straight as an arrow. He was adorned in flowing blue robes and a white tunic. His regal appearance commanded respect, and so she lowered her sword – though not by her own choice. Something inside her had taken over and made her do it.

"And who is this warrior?" the man said.

Gavin walked up to them, casting a wearily glance around the destruction that she had left in her wake. He drew close to the group and was joined by Vladamir before answering, "This is Andrea. She's Caleb's girlfriend. She was with Catrina when she died."

The man's eyes grew large as they reflected the shock inside. "She's dead? How?"

Gavin shook his head and walked away, collapsing to the ground in a combination of exhaustion and internal pain from the loss of his love.

"The goblin camp was attacked... how long ago?" Vladamir directed the question to Andrea.

She looked down at the blade that was dripping with the crimson blood of the goblins. It was mixed with a silvery substance that she assumed was the equivalent of blood from the Draith that she had slain. She shook her head, trying hard to get rid of the memories of leveling the entire village with her rage. As she looked up and scanned the new layer of carnage brought on in the aftermath of her rage, she was starting to understand Catrina's wish for her to leave her boys alone.

"Andrea?" the warm voice of the man asked.

She looked up and felt that calming sensation as she looked into his eyes again, "Before Vladamir, Nate and Gavin arrived."

The man looked around, taking in the ruins. "To my knowledge, there are few forces capable of this type of destruction. Draith are one of them... but to attack the goblins who were working for them makes no sense."

"Unless the goblins refused to turn the boys over. That could have brought on the retaliation," Vladamir said.

"Perhaps," he said. The man looked back into her eyes and then said for only the two of them to hear, "You are very able with the sword. Tell me, where do you come from? You have the eyes of an Angellian and the fine hair of one, but I do not know you."

"Marcause," Gavin said as he rose to his feet, wiping the tears from his eyes with weary hands. "Enough with the questions. My boys are out there and we need to go and find them. Tell me you have news."

Marcause continued to look into her eyes. He seemed to be studying her – but why? Was this yet another part of the story that she was not aware of?

"Marcause!" Gavin's voice was short and filled with urgency.

"I already know of their whereabouts. I tracked them to the far south region of the mountains. Word just came to me that the River Bottom Clan has found them and taken them into their care. However, time is of the essence because the bounty hunter and a small team just raced past here and are in pursuit."

"Then time is against us," Vladamir said. "I watched them ride off on horses just before the battle broke out. If we are to continue going on foot, we will fall behind very quickly."

"Where do you find a horse big enough to carry a beast like Mideon?" Nate added as a side note to the discussion.

"Bred by masters of the dark arts," Vladamir said. "Is there someplace where we can acquire horses, Marcause?"

"Perhaps. There is a village just a day's walk from here. My team and I can go off ahead through the air, procure enough horses for you three and then ride back to meet you. We will then go off ahead and try to slow down Mideon's advance. We have already dueled once before," he said as his hand seemed to instinctively move to the side of his abdomen and sooth some sort of aching pain. "I'm more than able to delay him."

Gavin was quiet, staring off to the south. He was distant now. A wave of guilt washed over Andrea as she watched the man slip farther away from reality. She always knew him to be strong.

He was broad in the shoulder, always standing tall and upright with a walk of confidence. Now he seemed to be thin and frail. His shoulders were slumping and he looked as if he had just been rescued from a concentration camp. His life was quickly draining before her eyes.

She moved over to him and rested her hand on his shoulder. At first it felt awkward and she pulled away. But that glancing touch felt right and so she rested it there again and then laid her head on his shoulder. Tears ran down her cheeks.

How could she ever explain what had happened at the camp? Would she have to live with this guilt forever – never be able to tell anyone that it was her actions that had killed Catrina?

"We're going to get them back," he whispered. His mouth was dry and the words croaked out. He moistened his chapped lips with his tongue and then cleared his throat before trying to sound more confident, "We're going to get the back. I can almost see them now."

"I know. I know we will."

She looked over and watched as Marcause and his handful of Angellian soldiers dissipated into glowing balls of light and shot off in a southern direction. It looked just as Catrina had described it.

"We need to get moving," Vladamir said.

Gavin answered with a nod of his head. He walked back and picked up the sword that she had dropped and then looked over to his wife who was still rolled up in the fabric.

"Nate, could you please help me cover her with rock to protect her from the animals. We will come back and give her a proper burial after we get the boys."

Nate nodded and went right to work. Andrea and Vladamir helped. As they prepared to leave the ruins of the camp, Andrea felt a part of her being left behind. They began moving quickly by foot into the woods and off to meet with Marcause and his men.

She chanced one glance back and she saw the make shift grave that kept Catrina's body safe from scavengers. She saw a mother and a friend being left there.

She also saw her innocence draw its last breath.

28

Clopping.

The rhythmic sound of horse hooves striking the ground were the first sounds that began to draw Lucas out of his deep sleep. Then he felt the floor fall away from him. The sound of metallic gear rang out. Then the floor raised back up and smashed into the side of his face – jolting him fully awake.

He sat up, anchoring his hands to the pitching floor to keep from falling over as his room seemed to be shifting in all kinds of directions. He looked around. Daylight was pouring through the wood bars that made up the walls of his cell. Then he realized the cell was moving and it all came together at once.

Lucas spotted Caleb stirring across the small box cell. He crawled over and shook him, "Wake up, Bro. We are in it now. I mean, really in it."

"Go back to sleep."

"No, Caleb. You need to wake up. We're in deep this time."

Caleb refused to get up. He rolled back over and continued his slumber until the mobile jail cell, or wagon, or whatever you want to call it – slammed into another rock or tree stump and sent Caleb smashing into the floor in a violent manner.

He floundered around and then got himself upright. Rubbing his head, he looked over at Lucas and said, "Okay… I'm up. I'm up."

"We're being transported somewhere."

"They betrayed us! That blasted Greactus, betrayed us!"

"No I didn't," came a voice from somewhere outside the cell.

Lucas and Caleb scrambled up to the bars and peered out in the direction of the voice. Greactus was running alongside the wagon. His neck was cuffed and the chain ran to the side of the trailer. The speed forced him to jog with the moving caravan. By the looks of his feet, they had been going for quite a long time. Blood covered them.

"What is going on? Why are they doing this to you?" Lucas asked.

"Why are they doing this to us?" Caleb countered.

"The Clan Elders made a deal with the man I warned you about,"

"Hathian," Lucas said.

"Yessem, Hathian. He promised that our people would have a prominent role in his New Order. That we would be redeemed. He convinced them that the prophecy was false and that only he could restore us to prominence in Carsonia."

"But Hathian will kill us. He needs us dead. That's what you said... right?"

Greactus jogged over to the wagon and leaped up on a little railing that was covered with dry blood. His long, lanky fingers grasped onto the bars for all it was worth. By the looks of it, he had been doing this off and on during the trip.

"You must understand. My clan has been hunted and persecuted for thousands of years. We are small in number and preservation is very important to the Elders. While some like myself hold out hope for the fulfillment of the prophecy, others have given up hope and are looking for any way to survive and restore our people. Hathian apparently convinced them that he was the answer to their prayers. I am truly sorry."

Lucas looked down at Greactus feet and then back into his heavy, brown eyes. "I take it you didn't go along with the Elders decision lightly."

He shook his head no.

"How long do you have to be punished like this?"

"Until we redeem ourselves and return to our homes. If I live, they will consider me forgiven by the Creator."

"How do we get out of here?" Caleb said as he surveyed the bars. "None of this seems strong. I would think we can easily break out."

"Maybe. But where would we go?"

"We take the green guy with us. He'll guide us back to the north."

"His name is Greactus."

"He's a betrayer. He led us right into a trap!"

"You have to understand… I had no way of knowing what was being planned. They sent me out to find you because Marcause asked them to. The Eyes of Hathian reported to him the findings of the Clan. Visitors came, proposed a path to redemption and everything was set in motion before we returned. But there is still hope."

"Yea?" Caleb said. "How so?"

"Before dinner, I sent one of my guards to inform Marcause that you were with us. He must be on his way by now. They will come for you. It is only a matter of time."

Caleb slumped down and disappeared into his own world.

"What's wrong now?" Lucas asked.

"I'm tired of waiting for other people to save us. I'm tired of being out of control of my own life and having to feel this way… weak."

"Greactus is right. Marcause will come for us. I bet he's with Mom and Dad." Lucas peered down at the goblin and asked, "How long have we been on the road?"

"Two sunrises."

Lucas drew back – stunned that he had been sleeping for that many days.

"In three days, we will arrive at a human village where you will be handed over to Hathian's men."

Someone shouted from up ahead. It was a high pitched

wail from a goblin. The clopping sound of the hooves became silent and the wagon stopped moving. Everything was quiet. Not even the chirping of a bird was heard.

"What's going on?" Lucas asked Greactus.

"I do not know. Perhaps something is blocking the road ahead? I cannot see from here."

Suddenly, there was an eruption of goblin screams and the woods came alive with a flurry of activity. From out of the foliage came swarms of goblins with metal swords – not the bone made weapons he had seen used by the goblins when they first arrived. These attackers were well armed.

Greactus ducked under the cover of the wagon while a battle broke out. Lucas looked around and saw the River Bottom Clan clashing with other goblins who were obviously not friendly to them. From what he could gather from a quick assessment of the situation, they were outnumbered. The only protection that Caleb and Lucas had now was the safety of being locked in a cage – which also served as a barrier from letting them escape to safety. Their lives now hung in the balance of the outcome of this battle.

From somewhere, there was a loud, stomp. It was like the clop of a horse – a very large horse. Again it thundered out. Soon there was a loud snort and both of the boys knew what was coming. Each of them had had their own interaction with the bounty hunter named Mideon.

Each footfall drew closer to them. The cage that was

offering some sense of security now had become a wrapped present for the Minotaur. He was about to get what he was after all along. The din of battle could not hide his ominous presence.

First, Lucas could see his horns and then the rest of his massive, bull like head. His broad shoulders came into view next followed by his massive arms and upper body. He was built like a walking tank and neither of the twins had any way to defeat him.

A metallic clank from below the wagon startled both of the boys. It was soon followed by a thundering blow of metal against metal. As they turned, they found Greactus using a battle axe to break the lock off the door.

He quickly swung the door open and Caleb and Lucas scurried out.

"You both need to run," he said. "Bring my people true redemption. The redemption that I know that only you two can bring."

"We're not leaving here without you," Lucas said.

"I fear I won't be leaving here. You both must go. I can only offer my life as an apology for the actions of my people. If they hadn't betrayed your trust…"

"We don't have time for talking," Caleb said as he began to move for the woods. He pulled Lucas by the arm but he refused to move.

"Please… go!"

Caleb yanked harder and Lucas took a reluctant step in his direction.

"For redemption!" Greactus cried out as he charged forward.

With one sweep of the mighty hand that he had used to crush the head of Lucas' grandma, he watched Mideon push the wagon out of his way. Greactus lunged forward with a swing of his sword. Mideon blocked the blow with the metal gauntlets that wrapped around his wrist.

He pushed the goblins sword out of the way with one motion and then backhanded the green scaled creature to the ground. He raised his hoofed leg up and then drove it down for Greactus' gut, but the quick goblin rolled out of the way and then drove his sword into the tree trunk sized thigh.

Mideon let out a roar and that was the last Lucas could see of the valiant efforts of Greactus as Caleb pulled him through the woods.

"You idiot! You trying to get killed?"

"He saved us. We owe him more than just leaving him to die. At least we should stand and fight."

Caleb weaved them through the scattered trees until he found a path that began to go uphill. The sky above was orange and looked like an old creek that ran through their woods. It was heavy with iron and reeked of rotten egg. If he took a chance to breath in his surroundings, he felt that was what this air would smell like.

They worked their way up the trail, but the trees began to thin out. The ones that were still standing were half dead. The farther on they went, the few standing trees were just remnants of a lush beauty from many years ago. They were just old stumps with a few branches still hanging on. The entire area looked like death and then they came to the end of the road.

Caleb stopped.

Lucas turned and looked at what was before them. His breath was immediately taken from him as he looked over the edge of the cliff that they now stood on. For countless miles – as far as his eyes could see – there wasn't a speck of green to be seen. The entire area was a wasteland. There was a city down below. Houses and larger structures and all of them looked sad and bleak. The sky cast an eerie orange glow over everything.

"What happened here?" Caleb asked.

"Grandma told me about this place. On the train ride the day she died. When the people rejected The Light, they began their journey into a dark world of death, destruction and slavery. There is no hope for those people because they have never seen a world worth living in. They just go about their day... doing as they're told. Nothing to dream about. Nothing to live for..."

The crunching of a tree as it was leveled to the ground caused both of them to spin around. Mideon had them cornered.

"You two have given me quite the challenge. I would be lying if I didn't admit how much I've enjoyed this here adventure. But the race is over. I have me a bounty to collect."

Lucas took a bold step forward. "All of this death and destruction... and for what? Money!"

"I have to earn my keep, boy. The death and destruction part is all on you two's. My hands are clean from any blood that's been spilt. If you both had stayed put... well, nobody would have had to die. Especially that old lady of yours."

Something snapped inside of Lucas.

He rushed forward and suddenly he could see a glow of light surrounding him. He didn't have a clue what to do with it so he just continued forward and suddenly, a tentacle of light jumped out in front of him and slammed into the chest of Mideon. He stumbled back and was just off balance enough for Lucas to tackle him to the ground.

Caleb rushed up to join his brother. He scooped up an old branch and charged in. using it like a baseball bat, he took a mighty swing and smashed the beast across his massive snout. Blood sprayed out and a tooth fell to the ground.

Lucas began driving his fists into the bounty hunters face, but he didn't allow it to happen for long.

He backhanded Lucas and he flew through the air. Slamming hard into the ground, he felt all of the air leave his lungs. He rolled to his stomach and tried to get back to his feet, but his body failed him and he collapsed back into the ground.

Looking up, he watched as Mideon grabbed his brother by the legs, picked him up and slammed him to the ground as if he were swatting a fly with a flyswatter. Caleb's body went limp and a cold rush of fear poured through Lucas.

Is he dead?

Mideon took a knife out from his back pocket and slit the palm of Caleb's hand. He then pulled out a glass jar with a wood cork on the end and removed the top. Taking Caleb's bleeding hand, he squeezed it hard and blood trickled out into the bottom of the jar. When he was satisfied with his take, Mideon tossed Caleb's limp hand to the ground, corked the jar, and then turned back to Lucas.

"Let's see if we can make you bleed. Huh, boy?"

29

They could hear the screams of war long before they got to the scene of the battle. On horse, they rode as fast as their steeds would take them. As they rounded the bend, they found the warriors of two goblin clans in a heated battle.

Marcause charged forward, his sword swinging in different directions as he severed the heads of those goblins who were dressed in the shabby earth toned outfits that were made from tanned leather and the skin of victims. The River Bottom Clan had adopted silk garments, woven from silk worms that were thick in their region of the forest. It was easy to tell who was fighting on whose side.

Andrea frantically looked around for any signs of Caleb. Were they even here? Where was the bounty hunter?

"We need to ride through this! I don't see Mideon!" Gavin called out. He was steering the horse while she rode along with him, her arms tight around his abdomen.

"The River Bottom Clan must have sent out scouts," Vladamir said.

"Or something more fiendish," Nate said. His head

motioned for the tipped over wagon. "Who were they transporting? And why were they going this direction?"

Gavin pulled his horse to a halt and got off. A goblin from the River Bottom Clan was bleeding out just a few feet away. He knelt down beside him and said, "I am a friend of your Clan. The father of the Twins of Prophecy." The eyes of the goblin grew big and as he tried to speak, blood rolled out of his mouth and then he went limp and died.

Gavin stood up and looked around. Andrea felt a surge of pain through her connection with Caleb. She screamed and nearly fainted, but quickly caught herself.

"Are you okay?" Vladamir asked as he rode up alongside her and rested his hand on her shoulder to stabilize her.

"He's close. Caleb is close... and in pain."

Gavin rushed over to her and said, "How can you be sure?"

"Catrina discovered it... a connection I have had with him since coming to Carsonia."

This caught Marcause's attention and he rode over to listen.

"I can almost see him... it's like being in the same room with him."

"But he's hurt?" Gavin asked.

"I think so."

She caught Marcause studying her. His eyes pierced through her own – as if he had the ability to read her mind.

She turned away from him.

Gavin maneuvered back onto the horse, "Hold on. We're wasting time."

With a hard kick to the horse's side, they took off up the trail and it began to slope upwards. The terrain went from lush green to a brownish orange. Dead trees made up the landscape and Andrea couldn't help but have a feeling of hopelessness wash over her.

"What is this place?" she asked.

Nobody answered as they continued up the trail. They rounded a bend of rock and then she saw the beast that had been haunting her mind since the night they were abducted. On the ground, not far from him, was the body of Caleb. In his grasp, she saw Lucas' hand bleeding into a glass jar.

The power rushed through her again. She felt anger and rage and it all channeled through her and rolled off her fingertips in the form of a gigantic ball of electricity. It hummed through the air and slammed into the chest of Mideon. He flew back, falling to the ground, but managing to keep the jar from wiggling from his grasp.

Gavin leaped off the horse and drew out the two swords he had in his possession. Fire burned in his eyes and she could see that all of his anger had boiled to the surface and either he or Mideon would be falling in battle today.

30

He charged for the bastard who had taken his family and shattered it beyond fixing. His entire life was in ruins and it all rested in the hands of this reject! Gavin hardly noticed the swarm of goblins that came pouring out of the woods behind him.

Marcause, Vladamir, Nathan and Andrea would have to take care of them. Gavin was out for vengeance.

Mideon got to his feet just as Gavin took his first swing. Raising his gauntlet, Mideon blocked the blow in a shower of sparks as the two pieces of metal struck with force. Mideon countered with a hard swing of his right hand, but Gavin ducked under it and just before the arm cleared, he drove up with his sword and drove it into the thick flesh of Mideon's forearm.

He screamed in pain as he spun away from his attacker. He pulled the sword from his forearm and tossed it over the cliff. Fire grew in the beasts eyes and Gavin couldn't help but coax up the fires a bit more as he said in a low growl, "That's just a small taste of the pain I'm going to share with you today.

You're going to taste everything I've felt since the night you ruined my life."

The bounty hunter snorted and then pawed at the dusty ground with his right leg. He snorted again and then charged at Gavin.

"Bring it, Mideon!"

Gavin charged forward and he began swinging his sword through the air. It met the gauntlets in a flurry of sparks. He spun around and came back again, attacking the other side of Mideon. Mideon blocked that shot as well and then drove a thundering fist towards Gavin's chest.

He rolled out of the way and came down with the bottom of his hilt, driving it into the tender tendon that stretched from Mideon's elbow to his wrist.

The beast howled in pain.

Gavin smiled.

He went back to work, slashing high and low. Mideon blocked each shot with his gauntlets and returned fire with his massive fists. Each blow skimmed past Gavin as he used his quickness to escape the shots that would seriously slow him down.

He leaped into the air, summersaulted in the air and landed on the other side of Mideon. With a mighty swing, he slashed the beast across his back, tearing flesh and shedding more blood. Mideon roared and spun around. He backhanded Gavin, who flew through the air and landed on his back.

Mideon leaped in the air and aimed his sharp hoof at the chest of Gavin. Gavin had lost his breath and struggled to regain it. He cleared his thoughts just enough to realize the doom that was coming down at him.

He rolled and felt his cape tear loose from his body as it became trapped under the thundering hoof of Mideon. He bounced back to his feet just in time to feel the full blow of Mideon's fist as it slammed into his face, throwing him violently to the ground.

Gavin looked down at the dirt and saw three of his teeth lying before him with a pool of blood quickly forming. He could hear the beast stomping towards him. He spit out the remaining remnants of his teeth and a wad of blood to the ground and then scrambled to his feet.

The Light gathered around him and he quickly summoned all of the tentacles and threw them at his attacker.

The powerful force lifted Mideon off his feet and threw him tumbling through the air and into a wall of rock. Gavin charged forward. He used three of the tentacles of light to pick up rocks nearby and throw them at the beast. He dodged the first two but the third one struck him in the leg.

As he struggled to get away, Gavin swung his sword down with a hard chop. Mideon blocked it with a gauntlet. Gavin raised his sword and chopped down again. Mideon again blocked it, but he fell to his knees. Gavin chopped again and again.

Sparks showered out with each blow.

Gavin repeated it again and again – waiting for him to lose his strength and allow a fatal blow to strike his neck. But the beast didn't let up. He continued to absorb every blow.

Gavin drew in an arm of light and used it to grab Mideon's arm and raise it out of the way. Mideon couldn't block – wouldn't block the next blow.

He brought his sword down for the kill.

Mideon used his overpowering strength and swung his arm, the tentacle of light wrapped around it, and Gavin, through the air. He spun around and around, taking Gavin for violent ride he had never expected.

Mideon snapped his arm like a whip and Gavin raised up into the air and then slammed down into the ground with great force. His sword flew from his hand. His head smashed into the ground.

Blackness drew in.

Gavin tried to lift his head up and defend himself – but all seemed lost. The darkness closed in fast.

He couldn't hold on much longer.

31

The goblins were falling.

Vladamir, Nathan, Marcause and his men, were all slashing and hacking their way through the small army.

They moved like lightning through the sky. Their swords stung like bees. The light that they summoned for strength danced around, picked up goblins and tossed them around like rag dolls. Some flew over the edge of the cliff. Others were tossed back into the woods from where they came. They didn't have enough size to overwhelm the trained Knights of Liberty and the highly trained Angellian Warriors.

Andrea didn't feel the presence of the power that had caused her to fight so well in her previous battles and so she did what she had been dying to do for so long. She rushed to the side of Caleb, who was being tended to by his brother.

She fell to his side and curled his head into her arms.

"Caleb," she looked up into the eyes of Lucas. She was looking for reassurance that he was okay. He gave her a nod of approval and she looked back down at him, patting his cheek lightly. "Wake up, Caleb. I need you to wake up."

Caleb's eyes fluttered open. They danced around, searching for something, but not focusing on her.

"Caleb, it's me."

"Do you hear them?"

She looked at Lucas. Lucas stood up and looked around, searching for whatever was drawing Caleb's attention.

Caleb appeared to bounce back to full strength and he stood up. His eyes were drawn to his bandaged hand before looking back up and searching the terrain.

"I heard them. The voices of the Draith. Did you hear them?"

"I think you're dreaming, Bro."

"No. No. They were close. Like before. Like at home. I heard them."

Lucas picked up a sword that was on the ground and then searched out another that he handed Caleb. He was about to pick up one for Andrea before she pulled a sword hilt that was tucked in the small of her back, under her belt. "I'm good."

"Dad's in trouble. He's going up against Mideon."

"Dad... Where's Mom?"

Lucas began frantically searching for her.

"She's not here," Andrea said in a low tone. "She didn't make it."

Neither boy spoke.

Whatever fight they had in them was suddenly sucked out. Both of their eyes bored into hers. She didn't dare tell them what truly happened. She had decided long ago that she would have to keep that secret till the day she died. It was a heavy burden, and as she looked into the pain in Caleb's eyes, she could tell that it had just become heavier.

"She didn't make it," she repeated. She collapsed into Caleb's arms as the tears ran down her cheeks. "I couldn't save her."

Caleb drew in a long breath and then stroked her hair with his good hand. She should be consoling him, yet she needed him to console her. "It's okay. None of this is our fault."

Lucas fell to his knees. She looked over and saw the pain roll down his cheeks and fall to the dead earth below – the first taste of moisture that this land had had in a long time. Her heart broke as she looked up and watched Caleb's eyes flood with grief and pour out as well.

What have I done? she asked herself.

His lips trembled and suddenly she felt his arms draw away from her. His hand tightened around the hilt of his sword and his jaw was suddenly set. He had the face of a wild animal about to strike and then he turned to the slope behind him and saw Mideon and his Dad disappear around the corner in battle.

"You're not to blame… He is!" Caleb broke into a dead sprint before Andrea could reach out and grab him.

Lucas rose up to his feet. He then fell back to his knees. Andrea knelt down and pulled him in close.

"I need to help him and Dad, but I can't. I can't move…"

She was to blame for the death of Catrina. She could never tell them what had really happened in that camp. All she could do now was try to be a rock for the family that had always loved her. While her instincts told her to go after Caleb, she also knew that the competitor in him could never be tamed. Lucas was always the weaker one when it came to that internal fire. For now, she would keep him safe – confident in the fact that Caleb was a fighter.

Whatever he was about to run into – he would survive.

She prayed that he would survive.

32

Caleb rounded the corner and saw the beast raise his sword up and take aim at the back of his fallen father's head. He screamed out a blood curling cry and then felt a powerful force surround him. He instantly knew what was happening as the world around him glowed.

He took greater strides and closed in on the beast. With a mighty leap, he soared through the air and then projected a solid blast of light from the palm of his hand. It flew through the air, struck the sword of Mideon and pushed him back.

The eyes of the raging beast shot a glance at him and he let out a snort.

"Is this it, boy? Is this where you try to become a man?"

Caleb began his decent and with a hard, downward chop of the sword, attempted to connect with Mideon's skull.

The beast raised his gauntlet up for a block.

The two pieces of metal slammed together.

The blade of his sword shattered into pieces, some of them embedding in Mideon and other pieces into his arm, while the gauntlet split into two pieces and crashed to the ground.

He rammed Mideon with the full force of his body and watched the Minatour stumble backwards. Taking the moment to strike again, Caleb took the broken hilt of his weapon and hurled it like a football. He watched as the jagged metal drove into the upper shoulder of Mideon.

He charged forward. Knowing that his mom was dead because of this creature, fueled his anger and gave him strength like he had never felt before. He slammed into Mideon like he was trying to break through a linebacker to pick up a first down.

Mideon fell backwards, crashing to the ground. Caleb came up on the beast's chest and then took aim at his face. He drove his right fist into Mideon's snout and then his left and then he repeated it again with his right, then back to using his left.

Over and over again he hammered out his aggression on Mideon until the freak of power fought back and hurled him through the air. Caleb crashed to the ground on his back. He felt the air exhale from his lungs but he didn't let the pain stop him. He didn't even know if he drew in another breath. He just bounced back up and charged back at the beast.

"You have moxie, kid. I'll give you credit for that." He let out another snort as he prepared for the attack.

Caleb felt the light wrap around him and he then projected it out again. The tentacles twirled through the air and then slammed into Mideon's chest, lifting him up and hurling him through the air. Caleb reached down, scooped up a sword and then jumped into the air.

Both of them flew through the expanse – straight for the edge of the cliff. Caleb began swinging his sword, trying to land a killing blow. Mideon used his remaining gauntlet to fend off the attack, but he couldn't move fast enough and the blade cut into his flesh.

He screamed in pain and tried hard to get away from the raging power of Caleb. He seemed to be trying to fall over the edge to escape and Caleb wanted to see nothing more than to see him fall to his death, but they had suddenly stopped moving.

Caleb and Mideon were locked in a giant ball of light – the very light that Caleb was using to attack Mideon was now trapping them both in a cage. A symbol that a final duel must take place.

Mideon jumped to his feet and swung a deadly fist at Caleb who ducked to the side and then chopped down with his sword. The blade cut into his arm and went half way through – lodging in the bone. Mideon ripped his arm away – taking Caleb's sword with him.

Caleb summoned a tentacle of light and threw it at Mideon, striking the beast across the face. He stumbled back and Caleb charged forward. He wrapped his arms around the waist of the beast and tackled him to the floor of the glass like globe. Mideon's head smashed into the dome and a spider web of cracks stretched out.

Caleb grabbed Mideon by the neck and began to choke. Mideon was about to grab him and throw him off when he suddenly saw his sword – still lodged in the beasts bone – draw close. He kicked out with his left leg and the sword dislodged and fell to the floor of the dome.

Mideon grabbed him by the scruff of the neck and tossed him into a far wall where he felt the air escape his lungs again. He slid to the floor and felt the hilt of the sword draw into his hand. He looked up and locked stares with Mideon.

Mideon wiped the blood from his snout and then turned his attention to the large gash on his forearm. He squeezed it tight to try and stop the bleeding.

Caleb got back to his feet and then, without any mercy, he charged forward.

Mideon blocked the first blow with his gauntlet. Caleb raised his foot and delivered a killer blow into Mideon's groin. The beast pitched forward as Caleb came back with a hard, upward swing of the sword. His blade cut through the equipment belt that draped over the chest of Mideon and cut through the leathery flesh. He reared back in agony as Caleb quickly changed directions and came back with another swing of the sword.

This time it sliced through the beast's right shoulder sending him down to one knee.

Caleb summoned another tentacle of light and let it wrap around his fist. He then summoned another tentacle and it gathered around his fist and the ball of power grew bigger. He summoned yet another one and suddenly the ball of light was three times the size of Caleb himself.

Mideon looked up with sagging eyes that had no fight left in them.

Caleb unleashed his wrath and struck the beast in the head, driving it down into the glass floor and watching with a smile on his face as Mideon exploded through the glass floor and hurled down towards his death in the deep, jagged canyon below.

His body flipped head over feet and the ground drew in closer to deliver a bone shattering blow that would kill him for sure. But the beast had one last trick up his sleeve. Mideon hurled something down towards the ground.

It exploded.

It revealed a portal that he disappeared into. He was probably going to be safe and sound on the other side. The satisfaction that Caleb had been feeling, escaped him.

Caleb watched the ground for a few more minutes, praying that he would suddenly see Mideon's body dead on the rocks.

No satisfaction.

He closed his eyes, concentrating on the ball of glass that had encased him and the bounty hunter. He could feel it in his mind and using his thoughts, he moved it to the safety of the land before him. Then he lowered it until it touched down on the ground. With one more command, the ball broke apart into tiny flakes of white – like snow drifting to the ground.

He looked up and saw his Dad being supported by Lucas on one side and Vladamir on the other.

Andrea rushed forward and wrapped her arms around his neck, squeezing him tight.

"It's over, Baby. This entire nightmare is almost over."

He closed his eyes and let the pain from the past month just flow out in tears. As he opened them and looked around, he saw broken men who had seen more death and destruction in a few days' time than they had probably ever seen in all of their lives combined.

He feared that there would be worse days ahead.

As he examined Marcause, Vladamir, Nate, his Dad and Lucas, he also saw hope. Perhaps there was still a life to go back to. Perhaps he and Andrea would get a chance to go to college and live the dream they had long talked about.

But even in that hope, Caleb realized one dark fact.

He turned his head and looked to the air above the cliff where he had just fought the mighty Mideon. He saw a side of him revealed in that battle that he didn't know existed. He saw a darker man. A more dangerous man.

The boy was clearly gone.

What now remained, scared him.

33

Lucas woke to the sound of wood snapping as it was engulfed in fire and the sizzling and popping of meat that had been placed in a frying pan. The smell tickled his nose and warned him that his stomach had been void of a good meal for too long. He sat up, stretched his arms and then looked around at the unfamiliar land around him.

The initial sense of normalcy that he felt at first, was replaced with the remembrance of the pain he had felt in the last 24 hours. He looked down at his bandaged hand and remembered the feeling of having his body pinned down and feeling the blade of a knife cut into his flesh. The tight squeeze as Mideon forced his blood out of his body and into the glass jar with his brother's.

No, this wasn't home. As he looked around at the lush vegetation, he realized that he was in a type of hell – purgatory even.

"Do you feel rested?"

Lucas looked behind him from where the voice came and saw Marcause standing there. He looked up and made quick eye contact and then looked away. He nodded his head up and down, but offered nothing more. He wasn't in the mood to talk.

He looked around the camp. They had traveled quite a distance after the battle. They had left the destruction of life behind, but he felt the stains of those events plastered all over his mind. He saw Caleb just off to his right. He held Andrea tight in his arms and her head was resting on his chest as it slowly moved up and down.

He remembered the feeling of her holding him just before Caleb rushed off into battle. He had never experienced the sensation of being so close to a girl. To feel her hair brush over his cheek and her warm tears splashing on his head.

Carsonia did an amazing thing to her. She was always beautiful, but now her pearl like skin and even the pointy ears, made her majestic. Breathtaking.

To him these became sick thoughts and so he quickly pushed them out.

"Do not allow your mind to travel that road," Marcause said as he crouched down next to Lucas. Lucas looked over to him and questioned his statement with a simple and innocent look. Keeping his voice low, Marcause continued, "She is dangerous. Your brother is not ready to hear this so I am trusting this to you. Stay away from her. For the sake of both of you."

"She's been a part of our family for years. Why would you

say that?"

"She is the fulfillment of an Angellian prophecy. One that speaks of a temptress who will lead the Twins of the Prophecy to bloodshed. I believe that she was once pure in heart; but that life is now over. You have all changed. While your father will attempt to take you home to return you to a safer life, he has not yet realized that none of you are the same as you were when you came through that portal."

Lucas understood that quite well. After watching Caleb unleash such a display of fury and rage, he feared what was contained deep inside himself. He had to admit that the idea of being a deliverer to the people of Carsonia gave him a sense of purpose. After seeing the price it would cost, he wasn't as excited as before.

Caleb stirred awake. His eyes fluttered and then he looked down at Andrea whom he held close. He gently placed a kiss on the top of her forehead and then began to gently wake her. Lucas felt a ping of jealousy course through him. His stomach twisted in a knot and he quickly turned away.

"You feel it. Her beauty has a hold on you already. She will use that hold to turn you against one another. Trust in my words. Stay away from her."

Marcause didn't say another word. He stood up and walked over to Vladamir, Nate, his dad and the other Angellian warriors and joined their conversation. He was left to ponder those words of warning.

When the food was done and everyone had eaten, they mounted their horses and started their journey to recover his mother's body and then head home.

He was shocked at the amount of grief his dad was taking when discussions veered towards his decision to return the boys back to the Earthly Realm. Both Vladamir and Marcause were very adamant that everything that had happened to this point was a clear indication that The Creator had brought them here to fulfill their roles in the prophecy. To attempt an escape would surely result in punishment.

"He is the true decider of our fates," Vladamir had said. "We have followed you and will continue to support you. But Gavin... we can see His hand at work in all of this. If you continue to defy Him... no good will come of it."

"I've lost my wife. The innocence of my sons have been stripped from them. This world is dying and worst of all, this prophecy wills for one of them to die. What good is there in staying in this wretched world? We're better off running and taking our chances."

"And running you will be doing. In the other realm, Draith still roam free."

"As do other Knights of Liberty. We will have an equal chance of survival because the Draith are outnumbered back there. Here... there are all sorts of evil trying to take my boys."

And no other words were said.

Everyone rode in silence.

Lucas rode up alongside Nate and cast a long glance at him before asking, "So what about you? Are you going to return to Tarrin?"

Nate snorted and then looked over at him, "No. I won't lie, there were aspects of your world that intrigued me. But I don't belong there... nor would I want to live there. My home is here and it's time for me to return to the Temple and complete my training."

"Will you be escorting us to the portal?" Lucas asked. Gavin knew of one last portal that had been a family secret since the dawn of the first one. He revealed this piece of information at breakfast and everyone stood in disbelief.

They had thought that the running was over and now they learned that Gavin had one more chance to get free of Carsonia forever.

Nate became distant. He looked straight ahead and then drew in a deep breath. He let it out slowly and then looked back at Lucas before answering yes with a slight nod of his head.

They rode on in silence some more.

They rested that night and early the next day they picked up his mom's body. It was painful having to open that wound again. His dad kept her strapped to the back of his horse. From time to time he would reach back and pat her with a gentle touch – as if telling her that everything was okay and that he would make it all right.

Lucas couldn't suppress the tear that rolled down his cheek.

The next day, as the sun prepared to set, they arrived at the final gate to make their final escape from Carsonia and leave this world behind forever. Once his dad sealed it up, there would be no way to return to this wicked land that had claimed their mother and altered their lives forever.

Lucas looked down at the ragged clothes he had been wearing since coming to Carsonia. They had been worn longer than any one piece garment should be worn and the condition of the material proved it. Holes had appeared in the knees, elbows and in random places on the back and chest. It wasn't the pristine outfit that his grandmother had given him all those days ago.

He didn't know where this portal would take them – what place in the world they would be delivered – but he was sure that they would have a hard time explaining to the locals why they were wearing these goofy clothes from an era long ago.

He heard footsteps approach him and he turned to find Marcause staring at him with those crystal blue eyes – like those of Andrea, now that he realized she was of the same race as him. He held out the hilt of a sword to him and Lucas shook his head no.

"The Draith walk in your world as they do here. You may find yourself needing this one day."

"Maybe. But just because I'm here doesn't mean I have to

be a warrior. I don't like what I saw here. I have no intention of living like this anymore," Lucas smiled and then continued, "Let's just say that the glamor of being a knight has already worn off."

Marcause didn't return the smile. As if he had already seen a glimpse of the future, he reached down, grabbed Lucas' hand and forced the hilt into it. "You will need this. I am not giving you a choice but instead, giving you an order. Do not suffer from the same issues of denial as your father. If you truly believe that you can escape the destiny that The Creator has chosen for you, then you are as stupid as he is."

Lucas drew back. He had admired Marcause since meeting him. Now he felt hurt by the words of a man who could probably be a mentor to him in a different life.

"Another thing," Marcause continued, "Do not forget what I told you about the Lady Andrea. She is the temptress of our prophecy. She will alter the relationship of you and your brother and divide you two. Do not allow it. Avoid her at all costs. She brings nothing but darkness to your future."

Lucas didn't answer. He was hurt by the words of this man and half ignored the warning. Reluctantly, he pulled his ruck sack off and tossed the hilt of his sword inside. He didn't make eye contact again. Instead, he turned to find his dad and aided him in removing his mom's body from the horse.

Caleb joined them and for the first time in days, he felt a slight feeling of hope. As they worked as a family to bring their mother down from the horse and then draw her close to the portal, he felt as if there was a chance that normalcy could return to the family.

Vladamir walked over and embraced each of the boys before turning to his dad. "I wish you the best, Gavin. You fight like your father and for a while, I felt as if he and I were together again."

His dad smiled.

He had aged quite a bit over the past month. He had new scars and wrinkles in his face. His skin was hard and leathery and his eyes drooped and looked lifeless – as if much of his spirit had died when his wife – Lucas' mother, had died.

He reached out to shake Vladamir's hand and instead the brute of a man wrapped his arms around his dad and drew him in for a huge hug. "I am so sorry for all of your losses. While I wish you would reconsider your decision… I will honor your wishes to the end. Perhaps this is what your father would have wanted."

His dad nodded his head as if to validate Vladamir's statement and then turned to the portal. He made eye contact with Lucas, Caleb and Andrea and then nodded in the direction of the glowing wall of light before them. Nathan had cleared away the vines and branches that had concealed it from the view of anyone who happened by the area. It wasn't hid that well, but the location was so far off any beaten path, that nobody had stumbled across it all these years.

Gavin reached down and heaved Catrina up on his shoulder and waited for them to take the lead.

"So long," Vladamir said.

"So long," his dad said as he smiled at the man with the Russian accent – who now that Lucas thought about it, really wasn't Russian at all.

Gavin smiled at Marcause, who did not return the gesture and then nodded a silent goodbye to Nate, and turned to join his boys who were now preparing to walk through the gate.

Lucas stopped in front of the light. He drew in a long deep breath. He could remember the feeling the last time they had passed through. It felt like sticking your fingers into a jar of jelly, except the jelly would grab hold and pull you through. It didn't hurt, but every instinct inside pleaded to resist and get away.

He reached out slowly and let his fingers touch the glowing, silver plate. Little ripples, like those in water caused by a single drop of rain, circled and moved away from his fingers as it touched. He felt the little suction begin pulling lightly on him, coaxing him in further. Lucas closed his eyes and let all of the past months events just wash out of his mind. He hoped to leave them here in Carsonia and never think about them again.

Then he heard a slurping sound – like the sound of a foot getting sucked into the mud and then pulled out – followed by a grunt.

"Nathan! No!" he heard Vladamir cry out.

Lucas turned and found the end of a sword sticking out of his dad's chest. He watched, unable to move as his dad dropped his mom to the ground and fell to his knees. His attacker stood behind him and Lucas was helpless to say or do anything.

Nate reached down and tore the necklace from his father right before he collapsed face first into the ground. He pointed at Caleb and Andrea and with the utterance of a spell, he lifted the two of them into the air and then with a sweeping motion of his hand, he threw them out of his way.

Nathan rushed forward, pushing Lucas out of the way and then tossing the necklace into the portal, he cried out one last spell and the light sealed up with a scream. Their final chance at escape was now gone.

"What have you done?" Vladamir cried out as he charged forward. "How could you do this? I trusted you! You are a Knight of Liberty!"

Had the Knights of Liberty ordered this hit? Lucas thought to himself.

Nathan shook his head no and then said, "I left the teachings of the Order a long time ago. Once you strike me down, I will be one with the Draith – as we will all be one day."

He raised his hand and fired a bolt of electricity at Vladamir. The Light surrounded the older man and one of the tentacles reached down and grabbed the electricity in the air and threw it into a tree.

Vladamir rushed forward. Nathan raised his hand to strike again and Vladamir chopped down with his sword, cutting off his apprentice's hand. He spun around and brought his sword up to head level and swung again, slicing through Nate's neck and stopping to watch the limp body of his friend fall to the ground – his head rolling away.

Vladamir just stood there and said nothing.

Lucas rushed forward and fell to his knees. He held his dad's body tight while Caleb pulled the sword out of his back. They rolled him over, but his eyes had already become empty. Like their mother, they didn't get to say goodbye. He was simply…

Gone.

34

To honor the last wishes of Gavin McGregor, Vladamir and Marcause didn't take the boys back to the Temple of the Knights of Liberty. Instead, they trekked North through the mountains and went to an old farm house out in the middle of a lush, ever reaching field.

With all of the portals closed and both of their parents gone, there was nowhere for the boys – and Andrea, to go. They were orphaned. They were nearly adult age and so on the surface, it might not have seemed so tragic. Yet what they suffered in the course of this past month was greater than anyone should ever have to bear.

The old farm house belonged to Vladamir. It was here that Vladamir had grown up as a kid and it now served as his getaway when he needed time away from the Order or to train an apprentice. A place where he had taken Nathan quite a few times for lessons on being a Knight. How he had failed to see Nathan's betrayal was eating at him the entire journey.

Nobody spoke of Nathan during their venture. The boys hadn't spoken a word since burying their parents at the site of the last portal. Andrea spent a great deal of time comforting the boys. In many ways, she seemed more like a sister to them. Perhaps it was from being such a close part of the family.

However, Marcause had shared with Vladamir about his discoveries of who she really was and the danger she posed to the Twins of Prophecy. While the two boys and she were oblivious to the ramifications of her fulfilling her role, Vladamir was very much aware. He understood the dangers she posed. If he was to honor the wishes of his best friend and the wishes of that best friend's son, he would have to evaluate the risks and make some bold decisions.

Marcause was alarmingly ready to kill her. It was too harsh and Vladamir forced him to make a vow never to end her life. The boys would surly flip to darkness over such an act. Plus, they had both just lost their parents. They couldn't handle yet another loss of life.

"She is an Angellian," Marcause said as the two of them sat by a fire that night. "She belongs with her people. I could coax her to venture back home with me. She should learn of her true ancestry and how to use her abilities. I can do my best to keep her away from the boys and hopefully prevent the prophecy from being fulfilled."

"Catrina's parents are still alive and at the academy. I can place the boys with them and at least they will have some family to give them support. I'm guessing that Andrea has family that you can connect her with?"

Marcause nodded yes.

Vladamir shook his head. He was turning around many things in his mind as he chewed on the end of a long blade of prairie grass. "Why is this part of the prophecy not in our scrolls?" he asked.

"I believe that every race of Carsonia has a part to play in this prophecy. My guess is that there are many parts to this story. Man holds the story of the Twins. Our race holds the story of the temptress who will divide the twins. If we spoke with the Aquarian's, I am sure that they have a piece of the puzzle in their possession. The goblins... or at least some of them... look at the Twins to being their redeemer. And who knows what role the dwarfs are to play in all of this."

"One world bound to one fate."

"Exactly."

Vladamir pulled the grass out of his mouth, looked at it and then tossed it into the fire. He mulled over the fates of Catrina and Gavin and then spoke, "Their parents believed that they could prevent the prophecy from coming true. Now both of them are dead. Is it possible that no matter what road we travel, we will fail and the prophecy will play out just as it's supposed to?"

Marcause picked up a stick and poked at the fire before answering, "I'm sure it will play out as The Creator has planned it. The scrolls we have cannot be verified for accuracy. Some of what is contained in them is dead on and other parts are legends written by man for entertainment purposes. Nobody has ever verified what parts are prophetic and which parts are false.

"One way or the other, we will see this played out. Possibly, everything that has happened did so as it was supposed to. Did it cost Gavin and Catrina their lives? Probably. Yet we can be sure that it was of no surprise to The Creator."

"So do we fight against what we know? Do we hide the Twins or bring them to the valley so they can begin their training?"

"Perhaps the best solution is to put all of the decisions in their hands. We can guide them as best as possible, but in the end, this prophecy is about them. We should allow them to choose the roads they want to take."

Vladamir nodded his head in agreement.

The next morning, Marcause and Vladamir took Andrea off to the side for a discussion. Marcause explained the prophecy to her. Her face was void of emotion. She had witnessed the death of her own parents, the death of Catrina and Gavin and now, in an unfamiliar world, she was being asked to leave the only two people she knew.

"Caleb needs me," she pleaded. "I can't leave him now."

"It won't be forever," Vladamir said. Marcause gave him a look of warning. He was in favor of separating them from her forever, yet Vladamir knew that love rarely worked that way. At some point, Caleb would be drawn back to her and nobody would be able to prevent such a thing. "It will be temporary. Give the boys time to grow, learn their powers and then be prepared to make those decisions. If we have any chance of altering the prophecy..."

"I get it!" she said. "I understand. I don't agree with you, but I understand. I'll do it. Not because you asked me to, but because I love Caleb. If this gives him a chance to survive..." she let the words trail off.

"It's the right decision," Vladamir said as he rested a hand on her shoulder and offered a warm smile. "Marcause will escort you back to the land of your people. A majestic city in the sky that will take your breath away. You will learn about your powers and heritage. When the time is right, there is no doubt in my mind that the two of you will be reunited."

She smiled back. It was clear that she trusted him and he appreciated her for it. He needed that type of relationship so he could speak into her life and help her make good decisions in regards to her and Caleb.

"I need one more favor, Dear. I need you to speak with Caleb. Please tell him that this is your idea, that you want him to have time to concentrate on his studies and you want to learn about your family. If you show him this is your idea..."

She nodded her head. "I can do that. But if he chooses not to let me go..."

He shook his head up and down. He understood and together, they would all cross that bridge if they had to. "Now run along."

When they were alone, Vladamir turned to Marcause and rested both hands on the man's firm shoulders. Staring into his eyes he said, "I have your word?"

"Yes. I will not kill her. Though I must warn you, no good can come from keeping her alive."

"If she was meant to be dead, she would already be gone."

Marcause nodded his head in agreement and then went off to prepare for the journey.

Vladamir had his final discussions with Caleb and Lucas. In them, he saw great hope for Carsonia. When they both agreed to go, he saw bravery unmatched. There was no doubt in his mind that this was the beginning of an incredible journey that would be talked about it until the last days.

It would be the story of…

The Twins of the Prophecy

EPILOGUE

Marcause was not the friendliest of sorts. He didn't offer a smile or any comforting gestures. Compared to Vladamir, he was very distant. He didn't offer much in the way of conversations. He pushed her past exhaustion. He criticized her for having to take extra bathroom breaks and not understanding how to fly so they could get home quicker.

He rushed her through meals. Woke her before she could get any sleep of any value. He didn't understand her crying outbursts when she found herself feeling lonely or having nightmares of all that had happened. If anything, he made her feel like a serious inconvenience.

They rode on in silence as a fine mist settled on them. Her clothes were feeling damp and heavy. She wanted to find shelter and start a warm fire, but he showed no signs of stopping. The sound of the soft clopping of the hooves of the horses was the only soothing part of this journey.

Just when she had lost all hopes of Marcause ever being kind to her, he pulled back on the reigns and brought his horse to a stop. He looked around the mountainous area. Full of green trees, high peaks and chirping birds.

"Are we stopping for the day?" She asked.

He shook his head yes and climbed off his horse. She climbed off and began looking for a place where they could find cover. Perhaps if she showed initiative that she could be helpful, he would loosen up a tad bit.

"There!" she said. "We can set up a camp spot there. I'll gather some wood and we can warm up."

He whispered something into the ear of his horse and then slapped it hard on the butt. It reared back and then took off down the road and disappeared around the corner. He then did the same to her horse.

"What are you doing?" she asked. "Will they come back?"

"Not with the command I gave them. They'll return to their masters – where they belong."

"How will we get home? You can't expect us to walk all the way."

"Nope," he said. "We can't walk."

He took her back pack off her shoulders. It was the first nice gesture he had shown her since they left Vladamir's home. She ran her fingers through her hair to shake out the water and then asked, "You're going to teach me to fly?"

He shook his head no. He laid her backpack on the ground and then pulled out a metal device. He snapped it down towards the sack and a flame leaped out. It ignited her back pack.

"What are you doing?" she cried out.

"I promised Vladamir that I wouldn't kill you. But that doesn't mean that I have to protect you. I'll leave fate to make the final decision."

"What are you talking about?"

"You are dangerous. I saw in your eyes what really happened to Catrina. I have no doubts that you will be the undoing of the prophecy. You will bring Caleb and Lucas to blows. I can't allow it."

She reared back. Her hand went straight to covering her shocked expression.

"There is too much at stake. You cannot be allowed to live. You are a risk to Caleb and Lucas."

"But I love Caleb. I promise to do whatever you tell me in order to protect him. I'll do it. I promise!"

"Then just close your eyes and die. If you really love him… just die."

The tears streamed down her face. She realized now that he was going to leave her here to die.

His body began to break into balls of light and soon he lifted up into the sky. From the glowing orb he said, "We will let the hand of fate decide your future. But I will not willingly allow you to threaten the future of the Twins of Prophecy."

And then he was gone.

Andrea was alone, wet, tired and completely lost.

She fell to her knees, sobbing.

How long she sat there, she could not remember. But then she heard the sound of hooves clopping on the ground.

Her head snapped up. She turned around and saw a group of men riding down the road. They stopped a few yards away. The lead man, dressed in a long flowing, black robe, hopped off. His face was concealed by a hood that he drew back so she could see his old and weathered face.

He walked up slowly and with gentle eyes and a kind voice he asked, "And why do we cry? Are we lost?

"I am." She said.

"Now, now. You are safe with me here. And who might you be, Child?"

He looked harmless and so she didn't hesitate to answer, "I'm Andrea."

"My dear, Andrea. Let us find a dry place, some good food and then we can talk about your future. I believe you are meant for great things here in Carsonia."

"How do you know that?" she asked. She felt safe with him and yet something about how he said that, startled her.

"Because I am a seer – like you. But I am much more powerful than just a seer. I also know the secrets of old magic. From your eyes, I can see that you know them as well. You only need a guide to show you how."

Vengeance was the first thought that flowed through her mind. Marcause had betrayed her and she wanted nothing more than to see him pay for trying to kill her like this.

"I would like that," she said as she tucked those wicked thoughts away. "And who are you?"

"My name, dear Andrea, is Magdoff. The trusted aid of Hathian."

ACKNOWLEDGMENTS

Books don't write themselves. They take time and anything that takes time means that some sort of sacrifice is involved. I want to thank my wife Becky and both of my kids; Mackenzie and Zachary, for their willingness to accept that sometimes I just need to lock myself away in order to crank out a few written pages. When I went into hermit mode to write, you accepted the burden without complaint. Thank you so much for your encouragement, love, support and understanding.

I want to thank my friends at Walmart DC 6025 (my full-time job that supports my love of writing and publishing – hey, you gotta do what you gotta do if you're not a New York Times Bestselling Author) for all the excitement you have shown for this book. I am very bad at self-promotion, yet when you all caught wind of what I was up too, you all showed more excitement for this work than I did. It's infectious and I'm excited to have a great group of friends who support my work. I hope the book doesn't disappoint.

Thank you to Paul Maitrejean who was an integral part of the writing process. Many of the tid bits of insight that you gave me on writing shaped this final work – which has deviated greatly from the original manuscript you had read so many years ago. This is a better book because of your guidance.

I want to thank Mike Green for coming to me with a proposal to paint this stellar cover. I had a generic idea and you brought your artistic talent to the rescue and gave me an original piece of art that inspires me every time I look at it. I'm excited to have you work on other projects with me.

Finally, I want to thank you the reader. You have taken a chance on my storytelling ability and devoted the time to learn more about this world I have created. I hope I didn't disappoint and I hope you'll be back for the next installment.

Thank you everyone!

Jason M. Brooks

About the Author

Jason M. Brooks has loved writing since the day his third grade teacher read *The Lion, The Witch, and the Wardrobe* to his class. Since then, he has pursued a dream of creating his own magnificent worlds that readers could get lost in.

Jason enjoys helping other writers bring their dreams to print which is why he founded his own publishing company. He also blogs about the art of self-publishing on his website, www.jasonmbrooks.com.

When he's not hard at work publishing a book or writing his own, Jason enjoys spending quality time with his family, reading and watching movies. Jason and his family reside in Wisconsin.